Sara George is the award-winning author of the acclaimed *The Journal of Mrs Pepys*, which was serialised on Radio 4's *Woman's Hour*. She lives in London.

Also by Sara George

The Journal of Mrs Pepys

The Beekeeper's Pupil

Sara George

review

First published in 2002
by Review

An imprint of Headline Book Publishing

First published in paperback in 2003

10 9 8 7 6 5 4 3 2 1

Cataloguing in Publication Data is available from
the British Library

ISBN 0 7472 6663 8

Typeset in Weiss by Palimpsest Book Production Limited,
Polmont, Stirlingshire

Printed and bound in Great Britain by
Clays Ltd, St Ives plc

Headline Book Publishing
A division of Hodder Headline
338 Euston Road
London NW1 3BH

www.reviewbooks.co.uk
www.hodderheadline.com

To Ruth and Daisy

24 rue St Jacques
Paris
15 October 1832

Dear M. Burnens,

   You will have heard, I am sure, of the death earlier this year of our esteemed friend François Huber, at the age of eighty-two. The *Revue Britannique* has asked me to write a memoir of his life and his work as a naturalist.

   May I call on you for your thoughts? I know from my visits to Pregny all those years ago how much he depended on your invaluable assistance – and how your leaving him was a crushing blow to a man not unused to enduring misfortune. The circumstances of your departure have never been clear to me, although I know it was without rancour and that M. Huber and his family never spoke of you but in the most glowing terms.

   I have always remembered how you once said to me, when I was a very young man, that yours was the sight and his the vision.

If you are able to send me any account of your time with him I should be most grateful.

I am at all times, Sir,

Your most humble and obedient servant,

Augustin de Candolle

33 rue de la Cluse
Geneva
10 November 1832

Dear M. de Candolle,

I write as the niece and sole beneficiary of the will of my uncle, François Burnens, who died in July 1828 at the age of sixty-two.

Thank you for your kind words about him. After he left M. Huber's service he returned to his native canton of Vaud, where his countrymen recognised his merits and he became, in due course, a magistrate and eventually a Councillor in Geneva.

Among my uncle's effects I found the notebooks which I am sending to you. You will find that for a long time he maintained his resolve to record everything; consequently there are many pages which contain very little, I think, that would interest you. I have taken the liberty of marking the parts which may be worth your attention. I should confess to a particular interest here: I have followed in the footsteps of the admirable Mlle. Jurine, and have become something of a dissector and observer of nature myself.

Since you are interested in the reason why my uncle left M. Huber's service I have also marked some passages which are not strictly to do with their study of bees. There are details of daily life here which evoke the nature of the Huber household, details which might shed light on my uncle's decision to leave M. Huber's service after so many years. I believe that if you read these pages you will understand the reason, although you may not find it pertinent to your memoir.

I have also made occasional comments on what may seem remarkable to us at this forty-year distance. You will find some references to yourself as a very young man. I hope you will not find these objectionable – I cannot think you will, for they show the esteem that M. Huber had for you, even at such a young age. I know that you have repaid this esteem by naming a genus of beautiful trees from Brazil as *Huberia laurina*.

Please let me know if I may assist you further. My uncle always spoke of M. Huber with great fondness and I know that he had immense respect for your family and for your own work as a naturalist.

I look forward to reading your memoir in the *Revue Britannique*, and am at all times,

Your most humble and obedient servant,

Alise de Moivre

1785

14 June

When I left the village this morning I was still a peasant, despite my family's pretensions. When I returned late tonight it was as manservant to a gentleman of independent means. With my own room in a pleasant house and a salary that is modest but more than any wage I can earn here.

It was new moon and the sky was dark when I left. I could still make out some constellations: the plough, the archer, the bow, fading in the sky now. And then the sunrise was very clear, and the meadows glowed pink and gold. An hour or so, and five miles later, it was early morning and I was glad of the warmth in the coach. My fellow travellers were a farmer in a heavy woollen cape – even in June – and a young woman clucking after her chicks, which were travelling outside in wooden crates.

It seems a world away now, that day when Maman came back from meeting Ursula. The news was that a gentleman in the family she served had need of a manservant, someone honest and used to country ways, but not stupid. Ursula promised to mention my name. My mother returned glowing at having been abroad (although it was only to the next village where her old friend was visiting her family, but never mind, it was a great excursion). As she spoke of the position, her eyes were lively in a way I had almost forgotten, and I longed to obtain it, to keep the brightness there.

And for myself, I hoped with all my heart that it might be my honourable discharge from the village. That day I began to grow a beard, wanting to look older, weightier.

Monsieur Huber, the gentleman concerned, has an establishment at Pregny, in the countryside outside Geneva. His wife is soon to bear their second child and has not as much time to devote to his needs as formerly. I am to be his servant not only in the matter of bathing, and dressing and clothes, but also in the matter of books and papers. For he is a man of cultivated interests who will need help with his secretarial work. He has immense interest in the study of the natural world, observing the life of God's creatures. In this he particularly needs assistance, for he is stone blind.

15 *June*

I met him at his father's house, which was nearer to the centre of Geneva, so that I could return home the same day. I wasn't sure what to expect. I had a picture in my mind of a blind man on a street corner playing the fiddle but I knew it wouldn't be like that. In the event what struck me most was his way of talking as though he could still see. I suppose it's a habit of speech, for he was nineteen when he lost the last vestige of his sight and I believe he's thirty-five now.

A maid showed me into a finely proportioned room which seemed to me in every way perfect. There was comfortable furniture and fresh flowers, a large bookcase, pictures, a cabinet of curiosities, a harpsichord with sheets of music scattered on it. I've never been in such a room before. Even the pastor's house, which has always seemed well enough to me, paled in comparison. (I don't mean to belittle my past, but the impression of generosity, abundance, was overwhelming. If a room can be said to be generous.) I felt as though I'd dreamt of a room like this and now I saw it in the light of day.

M. Huber came into the room on his father's arm, but once through the doorway he found his own way to a chair. Always the same chair, I guessed, always the same number of steps and nothing in the way. He smiles readily, a young man's smile, as it might have been before he went blind. He's a big man with dark, wavy hair, a large brow and full lips. A noble face, I thought, but an air of gentleness as well. His father is quite a fidget, crossing and recrossing his legs, tapping his hand on his thigh for no apparent reason. The son, in (deliberate?) contrast, is calm and economical in his movements.

After the usual formalities and inquiries about my journey, Monsieur asked me which route I had taken from the coaching inn and I told him I'd walked along the rue du Rhone. (I'd taken careful note of the name so I could find my way back.)

'And did you see how the light falls through the linden trees, making a beautiful dappled shade?'

'Why, yes, sir,' I said, although in truth I hadn't been particularly aware of it, being too preoccupied with the interview that lay ahead. But I remembered that there were trees and it was sunny, so there must have been dappled shade.

He smiled. 'So from which direction did the shadow fall? From the left or from the right?'

I had no idea. I felt a hot prickle of shame beginning but I tried to think coolly. Rue du Rhone ran east-west. It was midday in June so the sun had to be in the south. I'd been walking east so the sun must have been on my right. 'It fell from the right, sir.'

'You saw that for yourself? Are you sure you remember noticing that?' He looked at me with his opaque eyes. (And I'll say 'looked' although I know he can't see.) There was a crinkling at the corners of his mouth which made me wonder if he was teasing me.

I knew my answer was correct, but I could tell he'd found me out. It didn't occur to me to do anything but come clean with him. 'No, sir, I'm sorry, it's not true that I noticed it. I worked it out just now.' I was afraid it would mean the end of my interview and my prospects. I'd thought of many questions he might ask me, but which direction the light came from was not one of them. I expected him to tell me – probably quite kindly, judging from his manner so far – that I had failed and the position of his manservant would not be mine.

Instead, he nodded slowly. 'Good. I prefer you to be honest. It's very important to me to have eyes about me that I can trust.'

I felt a great wave of relief and then a deep resolve to be entirely worthy of that trust. There's something honest and solid about him that makes me want to please him and earn his regard. Even in those first few minutes he taught me a lesson: to know the difference between what I can really see and what I think I should see, or expect to see, or want to see. I believe that I can learn from him as I learnt from Pastor Rigaud, but even more, for it will be in the outside world.

'My wife,' he was saying, 'I trust my wife's eyes completely. God knows I rely on them for most of my world. Without her, I – well, it doesn't bear thinking of and I count myself the most fortunate of men. But now she's a mother, and soon to be doubly so and it's time for our household to grow.'

His father had been looking for a chance to join the conversation and he seized his opportunity now, turning to me. 'Your mother's family are known to my sister-in-law, I believe?'

'Yes, sir. My grandmother was her wet nurse and an old friend of my family is in service to her now.' I gabbled this, not knowing how much they know of my family circumstances, and not wishing to say too much on the matter in case it should prejudice things.

'Splendid woman,' he said expansively, referring, I assumed, to his sister-in-law rather than her maid.

Monsieur said, 'My father read me the letter from your pastor. He speaks very highly of you.'

'That's kind of him. Pastor Rigaud is a good man.'

'It would be a poor thing if he weren't,' he said, and I didn't know what to make of his expression. I've only heard such views expressed by men in their cups.

'How old are you, Burnens?' he asked.

'Nineteen, sir.' I was embarrassed, knowing that was the age when he lost his sight. I felt absurdly privileged beside him.

'Ah, I remember being nineteen.' His voice was quite steady and he spoke lightly, even fondly, but I was seized with a great pity for him. At my age, now, the loss of my sight would feel unbearable to me but the man before me had borne it, and with dignity.

He paused for a time as though aware of my feeling. 'Do you realise we share the same name? We're both François. Our saint is the man who loved animals. Are you fond of animals, François Burnens?'

'Why, yes, sir, very much.' But then I worried about making a false impression. 'Although not as much as Saint Francis, I'm afraid.'

He laughed. 'And now I need to hear you read. Marie-Aimée reads so intelligently, with such understanding. Sit down.' He indicated a book on the small table next to his chair. I picked it up and sat on a chair opposite him. His father was to one side, watching quizzically. I wondered whether this position might involve serving two masters.

At first I was ill at ease sitting in such company but I tried not to show it and braced myself to match the wife I already imagined as formidable. The book was open at an account of the life of a great Dutch naturalist called Swammerdam. His name was unfamiliar to me and my voice trembled a little as I began reading. He had founded the true methods of scientific investigation, invented the microscope, contrived injections to ward off decay in specimens and was the first man to dissect bees. His discovery of ovaries determined that the 'king' bee, as it had always been regarded, was in fact a queen.

As I read on, his story enthralled me so much that I forgot my nervousness and read quickly and fluently, the better to enjoy it myself. Swammerdam made woodcuts and engravings so perfect that to this day they illustrate books on apiculture. But he lived in a turbulent, troubled Amsterdam and sorely missed what he called 'the sweet life of the country'. Worn out with his work he died at the age of forty-three. A century passed before his great *Biblia Naturae* was published in Leyden in 1737.

M. Huber gestured for me to stop. We said nothing. The account had stirred me: that a man could do so much with his life, even at such great cost.

Monsieur said, 'I see you're taken with our friend Swammerdam.'

'It seems to me like a perfect life, sir.'

'Though a short one.'

Not so short, I thought, remembering my father.

'You read very well,' he said, 'and that's important. I want to read many papers, journals, books. There has to be a good understanding of the meaning to read out loud, otherwise it's just painful to the ear. Where did you learn to read so well?'

'Pastor Rigaud, sir. He and my father were friends as young men. He took a particular interest in my education.'

'Ah, holy men can be holy. So you went to his house and he taught you and let you read his books?'

'Yes, sir, exactly.'

He smiled. 'I had a relative like that. We did alchemical experiments together. It was so absorbing I thought I could have spent my whole life on it.'

'Bertrand was an utter fool,' his father put in. 'Wasted all his time and money, never found a thing. Wasted your time too.'

'You didn't think so at the time,' his son said mildly.

'Well, I've learnt better over the years.'

Monsieur nodded, some private amusement on his face, and continued talking to me. 'And there were lectures at the university, and reading romances at night, by candlelight.' He stopped, sighing. 'And then suddenly there wasn't enough sight left to do it all. And then there wasn't enough sight to do any of it.'

He made a helpless gesture. 'But can you serve a blind man? I mean physically serve him? I'm so used to Marie-Aimée helping me. She'd show you what to do, of course. But can you – not dress him but place his clothes so he can easily find them and dress himself? And shave him, of course, I'm not a complete fool.'

I'd jumped up at the word 'serve': it reminded me why I was there. 'I'd do my best, sir. I believe I learn quickly and I'm very willing to work hard.'

'Good. There'll be plenty to do. I have some ideas . . .' His voice trailed off, his gaze – but of course there is no gaze – his eyes then, fixed on the light streaming through the windows as though the ideas were motes dancing in the sunshine. Then he roused himself. 'So. When will you begin at Pregny? It's Friday now and you'll have your arrangements to make. Will we find you on the coach a week from today?'

'Why, yes, sir, if I have the position.'

'Of course you have.' Smiling in mock bewilderment that I might have thought otherwise. I smiled back, wishing he could see my delight, surprised by how sad I was that he couldn't.

16 June

And so I've come back to the village to pack up my few belongings and make my farewells. With my sister newly married and me now assured of a permanent position – and how my poor mother wept and held me tight with joy when I told her – she can sell the cottage that was once our beloved home but has long been a burden and move into the almshouse where her wants will be met, if frugally. But now I can supplement that meagre fare from my earnings instead of seeing every hard-earned franc disappear to pay off my father's debts. I'm immensely relieved that she'll be among kind people, be warm and fed and cared for if she is ill. Even so, there's a wrench at leaving my earliest home, knowing that a new body will mould my haybed to a different shape.

But I'm full of the new life that I'll lead and not so sad to leave the old one behind. Village memories are long and I would always have been known as the son of Michel Burnens.

Like father, like son, was the whisper on my first and last visit to the inn. But now I have the chance to make my own mark, to be accepted, or not, on my own account. A modest farm, cows in the byre, were never going to be mine. Although I shall miss the meadows, their carpets of flowers, more than I can say, and the tinkling of cowbells and the pure, sweet air. And the milky skin, the full breasts of Heloise. But she was never going to be mine either.

17 June

When I visited the farm to bid farewell to Heloise, her father was affable to me for the first time, friendly now that I was going and was no longer a threat to his daughter's prospects. I was civil to him but no more.

'We shan't know you when you come back, living in Geneva, with fine folk.'

Do you imagine I would come back? I didn't say it.

Heloise herself was a different matter. We walked in the lane and she pulled a handkerchief from her bosom, beautifully embroidered with the initials F B in one corner.

'I made this a long time ago. And now I must make one for Joseph Picard.'

She wasn't crying but there was a sad resignation in her face that touched me deeply. Joseph is the son of the richest farmer hereabouts, and though we've had our scraps in the past I know that he's a decent, hardworking young man who can offer her far more in the way of wordly goods than I ever could. It wasn't a shock that he should be the one.

She braced herself and cocked her head. 'We've got plans to build the farm up.'

'I'm sure you'll do well together. And lots of children.'

'I hope so.'

We embraced and I had tears in my eyes, saying goodbye to this sweet-natured and beautiful young woman.

There were other goodbyes, not as heartfelt, to those who ignored us in our hard times. I have no regrets about leaving them.

It seems to me that in making my way in the world I can find my path well enough through a blind man's eyes. For although I'm a countryman I'm no fool, and I know that my master's vision, whatever it is, will condition my state. Better to serve a plain blind man than one blinded by corruption or the vanity of the world.

18 *June*

It was very hard to say farewell to the man who has given me my passport to a new life.

Pastor Rigaud was sitting at his desk, books open, pen in hand, and the familiar scene made my heart begin to ache. But this time instead of gesturing to the chair opposite he jumped up and embraced me.

'I've heard the news, François. I'm very pleased for you, my boy.'

'Thank you, Pastor.' I shuffled a bit, not knowing where to begin with my thanks. Sometimes, when there is intense feeling, words desert me.

'Sit down, sit down. We shall have cake and wine.'

He's the most moderate of men and that very moderation allows him to enjoy a glass of wine and thank the Lord for its goodness. But of course we had never drunk together before. It made me feel like a man.

'M. Huber said you spoke very well of me in your letter, Pastor. Thank you.'

'But it was no more than you deserve, François. You've worked hard in this room here, you've worked hard in the fields to support your mother and sister.'

'I want to thank you for all the lessons, all the time you've given me.'

'It was my pleasure. If you have a love of books, of learning, there's no greater joy than to pass it on to someone who's hungry for knowledge. It's almost a holy moment: we forget ourselves and explore the richness of the universe God has given us.'

'I enjoyed our lessons so much. Sometimes the work was difficult but it always seemed worth doing, even if I couldn't see the end of it.'

He laughed. 'The end of it, for the moment, is that you've learnt enough to find yourself a good position. There's never an end to it. You'll learn a great deal more. Don't forget, the

Huber family are distinguished for their intellect rather than their wealth. Marie Huber, your employer's aunt, spent years translating *The Spectator*. I don't have any copies myself to show you, I'm afraid.'

I doubt that he can afford to subscribe to it and I resolved that as soon as I have saved enough I will buy him a subscription. I looked at his study, with its books that I know so well now, and remembered when I was a young boy and it seemed to me the best room in the world. Although I've seen richer rooms now it doesn't make those walls any less precious to me. Something was forged there which I will have forever.

'I couldn't have had a life outside the village without your help. Unless it was the army.'

'And there were always good reasons against that.' He sighed but made no mention of my father. 'For a short while I thought you might be interested in the Church. Then I knew you wouldn't be.'

'When was that, Pastor?' The wine made me bold to ask. He's never spoken of this before and I had no idea he'd known of my interest or its abandonment.

He smiled drily. 'About the time you realised that your playmate Heloise had suddenly grown into a young woman.'

'Ah.'

He shrugged. 'The time's not right for you to marry. Joseph will make her a good husband.'

'I know, I know.'

He saw me to the door. 'There are no boys in the village at present who are interested in learning. I shall miss our lessons more than I can say.'

'And me, Pastor.'

'But you'll go on to learn new ones, and that's as it should be. That's why it was worth doing.'

We embraced. Halfway down the path I turned to wave a last farewell and caught the sadness in his eyes. God bless this good man.

20 *June*

It's the middle of the night. Or at least an hour before dawn on a midsummer morning. The cocks have begun to crow and the earliest birds are singing. I haven't slept yet.

Last Friday, walking back to the coaching inn, my position secured, and with such a man, I felt as though I walked on air. I noticed the way the afternoon sun fell – oh, how I noticed – and I saw a shop that sold paper. Charles Zwemmer and Sons. I had the tightly wrapped bundle of francs my mother had given me as the first half of my patrimony. If I'd had a fortune I could have spent it there: bound and unbound paper, pens, pencils, inks, penknives, blotting paper, scalpels, engraving tools. All the instruments of occupation that a man could ever need. And an intoxicating smell of new wood, turpentine, new paper. Gentlemen lingered over the goods, chatting to M. Zwemmer, and there was even a lady or two.

I wanted to stay all afternoon but I had to catch my coach home. I promised myself further visits when I was established in my new life.

In the meantime I made a grand gesture of commitment to my future by spending all my money on one bound notebook. I have never owned, or dreamed of owning, such a beautiful object. I tried to assume the air of a man for whom this was an everyday transaction, but my hands trembled as M. Zwemmer handed me the little parcel. I'm writing in it now. Every so often I have to stop and smell the richness of its blue calf cover. I feel as though for the first time in my life I have hold of something substantial.

Unlike the clothes my mother ordered for me from the travelling man. The suit is itchy and uncomfortable, but when I think of what it cost her to salvage even this much the discomfort is soon forgotten.

I want to record everything. Every word, every gesture, everything that I learn. That's impossible of course – but at least the best impression that I can manage, for I wish to lose nothing, waste nothing.

21 June

I was met off the coach by Jacques in a pony and cart. He's the Hubers' gardener and general man, stocky and ruddy-faced, but his eyes are shrewd. I was looking round in some confusion, finding it difficult to get my bearings in the hustle and bustle of a coaching inn and anxious not to lose sight of my wooden chest, which had been my father's.

He seized my arm. 'You'll be Burnens, then,' he said. I agreed, with relief.

'I didn't bring the trap – we needed provisions,' he said, a little belligerently, as though he were challenging me to find a cart below my dignity.

'I'm very grateful. It would have been a job carrying this all the way,' hoisting my box on to my shoulder.

'That's true enough,' he said, which seemed to establish some sort of equanimity. As we made our way through the busy streets of Geneva and out into the country he became more at ease and began to talk about his work. Growing vegetables seems to be his great joy in life. (He gave me some valuable tips about the cultivation of chard, but I won't write about them now for I'm fairly sure I'll hear them again.) He's married to Anna, the Hubers' cook.

He said, 'I do a lot for Monsieur. Mending things, and making things that he can't do himself because . . .' He let the sentence fall away and I was surprised that he couldn't bring himself to say the words. At the same time he gave me a sharp look and I realised that he was a loyal man, who might be suspicious of a newcomer. I didn't want him to think I was trespassing on his territory so I said something about not being good with my hands.

He seemed satisfied with this. 'They're good people. Although the wages aren't the best in the world, other things make up for it.'

'I count myself fortunate,' I said, which sounded stiff, but I truly meant it.

He nodded approvingly and we turned off the lane through a pair of crooked gates into a short drive. I had an impression of a substantial country house, not in the best of repair. In front of it was a disordered collection of clucking hens and ducks and geese being chased in a rather haphazard and ineffectual way by a young woman – Martha, the maid of all work, Jacques said. Now that I was more aware of how M. Huber 'saw' things I noticed particularly how the light fell, the geese running in and out of the shade under the trees, the maid now in bright light, now in dapple. A little boy was running behind her, waving his arms energetically and crying out, 'Follow me.' I had a lively impression of order and confusion at the same time.

Martha gave up chasing the birds and greeted us a little breathlessly, her cheeks pink and her curly hair in some disarray.

Jacques said, 'You'd better get them back before supper, young missy.'

She said willingly enough, 'Of course I will,' but as Jacques led the horse round to the side of the house he didn't see her raise her eyebrows and roll her eyes in exasperation. But she realised I'd seen her, and blushed a little. She led me into the kitchen, where she announced my name and Mme. Huber turned to face me.

It seems to me that the more her husband is blind, the more her eyes are sharp, and bright as a bird's. I'd thought of her as formidable from the way that everyone spoke of her, but I hadn't for a moment imagined the sheer prettiness that I saw now, the delicate features and pale, fine skin. It was a face that might be looked at again and again, finding some new beauty in it every time. Despite her advanced condition her frame was clearly slender and graceful. Her appearance made a deep impression but I lowered my eyes, for this was my mistress, and I couldn't be seen to feast on her face. Her beauty must be of no account to me. She is Monsieur's wife, the chatelaine of this house where I find myself.

She had been talking to a full-breasted woman in a starched white apron – Jacques' wife Anna, I assumed. Mme. Huber had the air of a lady absolutely confident in the smooth running of her household. Her evident maternal state gave it even more weight.

'François Burnens?' she said. 'Welcome to our home. François has spoken . . . but how strange that you both share the same first name.' We smiled, and I found a refuge in this because I couldn't think of anything to say.

She dispatched Martha to show me my room. It's in a spacious attic and I have it all to myself. It's furnished simply but robustly – and it has a table with drawers and a chair, where I'm sitting now, writing this. There is a candle-holder and a supply of candles in the cupboard so it seems that I can retire at night to a room well enough lit to enable me to read and write. Again I feel like a man that I can do this, no longer the boy in the haybed.

But the difficulty is that I could stay up all night now, writing every single new thing that happened today, but if I do that I will be of very little use to my employer tomorrow. And most of all I want to be of use. The more I see of this household the more I thank God for landing on my feet. I want everything to go well.

So finish for tonight.

23 June

Yesterday Mme. Huber showed me round Monsieur's dressing room and the linen cupboards. There were clean shirts and kerchiefs and hose, all neatly piled. The dirty clothes go in the wicker basket which Martha empties once a week. The household runs in an enlightened way, Madame says briskly, none of this nonsense of saving up the laundry for six months just to prove how much linen it has. Here, washing takes place every other Monday, and woe betide anyone who gets in the way. It's always cold meat for dinner that day.

The piles of clean, ironed, lavender-scented linen in the cupboards have an orderly, satisfying quality about them. She gave me clear instructions about how Monsieur likes his clothes to be laid out, so that he always knows which item will be where. Again there was a strong sense of orderliness.

'He's very particular,' she said, 'and so am I.'

I don't doubt it on her account. He seems to me particular about small things, the placing of objects and furniture, naturally enough, to avoid colliding with them. But when the butcher's boy was late with the meat today and consequently

SARA GEORGE

dinner was delayed, he didn't waste his time fretting over it, just asked me to carry on reading to him. (Although after half an hour he opened the glass face of the clock and delicately felt the hands. But on discovering the time he merely raised his eyebrows and shook his head a little.) We both heard Madame in the kitchen, making her feeling on the matter known to the unfortunate boy when he did arrive at last.

When Monsieur moves around I'm not sure when to guide him, when not. Madame does it very naturally, but then she's his wife, not a man, not a stranger to him.

In the morning, when the pitcher of hot water is brought up and poured into the bowl, he bathes himself, washing all his parts thoroughly. 'Face, armpits, privates, feet,' he intones. He can do all of this without assistance. I stand ready with towels. He dries himself and I help him dress by adjusting his collar and cravat and anything else for which a sighted man would use a mirror.

25 June

It's hard to put into words the effect he has on the household, being both its master and a blind man. I caught a glimpse of him this morning seated at the harpsichord, just beginning to play, with such pain on his face that I hardly dared look. For an hour the house rang with beautiful, sad melodies, and if any of us moving through the house caught another's eye we would look away. But when I saw him afterwards his face was serene, as though all his pain had been poured into the music. And everyone in the house breathed a sigh of relief.

I took some books that he'd requested into the drawing room and his wife was showing him a wooden spinning top that a friend had made for Pierre to distract him when the new baby is born. It was a beautiful object that must have taken many hours of work. This is a family which receives considerable objects of esteem – and already I feel myself part of it, and a more substantial person because of it.

Madame was sitting close beside him and with their fingers they traced out together the pattern of carving and she described the bright colours to him. I think she must be the perfect wife for a man in his condition, for she brings the world to him and makes it real. She gazed at him tenderly and it struck me that no mother ever looked at her children more fondly than Mme. Huber looked at her husband at that moment.

There's something about the sum of them together which is different from them apart. I begin to see it as three separate things: Monsieur, Madame, and the married couple. In each circumstance I find I behave a little differently. To him, as master, it's simple. To her, as mistress, there's something else, a feeling that as a sighted man I sometimes have to stand in for Monsieur, which makes me more than just a manservant. But the two of them together make their own world. They express their affection for each other quite openly in gestures and endearing words. It's a new picture of marriage to me. I've never imagined that a couple could behave so gracefully to one another. I'm as careful as I can be not to intrude.

27 *June*

When I shaved Monsieur for the first time I felt a little tremulous – after all, this is an intimate act to perform on another man. But when I'd assembled the bowl of hot water and the brush, soap, razor, and he was sitting with the towel round his neck, I realised that I knew perfectly well how to do it. I had a vivid memory of it, stroke by stroke.

When they brought my father's body home, Maria came in shortly afterwards. She was the one in the village who laid out the dead. They were waiting outside, with his body in the cart, wouldn't bring it inside because of the old superstition that you don't bring the body of a person who's been accidentally killed into an inhabited house. My mother walked out with a lantern and asked the men to bring him in. 'This is his home. Let him lie here.'

'He'd want to be clean-shaven,' Maria said. He hadn't shaved for a day or two. And she offered me the razor. 'Would you like to do it?'

I still couldn't believe this man was dead. I shook my head.

So she set to it herself, cradling his head against her breast as she made firm, smooth movements with the razor. 'He'd want to be looking his best.'

My mother sitting quietly, the occasional tear. My sister

sometimes weeping, sometimes looking blank. My own eyes dry. All of us knowing, and none of us saying, that he'd died because he was so drunk coming back from market that he'd had a foolish accident, losing the path, falling into the river.

And now I shave Monsieur Huber. I hold his head back against my body so that it rests securely and I know that the sweep of the razor is firm but secure.

I couldn't do it for my father but I can do it for him.

30 *June*

M. Huber suggested we walk to the hives. There's a path which runs beside the kitchen garden and through the orchard, marked by a rope at hand height, held by sturdy posts – Jacques' work. Every five feet or so there are knots in it so Monsieur can count them off and tell exactly where he is. I notice the trees have been pruned so that there are no branches sticking out where he might bump into them. Jacques' work again, I imagine, and I'm impressed by how much care he takes. We arrive at a warm clearing, partially shaded by trees, where six hives sit in sunlight. M. Huber tells me proudly that the household can produce more than enough honey for all its wants and plenty over as gifts for family and friends.

'But we only take a little from each hive,' he said. 'We never pillage one particular hive. That would discourage the bees so much that they'd abandon it. Bees only do that *in extremis*. Except when they swarm of course.'

He stood in the middle of the circle of hives in his loose light clothing, not moving when bees approached his face. One or two of them climbed over it. I became aware of sweating in my beard and then, it seemed to me, of something crawling in it. I stayed rigorously still, hardly breathing. It took all my self-control not to brush at my chin.

'I have a hat and veil you can use, but we're not here long enough to trouble today. And we're not opening the hives. But the reason we wear them is not so much to protect ourselves as to ensure the bees are not distressed by being caught in our hair. It's only when they're distressed that they sting. That's why you'll find very few bearded beekeepers.'

I wondered if he knew I had a beard. But more, I liked the way he thought about the bees. I liked his concern for the little creatures. In the sun it was very still and quiet, but for the humming. There were two old wooden chairs sunk into the ground unevenly but he was evidently familiar with the angle of the one he sat on. He gestured me to sit on the other.

Looking at the hives – I know he can't see – he said, 'They've all swarmed at least once, and the stronger ones twice. Don't you think a swarm is a strange thing, Burnens? Why do they abandon the honey it's been such an effort to produce?'

'I don't know, sir. I hadn't thought of it before.' The question of my beard, which had been preoccupying me, was suddenly unimportant.

'And then who leads the swarm out? Is it the old queen or a young one? Why would the old queen give up her colony to a usurper? Surely it must be the young queen, chased out by the old one. But I can't help feeling – and it's a strong feeling – that the bees wouldn't desert their old queen, their mother, after all, to follow a new one out. What do you think?' He cocked his head to one side, listening attentively.

I felt dazed by the stillness and heat. It was difficult to think clearly about his questions. 'I've seen swarms every summer in the trees at home but I always thought it was just something that bees did. I hadn't considered those things you said.'

'Things are very rarely "just" something,' he said, though in a tone of explanation, not reproof. 'I believe there's generally a reason and sometimes it might be possible to discover that reason. Which would be satisfying work. I'd greatly like to see a swarm forming inside the hive, to understand how it happens, how it comes about.' He paused. 'Although it might seem like an impossible observation to make.'

I knew that he didn't mean it was his blindness that made it impossible.

'We're all blind when it comes to what happens in the depths of the hive,' he said.

We walked back to the house, where his father was expected for supper. Monsieur's words had aroused my curiosity. I began to see that the swarming of bees, until now just part of the natural round to me, might be a fit subject for a man to study. And that through M. Huber, instead of being, so to speak, a peasant who cultivated bees, I might become a man who cultivated knowledge of bees.

I shaved off my beard this evening.

3 July

Monsieur is not a naturally clumsy man and Madame is very delicate and graceful in her movements, but the combination of his blindness and her advanced pregnancy means they sometimes bump into each other and when it happened for the third time today I saw a momentary flash of annoyance on her face. He never knew it though, because she spoke mildly, making a joke about being so big she didn't know her own limits. Monsieur smiled and gently stroked the bulge that her smock cannot pretend to conceal any longer. She covered his hand with her own, while her other cupped his cheek and she whispered endearments. He looked as contented as any man could ever be. And indeed why not?

There was a bit of a contretemps in the kitchen at supper. Martha had been looking mighty pleased with herself all day, playing the innocent when anybody asked her why, which clearly annoyed Anna (pursed lips). The reason became clear when Madame came into the kitchen and told us all that Martha was to become nursemaid to Pierre and the new baby. Her sister Sarah would join us within the week as the new maid of all work. Madame told Jacques to draw us all a glass of wine and left us to our supper.

'So it's nursemaid now, is it, Martha?' Jacques said. 'You'll be wanting us to call you Mademoiselle soon enough, I suppose.'

'Of course not, Jacques. I'm still Martha,' she said in a tone of voice that left plenty of room for the idea of being

Mademoiselle. She's inclined to airs and graces but she has a good heart and I understand very well her wanting to better herself.

'And how old is Sarah?' Anna asked. I have the impression she tries to keep Martha down. Not the easiest of tasks.

'Fourteen. She's a good girl but she'll have to be told everything.' She sighed: it was clear who would be doing the telling.

'And is the wet nurse living in? There's no point in you being nursemaid if the baby's not here.'

'Ah.' Martha glowed with triumph at possessing a most interesting and important piece of news. She leaned across the table and we all couldn't help but lean towards her across our dirty plates. 'There isn't going to be a wet nurse.'

'No wet nurse?'

'No.' She paused. 'Because Madame is going to feed the baby herself.'

'Well!' Anna cried, in a voice that said it wasn't well at all. Jacques put the piece of bread that was halfway to his mouth back on his plate and looked at it, bemused.

Anna clearly needed to say more. 'Well, I never.'

'Madame says it's not natural to give your baby to someone else to feed if you have plenty of food for it yourself.'

'What's natural got to do with it?' Anna exploded. 'Madame is a lady of standing. It's expected. People will think Monsieur can't provide for her, that she's forced to it.' (I think by 'people' she means her great friend and rival Catherine, who is cook in the big house in the village.)

Martha shrugged. 'Madame says it's quite the thing in England. Some of the very noblest ladies do it.'

'England!' (That pit of heathens and savages.)

'There's not a bottomless well of money, that's for sure,' Jacques said, trying to steer the conversation away from this embarrassing subject.

'A wet nurse doesn't cost that much,' Martha said loftily, as one who was on nursemaid's wages now. 'That's not why she decided.' She looked appealingly at Anna. 'She said it broke her heart being parted from Pierre when he was so little, and she won't have it again.'

'Even so. There's her husband to think of. Men like their wives to . . . to look after themselves. Men of a certain standing. They like . . .'

'Madame Huber doesn't have to worry that Monsieur has a roving eye,' Martha snapped.

'Pert,' Anna cried, looking ready to slap the younger woman.

'It's not for us to talk of such things,' Jacques said firmly. 'We should thank God we have our places and food in our bellies. Good food too.'

Martha mumbled a bit of an apology to Anna, who nodded. She and Jacques have never been blessed with children.

'Two weeks then,' Jacques said. 'Good. Everything is in place.'

Martha looked puzzled. 'How do you know that? The doctor isn't visiting until tomorrow.'

'Not that side of things,' he said hastily, 'my side. My sweet peas. As soon as we knew when the baby was due I planned when to sow the seeds so they'd be ready at the right time. I had to hold back, mind, and sow them later than usual. But in two weeks' time they'll be perfect.'

His love for his garden made us all feel easier with each other and we parted for the night on good terms. Or equable, at least.

8 *July*

Monsieur has been teaching me to distinguish between male and female bees. The females are smaller and lighter coloured and there are always many more of them flying out than males. At first I had some difficulty distinguishing them and I was reluctant to admit it but he simply said it's good to admit to this, now look harder. When I do, it doesn't take me long to be sure of my classification. I catch them as they fly out and turn them on to their backs, feeling them squirming, and sometimes they sting, which is painful. I examine them and arrange them in two piles: small females and larger males. I invite Madame to come and check my work. She sails out majestically, large with child, and looks the piles over carefully, then says, 'Quite correct,' and sails off again. For no good reason I feel resentful about having my work checked. After all, she's assisted Monsieur for many years, she has a considerable knowledge. Perhaps I fear I can do nothing for him that is independent of their intimacy. For all my wish to serve, to learn, it may come to nothing if we can't venture outside the boundaries they've set up for themselves — the loving boundaries, I must add.

'How many out?' he asks.

I must count the number per minute and keep a tally.

'What proportion of wax and honey is there on the comb?'

I must open the hive, smoking it gently, and inspect a comb. 'About seventy per cent of the comb made is filled with honey.'

'How accurate is that seventy per cent? Is it nearer sixty-five or seventy-five? Make rough measurements.'

I was fairly sure of my skills at estimating but I measured the comb. 'I can't be entirely accurate in my measurements, sir, but about sixty-eight per cent.'

'Good. Very close. Ask Marie-Aimée to come and confirm it.'

I asked her to come and check my measurements and she looked at the comb and agreed with my calculations.

Monsieur nodded in satisfaction and I sighed, very quietly.

He laid his hand on my shoulder. 'I must be sure of you, Burnens, and this is the only way. I know that I can trust my wife's judgement, so I have to measure you against that, for the moment. I can feel you straining at the leash, but you must satisfy these simple tests first.'

How did he know that was how I felt? I'm sure I've given no indication.

He 'looked' at me. 'I must have eyes about me that I can trust. And that means I must check your work, and check it again. And then I can trust you and we can get on with the work and I can have complete confidence in you.'

I know this is true and I grit my teeth and get on with it.

It's much harder for Madame, who has to give up her positions one by one. Assistant, helpmeet, chatelaine, all have to go as she approaches her time. She doesn't let any of them go easily. Some of them she'll regain with her strength, others are gone for good. We both know that I'm in occupation now of certain parts of a place that was once hers.

13 *July*

The baby was born at five o'clock this afternoon, a healthy girl, thank God. Madame is not one to scream, but there were occasional terrible groans. All through the day the midwife was upstairs with her, and the doctor for the last three hours. The rest of us were walking on tiptoe. I was reading to Monsieur about experiments in chemistry, both of us trying to concentrate on the meaning of the words, when there was a particularly heart-rending sound from upstairs and he shook his head in sympathy and jumped up and said we'd go and look at the bees. I believe we were both greatly relieved to be out of the house.

He led the way, along Jacques' string path, and I followed in his footsteps. It was early afternoon, drowsy, hot summer time. Another time we might have sat there and not said much, slow in the heat, but because of the great event in the house we felt we had to concentrate, had somehow to match Madame's labour with effort of our own.

'Let's look at the males today,' he said, 'see what part they play in it all.' We sat on our two crooked chairs, me with my notebook. 'So what do you see?'

This simple question is always difficult. What can I see? What should I be able to see? 'I see bees flying out from the hive. I see bees flying back, with pollen.'

'Bees flying out, bees flying back. Do you see any males among them? You're certain you can distinguish them?'

He knows perfectly well that I can. We both know the pains he's taken to ensure it. 'Yes, sir. The drones are much bigger, darker. I can't see any flying out, so far.'

'Let's observe for ten minutes.'

He closes his eyes and I know that he's trusting mine. The sun has moved so there's no shade and the sweat runs down my face. In the ninth minute a male flies out. 'One out,' I cry, and he smiles.

'One? They're energetic today. Where's he gone?'

'There's some red clover nearby.'

'It would have to be near, he wouldn't bother to go far.'

There is, not a cry from the house, we couldn't hear it this far away, but a feeling that there might be.

'He's finished now, he's flying back.'

'Oh, a good day's work. Can you catch him?'

'I can try, sir.' In truth I still have some difficulty overcoming my fear of holding a live bee. Whenever I've been stung, it's been very painful. What makes it possible for me to do it is my firm conviction that if he had sight M. Huber would undertake it himself. As he doesn't flinch from his blindness, so I mustn't flinch from a bee sting. The first time it happened I cried out in surprise but I think I'm alert enough now never to do that again. He knew at once what had happened and apologised that purely for his own interest he was exposing me to pain, but I said that I could bear a few stings well enough. And it's true, because the interest of the work is enormous and my new knowledge is great compensation. The second time I was stung I made no sound and I think I managed it well enough that he was unaware.

'The thing about studying bees,' he said, 'is that we must always accept the possibility of being stung, and in an odd way even welcome it, or the fear of it will overcome us.'

I nodded. I still find it hard to remember he can't see such gestures. But often I don't know what to say. His authority, our respective ages, his blindness, all make it difficult to find the right words. 'Every sting makes us stronger,' I blurted out.

'Very good,' he said. 'Although I fear that if we were to make serious work of it, yours would be the pain much more than mine.'

'It would be worth it.' I was carried away by some unexpected excitement.

'Perhaps.' He frowned. This is a man who has to think carefully about what is worth doing. His blindness means he must marshal his resources and use them wisely.

'So have you caught the male?'

'Yes, sir.'

'Now look carefully at the pollen sacs on his knees. How much pollen has he brought back for the hive?'

I was holding him carefully, turned over in such a way that he couldn't sting. 'Why, virtually none, sir. The sac on his left knee is completely empty and the one on his right has a minute trace.'

'So he was out for all of ten minutes. Fed himself and came back empty-handed. Let him back into the hive now. He'll eat some more from the comb then find himself the warmest place in the hive to sleep after his hard day. And meanwhile his sisters, the workers, are out hour after hour, flying for miles if need be, to bring home food. How they must hate him, the drone, the parasite.'

'But they seem to tolerate him well enough,' I ventured.

'Yes, indeed, they give him house room, put up with him being a burden on the hive. Reaumur saw that the female will die of bowel disease rather than sully the honeycomb but the male shits on it whenever he pleases. And the worker simply comes along and clears it up. Why?'

I find this difficult but I try to think clearly. 'The male must have a function. Some male animals have the function of protecting the young, bringing food.'

'But not the drones. As far as we can see they contribute nothing. They're a drain on the hive. But there must be a reason for them, there's always a reason in the end. It must be fecundation, surely?'

'Yes, sir,' I said, having no idea, wanting to be agreeable.

'But then why so many? In a well-managed hive of eighty

thousand bees we'll find five thousand drones. Surely it couldn't need that many to fecundate one queen? If they do. We don't even know that much yet.'

'She has a great number of eggs,' I tried, but he shook his head.

'Think of sheep, or cows. If you have a hundred sheep in a field, one or two rams will do the job perfectly well. I don't understand why there must be so many drones in a hive.'

'The female seems to have a harder time all round,' I said, thinking of what my mother sometimes had to bear from my father.

'What makes you say that?' he asked with mild curiosity, as though he half knew the answer already.

I couldn't say what I was thinking. I mumbled something about the pains of childbirth, which was true enough but not the whole story. And I could have kicked myself because the mention of childbirth caused a look of anguish to come over his face and we both pricked our ears towards the house. But there was no sound, no movement to disturb the heavy afternoon air.

He looked back to the hives. 'It seems you have an old head on young shoulders, François.'

It's the first time he's called me by my first name. It made me feel warm, but it also perturbed me a little, as though he'd seen some failure in my past which had driven me to this condition.

I said hastily, 'My father died when I was young, sir. I had to care for my mother and sister.'

'I'm sure you did that very well,' he said.

And then there was a cry from the house and we jumped up and I saw Martha running towards us, shouting and waving her arms wildly to beckon us.

'Give me your hand,' he cried, and I did, so he could run in my footsteps. And all through the orchard and along the kitchen garden I felt suddenly light and happy in a way that I hadn't since so long ago: those alpine walks with my father when I was a little boy, the fields succeeding each other in drifts of wild flowers, pink and yellow and blue, when walking up the track seemed like walking up the path to heaven.

16 *July*

The household wears a smile. Jacques' sweet peas have indeed been timed to perfection. It seems that it's been his interest for many years to cultivate these beautiful flowers. Every day, in the quiet time before supper, he makes his round of the plants, cutting out the poorer blooms before they can set seed and tying little screws of paper round the choice ones so none of the seed will be lost as it ripens. Pierre thinks this very comical and calls them the paper bag plants. Meanwhile the house is full of their delicate colours and sweet scent. Many friends have visited of course, but Madame declares privately that she doesn't value their florist's flowers nearly as much as the ones Jacques has laboured to produce. He basks in these kind words. It occurs to me (unkindly –

my peasant side) that this sentiment is worth a good few francs a year.

As he brought in another bunch today, Monsieur said to him, 'I know what these cost you, Jacques. Every flower you pick means less seed to sew next year. I know you'd rather see them on the plant than in a jug.'

'That's true, sir, but I'll make sure there's enough seed left.'

'Let me smell them. Beautiful.' His fingers ran delicately over the flowers. 'I see there's a deep frill on this one.'

'I'm very pleased with that one. The difficulty is that as the frill gets deeper each year so it seems to lose its scent. But there's a blue one here that's very nearly true blue now, hardly any pink in it at all. I'm pleased with that too.'

'You're a fortunate man to have such an interest. Colour, form, scent, to work on all three, so many possibilities.' His tone was a little wistful.

'Indeed I am, sir. I think my interest will see me out.' Jacques spoke robustly and Monsieur laughed.

'Not for a good while yet, I trust.'

21 *July*

Monsieur has not asked much of me lately. He spends his time adoring his little baby, leaving me plenty of time for reading and writing. He told me I could read any books I wished from his library, just to keep a note of the ones I took so he'd know where they were. I understood this as a wish to keep his dominion over his library, as any man would want to do. I tried to tell him what it meant to me to take these texts to my room but he just smiled and said the better read I was the better I could assist him. Every night without fail I kneel at my bed and thank God for my place here.

23 *July*

I think Madame finds the business of lying-in quite difficult, for she's someone who likes to be up and about. There's a constant stream of requests and orders from her room. The doctor has told her she must not concern herself with the household until her two weeks are up, but his words fall on deaf ears. Martha, as might have been expected, bustles everywhere with an air of great importance and refuses to dirty her hands with anything not directly concerned with the care of Madame or the baby. She does manage, however, to pour out a string of orders to little Sarah who is evidently in awe of her older sister and does her best, but she's only fourteen and doesn't have the strength or knowledge of a grown woman yet. Despite that, she's well aware that she's prettier than her sister, and in her young way she unsettles all the household.

Anna busies herself preparing light nourishing food for Madame and delicacies for the visitors, so the rest of us get what's going. I don't mind, I'm happy to eat bread and cheese and sausage at every meal till the cows come home. But there's a slight feeling of unease in the household that our mistress is present but incapacitated. It would be easier in a way if she were absent, because then different arrangements would be made. When I served Monsieur his dinner tonight he sighed and said he had no appetite to eat without Marie-Aimée to feed him. (She always cuts up his food herself.) I offered to take his food to her bedside but Martha said she was asleep and she needed it, poor thing (significant nod), feeding a baby was much harder work than Madame had imagined.

Sometimes I wonder how it would be different if M. Huber were not blind, so he had no direct need of me and I wasn't here. Then the household would consist of the Huber family, Jacques and Anna, Martha and Sarah. Would the household still need another male to balance things? And would that be a boy or a butler? It boils down to money. A butler would mean Jacques would be demoted, but a boy would mean he'd be promoted, as the oldest man.

I suppose I'm thinking about this because my own position is unclear – I spend more time than any of the others with M. Huber and he's the master of the house. I know that when we eat together I'll defer to Jacques because of his age and length of service, but I know also that Martha is not my equal, despite her closeness to Madame.

It's as though I'm assisting Monsieur in work which, although it doesn't bring in any money, yet gives the whole establishment a purpose, a seriousness of intention. Here is a living, thinking person, the blindness is incidental.

(Note: For the next several months my uncle describes how the household

gradually resumed its normal round as it became accustomed to the new arrival. There were one or two instances of Pierre poking at his little sister's eyes but these were dealt with gently. Martha learnt to take her new role as nursemaid responsibly, and not use it to make trouble among the other servants. My uncle continued to find great satisfaction in his new life and as he became more familiar with the family's routines and affections and values, so he became increasingly indispensable to M. Huber. Alise de Moivre.)

1786

30 January

For obvious reasons M. Huber does not walk out much when the ground is icy. We spend long afternoons beside the fire in the library. I can feel myself growing less hardy than when my life was spent walking the mountains day after day in all weathers. Where another man might spend the indoor months in reading, writing, painting, cataloguing his books, seeing to his business affairs, Monsieur finds himself with many long hours to fill.

But one thing he can do without sight is to rearrange his cabinet of curiosities and at these times Pierre loves to join him. The cabinet itself is a substantial ebony structure, well-crafted but plain, so that the objects inside attract the most attention. There are bronze medals, rock crystals of many colours, fossils, a medieval psalter, a wax tableau – the fisherman and his family – small stuffed animals and birds, alabaster reliefs, a mother-of-pearl crucifixion, nymphs and shepherds in tortoiseshell, a German limewood carving of Death as a drummer, an Italian silver lamp in the form of an ass with a man seated on it. The man can be tipped back to reveal the opening for the oil.

This one is Pierre's favourite. He enjoys tipping the man back, laughing at his indignity, but equally enjoying the way the man can be tipped down again so precisely, because the craftsmanship is perfect. Just as interesting, but more frightening, is the life-sized wax model of a diseased hand. Two of the fingers are curled so severely that they pierce the palm, and the remaining fingers look like claws.

'This is fourteenth century,' Monsieur says to Pierre. 'That means the thirteen hundreds. A very long time ago. It's called a votive offering. Someone with a bad hand would have paid to have this model made, and then they would have paid to put it in a chapel.'

'Did it make their hand better?'

'No, I don't think so. But perhaps it gave them hope, and if you have hope . . .'

There's something in the cabinet that Pierre's not allowed to touch because it's too delicate. It's a knife and fork whose blade and prongs are made of the finest, most delicately chased silver, and the handles are ivory, carved in the shape of Mars and Venus. Mars has a bow and its string is barely more than a hair's-breadth. Pierre accepts that he can't touch them, so he takes agin them.

'It's a bit stupid to make a knife and fork that you can't use.'

'Yes, I suppose it is. But sometimes people enjoy stupid things if they're very well done.'

There's a tension between them, something Monsieur can never bridge, at least not without great difficulty. I can see this and I can see that Pierre knows it. I feel . . . as though I don't want to betray anyone.

Monsieur can touch the knife and fork because his fingers are so light. He's learnt over the years to be soft and delicate in his touch – it would be all too easy to crush something fragile. He can't, of course, see if his son is touching them – something Pierre is well aware of. I can see his fingers itching, but in the end he simply edges the knife closer to the fork, a little mark.

But curiosities can't contain all of a man's attention and, when that palls, Monsieur's interest in science is a blessing to him, for it provides many hours of thoughtful occupation. Although there must come a time when he will have had his fill of theory and will want to be practising, and if his blindness prevents him he will be a frustrated man.

15 February

A bitter cold grey day. We've spent all afternoon by the fire studying the fecundation of the queen, something I associate with the heat of summer. I like the contrast between the icy dead world outside and Monsieur's burning interest inside. He has got – dare I say it – a bee in his bonnet on the question of how, when, where, and indeed if at all the queen is fecundated.

He told me which books to consult and I prepared a reading. That sounds presumptuous. What I mean is that I found the relevant pages and marked them with slips of paper so we could more easily move from one authority to another.

(Pastor Rigaud used to tell me, when I started a new piece of work, to 'make it your own'. He meant learn it so well that it's always yours. Then, it meant practising over and over. Now, it means keeping a record. So. Today is Sunday and I have leisure to write.)

There's great diversity of opinion about the queen's fecundation. The esteemed Charles Bonnet has included in his book extracts of everything that has been discovered up to this time. M. Bonnet is a friend of M. Jean Huber, but Monsieur wishes to deal with him on his own account.

According to M. Bonnet, Swammerdam observed bees assiduously but he never saw the mating of a drone with the queen and he was satisfied that mating was not necessary for the queen's fertility. What Swammerdam did notice was that sometimes the drones exhaled a very strong odour and he imagined that this 'aura seminalis' penetrated the body of the female to effect fecundation. This would also account for the large number of males in the hive – it would be necessary to have very many of them to ensure that the emanations were sufficiently intense and vigorous.

'He "imagines",' Monsieur said. 'He notices the odour. Good. But to claim that's the agent of fecundation is unjustified. Yes, it accounts for the number of males, but that doesn't prove the point. He didn't do the experiments, so it's mere conjecture.' He looked a little perplexed, as though surprised at himself for speaking so forcefully. 'Not that I have anything but the greatest respect for Swammerdam. His observations are heroic, an inspiration.'

I continued with the reading. M. Reaumur considered that the queen's fertility depended on actual mating, but his experiments did not provide conclusive proof of this. He confined a queen and some drones in a glass box but although she made some advances to the male he couldn't see any connection intimate enough to achieve fecundation.

'So nothing is proved either way, and the question's still open.'

The English naturalist Mr de Braw seemed to have made accurate observations and he believed that the eggs were fertilised externally after they'd been laid. He'd observed what seemed to be white liquid or, in effect, seminal fluid at the bottom of egg cells, and claimed that he'd seen males placing their posteriors into cells to deposit this liquid. He experimented by enclosing a queen with workers and a few drones. He saw the queen lay eggs which were apparently sprinkled by the drones and from which worms hatched. But when the queen was enclosed without a male she either didn't lay at all or only laid infertile eggs.

Monsieur nodded thoughtfully, tapping his pipe against the fireplace. 'Again, that would account for the large number of males needed. But there's a strong objection. From September to April there are no males in the hive, and yet the eggs the queen lays at that time are fertile. Are we to suppose that seminal fluid is needed at some times of year and not others?' He raised his eyebrows at me and I agreed it was unlikely.

16 *February*

Today we continued by reading about the Lusatian school, particularly Mr Hattorf, who thought the queen was fertile by herself, without the concourse of males. He based this opinion on an experiment where he confined a virgin queen without drones and after a few days he found eggs and worms.

Monsieur was pacing. 'How does he know that a small male didn't get in? Drones pass easily from one hive to another. What specific precautions did he take to ensure that no male could possibly get in? This is not a conclusive experiment.'

I was immersed in his argument but when he stopped speaking I had a vision of intelligent men, thinkers, groping their way to the truth, sometimes blindly. I suddenly thought that Monsieur's blindness was so well managed by his wife that he had to find another testing ground for himself and this searching for the truth was it. The impression was so strong that I must have started, made a sound.

'What is it?' he said.

'I was remembering, sir, being a boy and thinking that grown men knew all there was to know. As though everything which existed was understood. And now I find that something as simple as how a queen bee lays fertile eggs isn't understood at all. And I just think it's worth doing, finding out. But I never realised before how complicated it might be. I'm sorry, sir, this isn't to the point.' I added these last words because I'm not in the habit of revealing my inner thoughts to him. When all's said and done, I'm his servant, it's not fitting.

He laughed. 'But it's absolutely to the point. You've just described the birth of a natural historian. So . . .' He was pacing between the windows, low winter light catching his face every now and again. He thought as he walked. 'Four different ideas: it's an aura; it's copulation; it's post-fecundation; it's self-fecundation. Not one of them proved or disproved.'

Martha looked round the door to tell him that Madame was expecting to see him in the drawing room before supper.

'Yes, yes, I'm coming.' She left, and he said wryly, 'And whatever we may speculate about the bees' activity, there'll be honey on the table at suppertime.' He moved to the door himself, but there he stayed, as though he must complete the thoughts in his mind.

'This is a very simple question, it's straightforward, it's not complicated, it's just a matter of mechanics, but nobody knows what happens.' His face was animated. 'It must be possible to determine it by experiment. Or at least to know for certain how it doesn't happen.'

'François.' Marie-Aimée was calling.

'I'm coming, my dear.' He turned back to me. 'Imagine being the first to observe it, Burnens. This field is ready to be worked. It could be fruitful, a man could make his mark.' He nodded at me. I know this is something significant, that something really might come of it.

I have no idea which of the four naturalists might be right, if any. It could be that fecundation happens in a way that none of them has thought of yet. And now I want to know the answer, almost as keenly as M. Huber himself. He's right, it would be a wonderful thing to observe it, something worthy of a man.

30 May

Today M. Jean Huber brought the distinguished naturalist M. Charles Bonnet for dinner. Monsieur and Madame were on tenterhooks that everything should go well for their guest. I was in the kitchen a few days ago when Madame was discussing the menu with Anna who was shaking her head at the prospect of a roast joint.

'Why not?' Madame said sharply. 'The butcher's account is paid. We can afford a fine piece of meat.'

'He's an old gentleman, I believe, Madame.'

'In his sixties. Why?'

'It's the teeth, Madame. The old people still like the taste of meat but chewing a roast can be hard work for them. If I might suggest stewing something?'

'Stew? Surely we can do better than that?'

'As you wish, Madame.' (Slightly huffy voice.) 'Of course there's stew and there's rich, tender daube of beef. And that needs good quality meat. It's not cheap.'

In the end there was a pike tart, roast hare and the daube, which had M. Bonnet sighing with delight and eating a second and even a third portion. He declared he couldn't eat another morsel, but room was somehow found for the blancmanges that followed. There were many kind words for Anna, who took them graciously, as her due.

When they'd finished their meal Monsieur asked me to attend them in the library so that I could look out any books that came up in the course of conversation. The fire was lit in deference to M. Bonnet's age. The room smelt of wood smoke and beeswax polish and old books. And tobacco. Monsieur invited me to join them in a pipe but the truth is I haven't yet got the hang of it without coughing and making a fool of myself and I prefer to make my experiments with it in the privacy of my own room. Instead I concentrated on making myself useful and felt immense, unspoken pleasure at drinking coffee in the company of educated, scholarly men. A year ago I wouldn't have dared imagine such a thing.

They were talking about the fact that in July and August, when the last swarm has gone, the bees get rid of the drones. We can observe workers chasing males to the inner parts of the hive but we don't know what happens when they get there because there's no way of seeing into that darkness. At the same time many dead males are found outside the hive and it's evident that the females have stung them to death.

'It's true they sting a good number outside, but they've never been observed to sting them when they're on the comb,' M. Bonnet said, gesturing with his pipe. 'And they'll have their reasons for not stinging them inside the hive.'

'If the male dies on the comb they'll have the trouble of removing the bodies to keep the comb clean,' Monsieur said, gesturing with his own pipe, and it was uncannily similar to the way M. Bonnet did it. (He, too, is almost blind. Too much work with the microscope in his youth, it's said.) It was very apparent to me how much Monsieur wishes to be taken seriously by M. Bonnet. While his father, leaning back in his armchair, had the air of a man who might talk about this as well as anything else, Monsieur was sitting on the edge of his chair, listening carefully.

M. Bonnet went on, 'It must be that the bulk of them are herded down to the very bottom of the hive to die of starvation. The bodies wouldn't matter down there, it's a long way from the comb. It's reasonable enough on the workers' part: after the last swarm the hive must conserve its supplies because the season of nectar is over and winter lies ahead. The males contribute nothing and new ones will be born next year – let them starve to death so they can't pillage the stores.'

Monsieur nods enthusiastically. 'It's entirely reasonable, Monsieur. But it would be something to know it for sure, to see them in the depths.'

M. Bonnet smiled. 'Indeed, my friend, but none of us can look down that far into the hive. I fear the details will remain obscure.'

Monsieur nods, but I know that he longs to know what really goes on there at the bottom where, as M. Bonnet truly says, none of us can see. He can't question M. Bonnet's assertion that the males are starved to death because he has no evidence of it being otherwise, and M. Bonnet's eminence in the field, his exemplary work on greenflies thirty years ago and in general his prodigious knowledge of insects makes Monsieur very respectful of his opinion. But I must confess to a kind of contrariness because he seems so old to me, and the work he does now is more of editing and collating than making incisive experiments such as I know Monsieur wants to do, although he hasn't found the means yet.

After M. Bonnet's carriage had come to take him home, M. Jean Huber remained, in the way that family do, and came into the kitchen. He's a man who likes any sort of company. He was jovial – perhaps the wine from dinner – and showed off his party piece.

'Watch now, Burnens.' He has a good thick wedge of cheese and he holds it to the dog's mouth. 'Watch.' The dog, naturally enough, bites at the cheese while M. Huber turns it rapidly, and the dog bites whichever side is presented to him. I've never seen this before, but I'm aware from their comments that Anna and Jacques have, for they encourage the dog and then M. Huber flourishes the piece of cheese with 'Look, look!' and there is a perfect profile of Voltaire. Everyone applauds. At this point Monsieur, his son, comes in with an expression that says he's seen it all before and gently tells his father that his coach is waiting for him, and his father takes the point and makes his farewells.

15 June

We were at the hives.

'It was all very well sitting by the fire in February, speculating about fecundation, but now here we are and the bees are going about their business utterly indifferent to our interest and keeping their secrets well hidden.'

He makes as though to stamp on the ground in frustration but he restrains himself – it would alarm the bees. A swarm flew out at the end of May and settled in an apple tree in the orchard. I was fascinated to watch the tens of thousands of them clustered in a great dense mass. While I was marvelling at their sense of purpose, at the way they flew out together to this apparently predetermined spot and stayed there, albeit with great comings and goings of some individuals, he was pacing the ground with 'How? Why? Ten minutes ago the hive was full of bees going about their usual round. And now they've abandoned it, cast themselves upon the wilderness. How did that happen? What was it that made them all fly out at the same time? What's happened in the hive in the last twenty-four hours? It goads me to distraction not being able to see.'

His frustration is concentrated on the interior of the hive, on the one thing that's veiled for others as much as it is for him. Our coiled-straw skeps, as Jacques calls them, are made in the traditional round shape but with the addition of a cap on top. When I remove this I can see one or two inches into the hive but no more.

'Could we make a glass hive?' he wondered. 'Reaumur says Swammerdam couldn't possibly have done his observations without a glass hive, though he's left no word about how he made it. I've read that Aristotle made an observation hive, but the bees were indignant at his prying and smeared the glass with clay to cloud his view.'

I smiled at this but something more practical occurred to me. 'Did the Greeks have glass at that time?'

'Good question. I think not, although Pliny talks of a lantern-shaped hive made out of horn, which is transparent when it's shaved very thin. But a lantern only has small panes of glass, we still can't see into the depths.'

'I've been reading Reaumur, sir, and he says he made a hive completely of glass.'

'Yes, yes, I know, but look at the dimensions he gives – eighteen centimetres high and eleven centimetres square at the base. How can bees live their accustomed lives in a space that small? What could a man do who lived from his earliest days in a tiny confined space?'

'He'd never learn to run. Perhaps not even to walk.'

'Quite so. I'm certain that the most important thing, always, is to conduct experiments in circumstances as near natural as possible. The further the bees are from their natural way of life, the less we can trust the results. Yes, Reaumur saw them build comb in his hive but they won't do the things that only happen in the depths because there are no depths. The fecundation of the queen, for example. We know something must be going on between the queen and the males, but I don't believe that whatever it is, it could happen in a hive that small.'

20 *June*

We've read further in Reaumur and found that he'd made a different sort of observation hive: two sheets of glass within a wooden frame with space for a single comb between them, the whole thing about fifty centimetres high and sixty centimetres long. Monsieur considers this a much better proposition and has asked me to write down the measurements so we can make one ourselves.

2 *July*

Jacques has returned from buying supplies in town with the wood and the glass that I asked for. He stacks them carefully against the kitchen wall and asks where I would like them to be put. He speaks in an entirely neutral tone, as someone who doesn't regard the making of frames as in any way his province. This is a moment I've been dreading, for although it is not in itself a very complicated construction, my carpentry skills are unproven. I have seen Jacques grimace (and curse) when a pane of glass in a cold frame he was building broke during the work.

I said I'd take the materials into the workshop, but even as the words came out of my mouth I knew he'd take offence that I hadn't called it his workshop. It's a somewhat decrepit wooden outbuilding and Jacques is the only one who uses it. I felt half embarrassed at my own ungraciousness and half defiant because the workshop belongs to M. Huber's household and I might do work there for Monsieur without asking Jacques' permission. He turned away and began talking to Anna. I took the things into the workshop and looked at them for a while. I looked at the saws and drills and vices neatly stored and then went to the library and took another note of Reaumur's measurements – which were no different from when I first wrote them down – and confirmed my belief that he supplied no plan or picture of the finished piece.

I went back to the workshop and looked from the piece of paper with its measurements to the wood and the glass, wishing they would all join together in some alchemical way. But everything stayed just where it was and I knew there wasn't going to be any miraculous metamorphosis. I thought I could design it well enough but I wasn't sure about my skill at the joinery and I was very afraid of breaking the glass. At the same time I was desperate not to let Monsieur down for he was relying on me to produce this so that he could make his observations.

'Why, you haven't started yet,' Jacques said when he came in (just looking for something). He sounded only a little as though he was having a dig at me, more as though he was honestly surprised.

'I'm thinking, trying to figure the best way of doing it.'

'It's to be a hive, isn't it?'

'Yes, but we only have the measurements, no plan.'

He looked at the figures. 'Strange shaped hive, whatever.'

'It's just to observe the bees, it's not for honey.'

'So how is it supposed to look?'

I began to feel a stirring of relief, for he was no longer talking of it as something that was my business – and perhaps a bone of contention – but as something that had a life of its own, its own difficulties and solutions.

'There need to be two panes of glass fastened inside a wooden frame, mounted on a base so they're stable. Exit and entrance holes for the bees at the top. Then the bees build their comb in the middle and we can watch them from either side.'

Jacques nodded slowly and pulled out a stub of pencil and licked it and began drawing directly on the workbench. A design emerged, crude but sufficient. 'This sort of thing?'

I nodded.

He looked over at the materials. 'Are you sure you're not short on wood?'

'I wasn't sure how much to allow for . . . joints and things.' I was willing to eat any amount of humble pie if it took the responsibility from my shoulders.

'Well, here's a good piece for the base.' He picked up a rule and began to measure and mark the wood, referring to the figures as he went. 'I'm surprised you weren't up and at this yourself, seeing you seem to know so much about everything else.'

And I thought, but I'm learning that I know so little about

anything at all. I said, 'My father was away in the army for most of my life. I never had the chance to learn carpentry from him. I suppose that's how most people learn, from their fathers.'

He said, 'Some people are good with their hands. I mean they can work neatly, and they can take figures like these here and imagine what they would be like if they were turned into a table or chair or, come to think of it, an observation hive. I can do that, if I say it who shouldn't. Others are better at reading and writing. That may be your sort.'

I didn't say anything because I didn't want to interrupt his absorption in the task at hand. He was picking up various pieces of wood, turning them this way and that, considering them. And then he stopped, and just stood there, and said, 'But Monsieur Huber, you know, he could have done them both. He's got the mind to see how to make things, and he would have had the skill – he could paint, couldn't he, before . . . And he can still play music.'

'If he had his sight he'd be here doing this himself.'

Jacques nodded, satisfied. 'I'll have a look at it. See if I can give you a hand.' He moved to take up my position at the bench and the set of his shoulders indicated that far from just giving a hand, this was his undertaking now, and I was in the way. Greatly to my relief.

Martha appeared to say that Monsieur required my attendance. I found him wanting me to help him bathe and dress, for guests were expected for supper. As he picked up the bay rum to splash on his face I told him that Jacques was more capable than I was of making the hive and he shrugged and said it didn't matter who made it as long as it was done. I realised I'd been thinking the whole enterprise depended on me when it didn't at all.

9 July

Jacques proudly produced the new hive three days ago. Monsieur told me to place a piece of comb in the middle of it, at the top. We introduced a swarm and waited for it to build comb from this foundation. They always build a parallel comb, two cells deep and sharing a common base, and if they'd built down from the middle, as we intended, we would have been able to see them at work from both sides. Unfortunately, today I saw that the space between the two sheets of glass was too wide, enabling the bees to build two parallel combs so that their activity in between these combs was hidden from us. The whole point of it being an observation hive was lost.

Monsieur's face fell when I told him but he spoke levelly. 'That's a disappointment. We'll have to try again, making the gap smaller this time.'

I told Jacques and he's set to again, willingly enough.

20 *July*

The second hive is also unsatisfactory. This time the space was too narrow and instead of building one double comb in the middle, they've made a single celled comb at each side. Once again their working inside can't be observed. I can see Jacques' frustration that good workmanship isn't enough to answer the situation. Monsieur is frustrated too. 'But we must be patient. Rome wasn't built in a day. Perhaps it will be third time lucky, if you can bring yourself to make another one for me, Jacques.'

Jacques said of course he could and Monsieur has worked out a new set of measurements.

30 *July*

We've been working on the third observation hive, and yet again it has proved to be the wrong size and shape. This one was thinner than the first and wider than the second, but even so they built two combs and we couldn't see what was happening between them. I saw the look on Jacques' face when Monsieur pronounced this third experiment a failure. It was a hot, sultry day, which didn't help the atmosphere. I hastened to reassure him that it was nothing to do with his workmanship, which is perfect for our purposes, but purely a matter of the design, for which Monsieur and I must stand responsible. Monsieur heard my tone and reached for Jacques' arm.

'Dear Jacques, your craftsmanship is superb. If I've specified the wrong measurements that's none of your fault. I hope you'll still be able to help us on our next attempt.'

'Well, of course, sir, whatever you need.' He lays his hand on Monsieur's arm, gruff and clumsy.

'But I think we might postpone it until next year. It's nearly August now, too near the end of the season to make another try worthwhile. I'll think about it over the winter.'

I think we were all relieved that there will be no more disappointments this year.

'And now what we all need is a swim,' Monsieur said. 'Let's seize what pleasure we can from the day.'

It was a very welcome idea. I went to find Pierre and we made our way to the swimming hole, Pierre guiding his father over the rutted field, Jacques and I enjoying our unexpected break from work. The hole is about six feet deep and fifteen feet or so across. Willow trees hang over the edges. There was a distant rumble of thunder as we stripped off our clothes and plunged in.

Monsieur swims like a fish and we all splashed about and bumped into each other, and it made not a jot of difference his being blind. It began to rain, a light summer rain, as we were swimming, and there was something unexpected and exhilarating in having water underneath and rain on top, as though we had twice as much as we'd asked for. Then the rain stopped but the sky darkened ominously and we hauled ourselves out and pulled on our clothes and ran back to the house laughing and reached it just as the first enormous clap of thunder sounded and the sky was ripped apart by a jagged fork of lightning.

5 *August*

Mme. de Candolle has come to stay with Madame for a few days. Her son Augustin is considered delicate and it's true he has a much slighter frame than Pierre, who has inherited his father's robust build. Augustin is just a year younger than Pierre and the two boys are inseparable. When it comes to it, Augustin seems to have little trouble keeping up with Pierre in the matter of tree-climbing, chasing rabbits, and more often than I would have expected in boys of this age simply standing still or squatting down and observing: ants, bees, birds, beetles, spiders, ladybirds, whatever crosses their path.

Mme. de Candolle is the great-niece of a senior minister of Czar Peter. Although Madame's ancestry isn't quite as distinguished, nevertheless her father was a Councillor in Geneva, a man of eminence and wealth. They're distantly related, I believe. The two ladies walked arm in arm in the garden, talking of husbands and fathers and sons (from the fragment I overheard).

They came in, animated, and Madame introduced me as 'Monsieur Burnens, my husband's manservant, who's so much more than that'.

Madame said, 'Madame de Candolle was the only person to stand by me and attend my wedding when I married François.'

'You were my dear friend. Would I have abandoned you? I knew your father would relent in the end, but if he hadn't, our friendship would have been all the sweeter. These things are above price.'

They squeezed each other's arms and walked into the library to greet Monsieur, who rose from his seat with great joy.

I felt rather pleased with that 'so much more than a man-servant'. And the little detail she disclosed about her wedding, even though it wasn't in any way private, made me feel something of a confidant. She's my master's wife and I try not to think of her in any other way. She's a beautiful woman whose husband has not the eyes to see it, but I see it every day. Sometimes it seems as though she drops me a titbit to keep me content with my place. Dare I say it suits her to have me here?

10 *August*

'It's a shame about the observation hives,' M. Huber said. 'But at least now we know that Reaumur's measurements can't be accepted. We'll write to M. Bonnet and seek his advice.'

But I was still frustrated – I want to see the fecundation of the queen, the formation of the swarm, the death of the drones – and we've seen nothing, only that the dimensions of our observation hives are wrong.

Monsieur seemed to hear my unvoiced frustration. He settled down on his chair next to the hives, with his pipe.

'Did I ever tell you how it was that I came to the study of bees?'

'No, sir.'

'I think this must be why.' He paused, his head on one side as though listening for a dissenting voice; not hearing one, he continued. 'I was living in the country, near Paris, working on a farm. It was to help my recovery from consumption. My sight wasn't perfect.' He smiled. 'Though a great deal better than now. But still not very good. And this particular day – I was a young man – I was being foolish, running quite fast while I turned my head to shout out some funny remark to the maid who was giggling behind me. I wasn't looking where I was going. And the next thing I knew, I'd run into a swarm clustered on a branch. The branch hit my face and I heard the sound of the swarm, a huge hum, filling my ears.

'When I staggered away, there were bees all over me, in my ears, my hair, up my nose, in my shirt. They were stinging and I was scared. I could see well enough to know where the stream was and in only a few strides I could throw myself under the water – which took some doing, because it wasn't deep, this stream, no more than a foot or two at most. I held my breath as long as I could and when I came up for air I thought they'd all be gone but they weren't and in the end it took five plunges before I was rid of them.'

'It sounds like something which would make you want to stay away from bees, sir, for the rest of your life.'

'But that's the point, Burnens. It was a dreadful experience, but all the time that they were stinging me I felt pain, yes, but at a distance. Much stronger was the feeling of a great sense of calm. Above everything I knew that there was no personal business here, I'd blundered into them and they'd reacted quite naturally. They hadn't come looking to attack me until I disrupted their home. And when I did they reacted dispassionately. And whether I could see them or not was neither here nor there.

'That night was very painful, but I liked the idea that they were impartial. And when I came to read about them in a general way of reading about natural history, that experience seemed to fly in through the window and make the bees intensely interesting. And I saw what a wonderful, rich field of study it could be.'

'Did you begin your study then, sir?'

'No. I wasted – no, that's not true.' He sighed and shook his head. 'It took me a long time to accustom myself to being blind. I spent many, many hours railing against my fate – only to myself of course, not out loud. Marie-Aimée saw the truth of things. It was she who began the serious reading. She who inspired me to think I might do serious work.'

He smiled. His smile is quite mischievous sometimes, very attractive to a young woman I imagine. 'But early married life – there are very pleasurable distractions. And then Pierre was born and then we moved here. All these things take up a lot of time, which I don't regret, for they were the happiest of days. It wasn't until two years before you came that I began steady work on the bees. Before that it was anything and everything. And I don't regret that either, because it's all grist to the mill.'

He shrugged. 'So here we are. We haven't achieved much this year, but we can wait for next spring. The hives are here, the bees will still be here. And I have a lot more to understand before I can undertake my own work with confidence.'

He stood up, began pacing. 'We have to start from the base of all the knowledge there is up to this day. And then . . .' He opens his hands, as if to say, who knows what might happen, raises his eyebrows. I'm burning to know – and I marvel at his patience.

25 December

The house is decorated with holly and ivy. Martha has grown more serious with her responsibilities while Sarah seems to have grown overnight from a little girl to a very pretty young maid. Anna provides a sumptuous dinner for us. God keep us all.

(Note: And so the household continued its round. M. Huber studied his subject and determined that come what may he'd start practical experiments as soon as possible the next spring. Marie-Aimée continued, as always, to be an exemplary wife and mother. A. de M.)

1787

30 March

There's unrest in the cantons, particularly my own Vaud. I have some sympathy but I feel too much of an outcast already to support it. My mother makes no mention of it in her letters and neither do I, for I don't want to alarm her in any way. My sister writes that her husband is keen to be known as a republican. This doesn't surprise me, although from what I've seen of him I don't think his support would be a great asset to any cause. Sometimes the house here at Pregny seems like a wonderful refuge where we can engage in serious work while the world outside rages by. When we examine the life of the bees it's timeless, not affected by wars, treaties, alliances.

But there are always wars I suppose, and becoming a soldier would have been an obvious way for me to earn my passage out of the village. While my father was away, there were boyish dreams of valour and uniforms and horses, but I was older when he returned and the dreams soon turned to disillusion. I admired the Swiss Guard but I didn't want to be part of it. I wanted more chance to steer my own life.

I found a blackbird's nest last week and today I asked Pierre

if he'd like to come to see it. He's his father's son through
and through, and his eyes lit up. It surprised me though when
Madame said she'd like to come as well. Little Marie (who
is an enchanting two-year-old version of her mother) would
do perfectly well with Martha, she said, so we set out over
the fields to our neighbour's hedge, where I'd found the nest,
unusually low. It was a bright, cold spring day, an unforgiving
light, but Marie-Aimée's skin was translucent, perfect. We
picked our way along the path which was almost clear of
snow now. Pierre ran on ahead.

She kept her eyes on him and I knew she'd decided to come
on the walk because she had something to say – or had to say
something. We talked about the signs of spring and Easter
being late this year.

She looked up at the sky. 'The weather was just like this when
I had the letter from François telling me it was certain he would
go blind. It only took me a minute to read it. But then it took
months to be able to read it again. Every time I tried, my eyes
filled with tears and the words were too blurred.' She stopped
and wiped her fingers under her eyes. 'This east wind.'

I gave her my handkerchief, feeling very much the gentleman
that I could produce one at this moment. And feeling almost as
though I were standing in for Monsieur, doing what he would
have done. Except that he wouldn't have made that gesture,
because her voice was steady and a blind man couldn't have
seen the tears in her eyes.

I suddenly realised there could be a loneliness within their
intimacy.

Pierre looked back, concerned for her, for some reason, and she said, 'I'm all right, my dear, it's just the wind making my eyes water.'

I wondered why she was telling me these things.

She smiled. 'But that was the very worst time. It was never as bad again. Because once he was back in Geneva, it was always a question of dealing with the practical things. How much could he really see? How much assistance did he need? He made this great pretence, heroic really, that he could see, when I knew he was virtually blind. We'd walk arm in arm like any other couple, as though affection was all there was to it and there was no question of me guiding him as well. And then there was the day . . .'

She was silent and I couldn't think of a thing to say. I may imagine myself, handkerchief at the ready, to be a gentleman, but when I find myself tongue-tied at such a moment I know I'm still a peasant, not having easy phrases at my fingertips. I felt awkward and while I groped for words she braced herself against the wind and she was a strong figure when she spoke again.

'To tell the truth, as soon as he admitted he was blind, everything was much easier. We used to go for wonderful long walks. I'd go in front, holding one end of a stick, and he'd follow, holding the other end. It gave us much more freedom. I'd describe the wild flowers and he'd tell me their common names, and their botanical ones. The same with birds. He loved those things, and he'd always hear the bees humming and ask what blossom they were on. But my father was beside himself. I

was a well brought up girl. Every accomplishment lavished . . .
To throw myself away on a man who was blind. He couldn't
forgive it. But I didn't think it was a matter of forgiveness and
the more he opposed us, the more determined I was to stand
by François.'

She picked off the tip of some sticky willow and rubbed the
buds between her fingers, dropping them and looking at the
dark gum left on her fingertips. 'By then I was only three years
away from my majority. Once I was twenty-five we could marry
without my father's consent and the family couldn't prevent me
receiving my inheritance.'

'Monsieur was a fortunate man – I mean in your loyalty.'
I felt a fool, as though I'd suggested he was just after her
inheritance.

She didn't take it the wrong way, just smiled, her head on
one side. 'When we were first married, when we had all the
time in the world, I used to mould battlefields out of flour
and water paste and I'd put pins in for the different armies so
he could follow the action in the American war. Lexington,
Bunker-Hill, Quebec, Saratoga. Things like that. There's no
time for that any more. The children, the household.'

The things she was saying weren't unknown to me – they
were the stuff of family legend – but it was the first time
she'd talked to me on my own about them, and there was
an impression of a confidence passing between us.

We were nearly at the spot. I warned Pierre to walk quietly
so we wouldn't disturb the mother blackbird on her nest.
Despite that, she flew up in alarm and we peeped at four

eggs, mottled the colour of an early summer sky. We left very quickly, to give her time to get back before her eggs cooled.

But I felt how fragile her life was, and her eggs. She'd made a mistake, she'd made her nest too visible, so we could see it, and she was lucky that we were people, all of us, who would rather leave her to hatch her eggs than steal them to blow and display in a collection.

Monsieur was gently insistent about this last year when Pierre, naturally enough for a boy of eight, expressed an interest in collecting eggs.

'Let the birds breed,' he said. 'We already have drawers full of eggs of any bird to be found round here. Sometimes we have to interfere with a creature's conditions in order to study it, but not in this case. And always as little as possible. Remember, Pierre, the nearer they are to their natural instincts the more value your study will have.'

It was characteristic of Monsieur that he spoke of his son's study of nature as seriously as he spoke of his own. And it was characteristic of Pierre that without apparent resentment he shifted his interest to beetles.

We'd turned for home, the rutted path freezing crisp under our boots. Marie-Aimée said, as stiffly as she had been confidential before, 'I know how my husband regrets not being able to do this himself with his son.'

'Of course, Madame.' The confidentiality was over. All I could give was some sort of clumpen assurance that I was not trying to walk on her ground.

When we reach the house and go in through the back door, her cheeks are pink from the cold.

She says, 'Come, Pierre, and tell Papa what you've seen.' She takes off her cloak and bonnet with never a backward glance and they walk into the drawing room.

I'm unclear whether she's inviting my presence or rejecting it. Oddly, I have the impression that it's unclear to her as well.

As I enter the kitchen, Sarah is laying the table for our supper and there's no uncertainty here about the invitation. As always I'm polite and friendly, but no more than that. She's a lively, pretty girl, but impetuous and a flirt. There are many things I can imagine enjoying with her, but marriage isn't one of them. And given that, I keep my distance so that neither of us falls into temptation. But . . . dreams . . . As Jacques put it, when out of domestic earshot, 'She's seventeen now and ripe for the picking.' Indeed.

3 April

Monsieur and Madame are sitting opposite each other at the library table, away from the noise of the children, and she's reading out the household bills to him – which would be her responsibility even if her husband weren't blind. She says the amount of money for the amount of goods, and produces a total and he questions her addition at one point and she starts, and does the sum again, and thanks him for pointing out the error, which is quite substantial, otherwise she might have carried it over for months.

I must have mentioned something at supper about how amenable she seemed, for Anna said, 'But don't misunderstand her. This is a lady who stood out against her father for seven years after she'd determined to marry Monsieur, and he was very unkind to her. Then her family tried to get the marriage annulled and she withstood that. Then they tried to dispute her title to the lands and she saw them off again. But she's amenable to her husband of course, no wife could be more. And that's as it should be.' There was a faint trace of a wry smile on Jacques' face as his wife spoke these words but he made no comment.

I find myself wondering whether Madame's start when he pointed out her mistake had not been a little dissimulated, whether she deliberately makes mistakes to give her husband the chance to be – oh, an ordinary man.

Easter Sunday

The new observation hive is ready, one without glass. It's a handsome device with a dozen hinged leaves opening like a book so any single comb can be examined in the minutest detail. The weather is warm enough for quite a few bees to be active, feeding on lime tree blossom and cowslips. M. Huber is almost skittish, for he has been waiting many weeks to begin the work on fecundation. He's spent so many months considering the form his experiments should take and I've noted his objectives and the methods he proposes, everything neatly written out and filed in the library. He is insistent that a truthful, accurate record of experiments and observations is the only foundation on which to base conclusions. (And essential, of course, if his work is to be successful enough for him to present it with any confidence to his fellow natural historians.) It's also necessary that he has complete confidence in the accuracy of my observations. I believe that he has, although sometimes his questioning has felt like a terrier worrying at a rat.

The first experiment was to establish whether Swammerdam was right in conjecturing that the queen is fecundated by the emanation or *'aura seminalis'* of a large number of males. Accordingly, I confined the males from one hive in a box perforated with very small holes. I'm proud to write this, for it sounds controlled and competent, but the reality was many hours of smoking them and then passing them through water to pacify them so I could examine them closely enough to identify the males. There seemed to be no limit to their numbers but in the end I think it was about five hundred. And the first sting of the season – I'd forgotten how painful they are, but I know the pain will be less as the season progresses and I get used to them.

The holes in the box were small enough to allow the passage of the odour but not the male organ – assuming it is larger than a pin prick, which is reasonable, although no one has ever seen the penis yet. The box was placed in a hive containing only females. Had the queen then begun to lay fertile eggs

Swammerdam's hypothesis would have become a possibility, but as it was she remained barren. The experiment was repeated twice, each time with the same result, and today M. Huber was able to conclude that the odour of the drones is not sufficient in itself to impregnate her.

He was delighted with the result. 'If we know for certain what's not true, it narrows our search for what is true.'

I agreed of course, though it seemed to me that we were as far away as ever from knowing how it actually happened.

'So that's Swammerdam refuted,' he said. 'Time to move on to Monsieur Reaumur.'

His words were mild enough but in his tone I recognised the feeling I had when I was fourteen and knew that I had to fight Joseph Picard if I were ever to hold my head up in the village again. Not so much a question of picking fights as having to measure up, in my case long ago with fists, in M. Huber's case by the utmost rigour of method and observation.

1 May

Reaumur thought that fecundation was the result of mating. Many times in the last few weeks we've repeated his experiment of putting males in a glass box with a virgin queen and I've seen her make advances to them and there appeared to be very short unions.

'Long enough for fecundation?' M. Huber asked.

'I'm not sure, sir.'

'Think about it, man. From what you know of such things, does it look likely that it's a sufficient conjunction to fertilise her?'

My knowledge is not great in this matter. My experience with Heloise, though deeply pleasurable, was very limited – but I have imagination. 'I think probably not, sir. It's very momentary. It doesn't seem . . . serious enough.'

He nodded. 'That sounds like a fair judgement.' We left it there.

15 May

We were at the hives, just generally observing, nothing in particular. He sat in the shade. I sat in the sun so I could watch more directly the comings and goings.

'Momentary conjunctions,' he said, smiling drily, and I pricked up my ears. I'm not any more the very young man I was when I first came to him and he acknowledges that now.

He stretched his legs out in front of him. 'There was a time – when I was labouring on the farm at Stein. There was a countrywoman – sweet Marguerite.' He savoured her name for a moment and looking at him I saw the shy, charming smile of the young man, still able to see.

'A year in the country to build up my strength.' He closed his eyes. 'She was a young married woman, very pretty, already had a child and her husband had just left to work in Paris for three months. He was a stonemason, very skilled. There was a haystack, a brief conjunction.' He paused and smiled again, in recollection. 'Well, two or three. Afterwards she was pregnant, but it could have been her husband's. He made a good living. He was a good provider and she loved him. She swore she was certain the baby was his. I was sixteen; my heart was already given to Marie-Aimée. I didn't argue.'

'I don't think I would have done either.' I felt worldly, expanded by this confidence.

'That's of course the great advantage of a married woman or, even better, one who's both married and pregnant.' This idea seemed rather a calculating one. I was disappointed in him.

'Take for example,' he went on (and suddenly I didn't want to listen), 'someone like Sarah. I have the impression from her voice, her bounciness, that she's a nubile young woman.'

I said nothing but my heart was pounding.

He went on relentlessly, 'But for Sarah it would be a disaster to fall pregnant. And possibly for the young man who impregnated her as well.'

'Yes, sir, of course it would.'

'And speaking of such things, let's confine the queen which, according to Reaumur's theory, appears to have had union, and see what happens.'

I attended to this task with relief.

15 June

Over the course of a month this queen has not laid a single egg, so Monsieur thinks it's safe to assume that momentary union with a male does not produce fecundation.

This left us with Mr de Braw's theory that the eggs are fertilised externally after laying. His observations were precise. He saw a whiteish liquid that looked like seminal fluid in the base of some cells. He further observed males putting their posteriors into cells, apparently depositing their masculine liquid in them. We've tried to reproduce his experiments. Today I pulled out cells with eggs and I looked at them in the sunlight and it seemed there was liquid in them, in fact I was sure of it, and so was Monsieur when I described it to him.

'It's not what I thought.' He's perplexed, pacing. 'And it still doesn't answer the question of how the eggs are fertile when there are no males in autumn. But if Mr de Braw has seen it, and so have we, it makes for a strong argument.'

20 June

Monsieur decided a few days ago that the argument against de Braw's theory was too strong. 'No males in autumn but fertile eggs in the hive. He can't be right. Dissect the cells. See what's really there.'

When I did, it became apparent that what I had actually

seen was the remnant of an old cocoon. There was no liquid; it was a trick of the light. I felt sick in my stomach because I'd believed that I'd seen it, and in believing that, I'd taken us up a wrong path, wasting time, and casting doubt on my ability to observe accurately.

Monsieur was unperturbed. 'You described what you saw, but we both chose to give it the wrong meaning. We assumed it was seminal fluid when there was no conclusive proof that it was. Nature has justly reprimanded us. We've learnt to assume nothing. That's a good lesson.'

'Yes, sir.'

'Let's not forget the law of Occam's razor: nothing can be presumed which isn't absolutely necessary. Let's shave away anything that relies on conjecture. Let's confine ourselves to what we can truly observe.'

But to be quite sure, we have enclosed a queen in a hive where we knew there were no males (because I had removed each one by hand) and made the entrance so small that no male could get in. The queen laid fertile eggs, proving that they do not need to be sprinkled with seminal fluid from the males to be fertile.

'And what has de Braw not made sure of?' M. Huber asked today.

'That there were definitely no males present?'

'Yes, his experiment wasn't rigorous enough to exclude that. But there's more to it than that. Go further. He didn't make sure that they were virgin queens. How did he know that they hadn't been fecundated already? He sees a queen in a hive with males, he sees the males sprinkle their liquid, he makes an assumption. But he doesn't consider the possibility that she was impregnated already by some other means. It's Occam's razor again.'

24 June

Monsieur was left with only one more theory to examine: M. Hattorf's, who claims that the queen is self-fertile. In his experiment he excluded all males from a hive but still the queen laid eggs from which worms hatched, so he conluded she must be fertile by herself. We repeated his experiment and found that our queen also laid fertile eggs. But to conclude that the queen is self-fertile it's necessary to make the experiment very exact, ensuring there is no possibility whatever of any drones being present. So I've checked our experimental hive by passing every bee through water, immobilising them enough to examine them, and have found that in fact there were four small drones present (although whether they were big enough to effect fecundation was open to question). But Hattorf had failed to do this.

I placed a virgin queen in a hive from which all males had certainly been excluded (without doubt – my effort, my stings) and she remained sterile. So M. Huber can tentatively conclude that a queen separated from all commerce with males remains infertile. But the results were still inconclusive: Hattorf's work, which was good, careful work, showed that sometimes the queen was fertile, sometimes sterile, and there seemed no way to reach a definite conclusion.

'I don't see how we can go any further,' he said today, and my heart sank. 'Everything is so inconsistent, we can't draw conclusions. All this work, so many natural historians concerned with it. There must be something being overlooked.'

At this moment Sarah came to call us for dinner, smiling in her pretty way. He heard her voice and suddenly a great smile broke out on his face. 'Ah, Sarah,' he said. Then he turned to me. 'What we've overlooked all this time, the key to everything, is whether the queens can be guaranteed virgin or not.'

Sarah gave a little start as she left the room.

30 *June*

We've removed all the reigning queens from our hives and substituted virgins, observed since birth and known to have had no concourse with males. Then we divided the hives into two sorts: in the first, we removed all the males and made the entrance large enough for the workers to fly in and out as usual but too small for males to enter; in the second, we made sure there were many males, and even added more, but once again we made the entrance so small that they couldn't get out. So we had two sets of hives with virgin queens: one with no males, and one with males of all ages. We followed them carefully and found that in all the hives, the virgin queens remained sterile.

'And from this we can conclude that queens remain infertile

even when surrounded by a seraglio of males, when confined inside the hive.'

M. Huber was slumped at the library table. He leaned back in his chair and ran his hands through his hair and it happened that the sun broke through clouds and his face entered a shaft of sunlight from the window and he turned his eyes towards it and luxuriated for a few moments in the warmth, while a smile began to break over his face.

'It's the haystack,' he said, smiling broadly now. 'Where do you go for copulation if you live in quarters with no privacy? You go outside.'

Until now no naturalist has ever considered the idea that fecundation occurs outside the hive: it confounds our notion that this ultimate mystery must occur within its darkest recesses. But Monsieur has done the experiments to show this can't be the case. I know his guess is right. A cloud is moving away and light floods across the meadow.

'We've tried every way there is inside the hive. It's not an aura, it's not a momentary conjunction, she's not fertile of herself, it's not an external fecundation. It must happen outside, in the air. It's the only possibility left. It's got to be.'

His voice was surging with excitement. I don't know how long he'd been nurturing the idea but at last he was free to voice it. I thought it was a beautiful idea, a rich, fruitful idea. And brave, arguing against naturalists he deeply respects. I want to commit myself to proving it true.

'How will you prove it, sir?'

'Good man.' He laughed. 'Straight to the business.'

2 July

It's in all of my mind. I write of it as it happened.

It is late morning, eleven o'clock. I've chilled my arms with a long dousing of cold water to numb them against the pain of stings. Monsieur needs no guidance to the hives for the path is etched into his boots and the ground is dry and firm after long weeks of sunshine. We arrive in the clearing and there is an immense hum.

'They're busy today, I see,' he says.

'They're stocking up. There could be another swarm in a few days.'

He finds his chair with no difficulty and I take up my own position within easy arm's reach of the alighting board in front of the observation hive that holds the virgin queen.

We sit quietly, sweating gently as the heat of the day increases. It's hot enough for even the laziest drone to consider leaving the comfort of the hive for the vagaries of the outside world. There is not the smallest breeze to deter them, the air is so still they can fly with the minimum of effort. A warm hour. If the drones are going to fly out, it will be now. So it's natural to think the virgin queen will appear at the same time if Monsieur is right and she needs to fly out to be fecundated. She's five days old, fit for it. There's busy activity near the entrance, all of them workers.

'Here we go. Three males out, five, twelve, thirty, oh fifty, must be a hundred. More now.' This must be the time. 'Oh, here she comes.' The queen at last.

'Eleven and twenty?' he guesses. I bring my watch up to my field of vision so that my view of the queen is uninterrupted.

'Twenty-two. She looks healthy. Good colour. She's not flying yet, she's promenading on the alighting board. Brushing her belly with her back legs.'

'How do the others react to her? Males, workers?'

'Nothing. No reaction.' This is the first time she has left the hive. She walks around outside as though learning the dimensions of her home. Then she flies a few feet away and returns to take cognisance again. None of the bees around takes any notice of her. I describe these details.

'Memorising her home so she can get back again,' he says.

'Now she's flying away again. Oh, so high.'

We both stand up and M. Huber faces the sun, a point that we always call south, regardless of its actual position and I call out, 'North-northwest.' We both turn to her direction as she flies up making circles in the air, twelve, fifteen feet, then higher than I can see. I watch her like a hawk but she's gone, beyond my eyesight. We move back to the hive and I stop up the entrance so it's too small for her to return and enter unobserved. We sit very still.

'It's all up to nature now,' he says. 'The queen depends on it for the fecundation, which will allow her to fulfil her purpose in life. And I'm dependent on it for the proof of my conjecture. Nothing more we can do. Let's sit here, then. We've cast our bread upon the waters.'

The Beekeeper's Pupil

We sit in the sun. I have a feeling of being involved in something immense – something beyond what we can write up in our observations.

Seven minutes later she's back and I seize her at once, telling her, as always, that there's nothing personal about the indignity. I examine her with the magnifying glass, turning away so the sun's rays can't burn her little body. She's in no different shape from when she flew out. I feel a deep disappointment. 'Nothing at all, I'm afraid. Not the smallest suggestion of any union.'

'Let her back into the hive. Don't worry, it proves nothing either way. All it means is that she didn't get fecundated on this particular flight. Let her back into the hive to rest awhile. She knows the deed still has to be done.'

We sit quietly in the companionable way of two men not needing to talk, contemplating the natural world. But I realise how much of my mind is taken up by simple looking – at the dappled light on the ground, at the bees on the lavender bush, its spiky grey leaves and blue flowers. There's such calm pleasure in it, a sense of marvel in the commonplace of sky, earth, tree. Troubling thoughts pale into the distance.

To have to do without this comfort, this refreshment, to be a vigorous man of thirty-seven sitting in darkness . . . He makes no notice of his loss. I see a preternatural patience, I know that it's been acquired painfully over the years. Its effect is that he can sit quite still at such a moment. I want him to have the reward of being right.

We have no idea what the queen is doing inside the hive, but fifteen minutes later she reappears. Again she brushes herself on the alighting board, takes off and comes back very shortly as though to learn her way perfectly. And then she's off. She circles higher and higher, far higher than we've ever seen bees fly before. I stop up the entrance again and wish every male from every hive after her, all the thousands from every hive in the vicinity, to fly that high, that fast.

'Everything rests on the consequences of this flight,' M. Huber says. 'Strange that the one serious piece of work my father has done is on flight. Albeit birds of prey.'

There is nothing I can say to this. I remark the moment when the seven minutes of her previous flight have passed. There is no sign of her returning. We sit waiting, hearing the buzz of insects all around, the distant sound of girls laughing as they hang out the washing, a cowbell ringing to call servants to dinner. 'How does he grab hold of her if it happens in flight? How can he keep his penis in when they're both flying? A strong pair of thighs would help. Just like men and women.'

'A very strong pair if they're flying at height when it happens,' I say.

When twenty minutes have elapsed since her departure I begin to worry that she must have lost her bearings. Clearly she must have flown much further this time.

'But there's no breeze to blow her off track,' Monsieur says. 'She learnt the hive's location the first time, there's no reason she shouldn't find it again.'

After twenty-five minutes he begins to fear that she might have been eaten by a bird – a small bird of prey, perhaps?

At twenty-seven minutes she returns – I grasp her and shout

out, and Monsieur jumps to his feet and I see a sudden rush of tears in his eyes and he cries out, 'What? What can you see?'

'She's very different. Her posterior filled with a whiteish substance, thick and quite hard.' I examine her more closely. 'Her vulva's partly open, filled with the same matter.'

'What does it look like?'

'Identical in colour and appearance to seminal fluid, coagulated.'

'Done it.' He breathed out in a great sigh. 'We're seeing something no one's seen before. What a day, what a day. God bless your vision, Burnens.'

'Mine is only the sight, sir, yours is the vision.'

But I exulted in our success.

We walked back to the house so lightly, great smiles breaking out all the time. 'It's been satisfying to disprove the theories I suspected were wrong,' he said, 'but as nothing to finding my own theory is right.'

Marie-Aimée and Pierre knew enough of his work to join in the celebration and the house rang to Monsieur's playing on the harpsichord, joyfully singing his favourite songs. In the garden Pierre played on his penny whistle, equally joyfully, though less tunefully. I smiled to myself and settled, with the greatest contentment, to writing up our experiment.

Marie-Aimée passed by and there was an intake of breath as she saw my work. I said nothing, just continued writing.

I suspect – more than that, I know – that there are some situations where she welcomes my presence and there are others where she doesn't.

She said, 'Ah, this is what we were working towards. I wish I'd been able to carry on for longer. But you've done it, Burnens. Well done, well done.'

It was spoken in the tone of a gracious loser. But underneath there was an intimation of a battle that wasn't over yet.

4 July

Of course we needed a stronger proof that this substance with which the queen was impregnated was really the fecundating agent. Accordingly we'd confined her to the hive on her return and today I found her belly perceptibly swollen, and a hundred fertile eggs laid in worker cells. It was no surprise, but it was a deep, deep satisfaction.

6 July

We can now account for the great number of males in the hive – if it's necessary for the queen to fly out for fecundation, then there must be enough males in the hive for her to have the chance of meeting one. If there were only one or two drones in the hive the chance of them emerging at the same time as the queen would be much less, and therefore many queens would remain sterile.

10 July

It's been a good season for the bees – warm, still and dry. Our best hives have swarmed three times and even the weaker hives have managed one. Now that the swarms have finished, Monsieur is determined to find out what exactly happens to the males. That they die in great numbers at this time is beyond dispute, but the manner of their death is not known, despite Reaumur's talk of a horrible slaughter, and Bonnet's belief that they are imprisoned and starved to death, and the fact that drones are stung to death by workers outside the hive. But all we have seen inside the hive is workers driving the males away, down to the bottom.

So to find out what happens in the depths, M. Huber has decided we should have a glass table on which to place the hives and I should lie underneath and observe what happens at the very bottom of the hive, where we could never see before.

15 July

Jacques has constructed glass tables and we've placed six hives on them, well stocked. I've been lying underneath them, waiting, sometimes falling asleep in the soporific heat. But today, on the third day of observation, I saw the workers in all six hives massacre the drones at exactly the same hour (eleven o'clock) and in the same way. The glazed table was covered with highly excited female workers in the depth of the hive. As the drones were herded down to the bottom they were seized, by the antennae or the legs or the wings, and dragged about so savagely that parts of their bodies were torn off. We might say they were quartered. Then the females pierced them with their stings in the lethal area between the rings of their belly. The moment when they were stung was the moment of their death; they stretched out what remained of their wings and expired. But as though the workers did not consider them dead enough they would strike them again and again, piercing so deeply that they had trouble withdrawing their stings, and would have to twist themselves around violently in order to escape.

'So much for the drones being quietly starved to death,' Monsieur said. 'It never seemed to fit with the workers' nature. If they're going to do something they do it with the utmost dedication, though I hadn't imagined quite such ferocity. But what a beautiful observation. We can describe exactly what we've seen and there's no uncertainty about its meaning. And no one else has ever observed it before.' He said this with surprise.

'No one else has thought to look, sir.'

'Indeed. Seek and ye shall find. Thank God for your eyes, Burnens.'

16 July

Today I saw the massacre repeated furiously with drones from other hives who had sought refuge in ours from the massacre occurring in their own. I also saw the females tear the few remaining male larvae from their cells – they sucked all the fluid from their abdomens and then dropped them outside the hive.

25 July

In the hives that have already swarmed twice there are no males left at all. M. Huber says, 'It's clear that nature has charged the workers with killing males at certain times of the year. But how does it incite their fury? How do the workers know the moment?'

It happens that, for different purposes, we have two hives with no queens, and one with an infertile queen, and I've noticed that in these hives no massacre occurred, indeed the drones were well tolerated and fed. I ventured to point this out to Monsieur.

'Excellent,' he said. 'Ah, Burnens, you're no longer a servant faithfully following instructions, you're an assistant who can think on his own account. Where would I be without you?'

He rubbed his hands in delight. 'So we can conjecture that the hive only massacres males when it has a fertile queen in place, when it has already swarmed and is well supplied for the winter. But if a hive needs a fecundated queen they'll retain the males, whatever the cost in food consumed.'

He's pacing now, as he always does when he's thinking. 'I'm very tempted to refer to a spirit of the hive. Individually, they can't possibly know, but collectively they're more than their sum, and that "more" is where their intelligence lies.' He waves a hand. 'But that's just conjecture – let's simply record the observations, that's what I'll be judged on.'

9 September

We can be sure of our observations of the massacre of the males. But we're still left with the failure of our attempts to observe fecundation directly. I've watched the queen soar time and time again, but whatever happens is always too far away.

We also have to acknowledge the failure of our attempts artificially to inseminate a virgin queen with some of the male liquid on the end of a pencil hair brush. (We both knew this wouldn't work but M. Bonnet had suggested it and M. Huber felt honour bound to respect his suggestion.)

We have to jump through every hoop. We have to go up every cul-de-sac. So that we can say we've tried it and we know that's not the answer. We have to examine every possibility. A blind man's work in this field, to be seriously received, must be twice as thorough as the next man's.

The effect of trying to inseminate the queen artificially was that we injured her, because it's difficult to expose her vulva without injury and those queens that didn't die remained sterile. We have an ample supply of queens because our hives are strong and healthy. I can generally find a royal cell with a nymph in it, and put her in controlled conditions to complete her metamorphosis. But this doesn't make them less valuable to us. M. Bonnet had also suggested that we try mutilating the queen so that she couldn't fly out so far in search of fecundation, but when I clipped her wings severely she couldn't fly out at all, and if less severely she flew out as usual. I feel in my gut this is crude stuff, but Monsieur insists we try it all.

We were awaiting the return of our tenth known virgin to fly back from fecundation.

'Ants do this as well,' he said. 'The female has to leave the nest to mate. Why has nature forbidden mating inside the hive?'

'It would be less effort inside,' I ventured.

'That might be important. If it was possible inside, the queen might be smothered by the number of males attempting her. But then why have so many males? Why not just have one or two?'

'They might not be able to find her inside at the right moment.'

'I'm sure if it were intended to happen inside she'd have the power to summon them. Perhaps the effort is the point. The drones lead such fat and lazy lives the rest of the time that if it were no effort to fecundate her a very poor specimen could manage it. But when she flies out she flies very high and very fast, so her mate must prove himself strong enough to match her speed.'

The queen's return interrupted our speculations. I reported her condition – fecundated – and we went back to the house where I would write a note of our observation, and a separate note of our conjectures, for Monsieur is adamant that he will only assert what can be observed.

On our return we met Marie-Aimée in the hall.

She kissed him on the cheek. 'How did your work go today, my dear?'

'Very fruitful, my dear, very fruitful.'

She smiles abstractedly and calls the children to come and play with their father. He'll go down on all fours pretending to be a bear and little Marie will sit on his back while Marie-Aimée holds her on and guides them round the room. Pierre will demand a turn as well and there'll be a rumbustious time on the floor. Monsieur loves this physical time with his son.

I'm envious, though I'm not sure whether of the father or the son.

10 *October*

While we've been conducting our experiments on fecundation, Monsieur has also been considering swarms. He likes to have several pots on the boil at once (to avoid melancholy thoughts?).

We'd observed that just before a swarm there is immense agitation in the hive and he wondered whether this came directly from the queen – as opposed to his notion of a 'spirit of the hive' which infused them all at the same time. So once the season of swarms was past, we imprisoned a virgin queen and I observed that every mid-morning, when the males would generally be flying out, she made frenzied efforts to escape and all the bees quickly became very agitated. After an hour or two it subsided until the next day.

On the thirty-sixth day we released her to fly out for fecundation. Oddly, however, she laid only males. This was a catastrophe for the hive, because without a great number of females to replenish the stores, the males would quickly eat themselves out of house and home.

We have now confirmed that when fecundation occurs after twenty days, the queen can only lay males. We have no explanation for this.

On our way back from the hives we passed Pierre, squatting on the ground, utterly absorbed in watching a column of ants. He was putting little obstacles in its path, a twig, a leaf, to see whether the column went over or round it. I described the scene to Monsieur who smiled tenderly. 'Another natural observer,' he said. Pierre smiled but didn't reply, enjoying his father's approval, but more interested in studying the creatures in front of him.

At the end of the season we can say that although we have not witnessed an actual mating between a queen and a drone we believe that this mating is essential for fecundation. Perhaps next spring I might be able to seize one at the very instant of copulation, to secure the final proof.

(Note: I have read with great interest M. Pierre Huber's work Investigations of Native Ants published in Geneva 1810 which established his reputation as a serious naturalist. My uncle followed his mature work with interest. He told me once that Pierre had confided to him as a boy that he thought ants were much more intelligent than bees (but don't tell Papa).

My uncle and M. Huber spent the winter carefully writing up the notes on the summer's observations. My uncle tried making enlarged clay models of his dissections so that M. Huber could appreciate more readily the proportion and positioning of the bees' organs. This had limited success and M. Huber decided he was content to rely on my uncle's descriptions. A. de M.)

1788

2 January

Monsieur and Madame went to friends for Twelfth Night, but Madame had ordered a mighty cake for us to have at home, delivered by the baker so that Anna didn't have the trouble of making it (at which Anna clearly didn't know whether to feel pleased or annoyed).

There was a bean and a pea in it, for the King and Queen. Jacques got the bean and Sarah the pea and we made a game of them being King Louis and Queen Marie Antoinette. They tripped hand in hand through the kitchen, blowing kisses at their subjects as we all drank wine and Anna made sure that nothing untoward occurred. We were all still singing – and Pierre clapping his hands – when Monsieur and Madame returned and for once we went to bed later than them. (A lot later.)

I was up in time to shave Monsieur but we both had sore heads and neither of us said much.

18 *February*

We sat in the library all afternoon, snow falling gently outside. Pierre lay on the rug in front of the fire playing with a toy coach and pair, a present from his grandfather and his pride and joy.

Monsieur was speculating on swarms. He's sure that it's the queen who decides when the flight will occur but the question is whether it's led out by the old queen or a young one. Received opinion is that it's the young queen, for why would the old one give up all she has? Why would she abandon all the pollen and honey her colony has laboured so hard to build up? It would seem more likely she'd chase the young queen out.

'But that's what men would do,' he says. 'What man would ever willingly abandon all his wealth and leave his house with nothing but the clothes on his back, to have to start again from nothing?'

'But if he were leaving it to his son?' I tried.

'Then he leaves it when he dies. He may give some of it during his life, but he doesn't leave himself destitute, not if he has any sense. Because then he'd be entirely dependent on the goodwill of his child.'

Pierre laughed. 'Don't worry, Father, I'll look after you.'

We smiled, slightly shocked at this child/man's comment.

I persisted. 'But if you were the rich man's son and he was jealous of your youth, and was cruel and promised nothing for the future, you might decide you were better off with nothing and make your own way in the world.'

'That makes good sense for the young queens, but I can't believe the bees would abandon their old queen – their mother – to follow a stranger out. Well, observation will tell the tale. The difficulty will be in distinguishing young from old with absolute certainty.'

19 February

There's a dispute in the kitchen: Jacques risks his life by claiming that Anna's indiscriminate use of wooden spoons taints the taste of a sweet dish with that of a savoury one. There is a tremendous amount of huffing and puffing before they reach an agreement that the spoons for savoury dishes will be painted with a red dot on the handle so there is no danger of the taste of onions in a strawberry blancmange.

M. Huber has walked in on the end of this conversation (after the heavy copper pans have been washed and safely put away instead of being hefted about in a threatening manner).

He says, 'But what an excellent idea.' And everyone is suddenly at peace and thinking well of themselves and their neighbour.

'We have such trouble identifying queens sometimes . . . A dot of paint could work wonders. Could we do it, Burnens?'

'There's no reason why not, on her thorax, if the paintbrush is fine enough.'

Anna and Jacques forget their animosities and with modest, disclaiming gestures make light of their humble contribution to Monsieur's work.

There's a transparent excitement on his face, and all of us who see it are moved. This is not a look assumed to solicit the good opinion of the world; it's an expression of, I might say, a good soul.

6 *May*

We've been waiting eagerly for the season to get under way and at last we've begun our work. I've marked a queen with a dot of paint. She is fertile, with a swollen belly, indicating that she has lots of male eggs to lay, as well as females. She's been introduced to a hive without a queen and the bees have accepted her. The workers have destroyed their previous royal cells and are building new ones. The queen lays alternately in male and female cells.

13 *May*

The queen has started laying in royal cells.

19 May

The hive swarmed unexpectedly. It settled in a nearby tree and I shook it into a sack and then into an empty hive. When I first captured a swarm I was nervous but I know now they're not particularly aggressive at this time because they don't have a hive to defend. If the swarm is kept together it doesn't mind being moved en masse. When I examined the swarm I could easily identify the old, large queen by her size, and I found no other queens at all.

25 June

We've repeated our observation of swarms several times, including hives where a queen had reigned for more than a year. Monsieur can safely conclude that it's always the old queen which leads out the first swarm – but only after she has laid eggs in the royal cells which will hatch into young queens after she's gone.

'But sir, I notice that the bees never build these royal cells until the queen has laid her male eggs.'

He nodded. 'The reverse, however, is not true. The laying of male eggs doesn't necessarily mean the bees will build royal cells. It's not a blind, instinctive pattern: sometimes they do and sometimes they don't.'

'It seems to depend on the size of the colony, sir. If the

hive's not heavily populated they tend not to build royal cells.'

'Which means the queen can't leave a royal brood to develop into queens, and without doing that she'll never fly out. So we might venture that the bees determine whether or not there are enough of them to cast a swarm. Might we call this the spirit of the hive?'

The more we study them, the more they seem possessed of intelligence and the fonder we become of them. That there should be some sort of guiding 'spirit of the hive' seems perfectly reasonable.

3 *July*

To my quiet pleasure M. Huber referred to me today, to a visitor, as his secretary (rather than manservant). It's true that Sarah has taken on a lot of Monsieur's personal care although I still shave him every morning and it's a pleasure to perform this service, and well, for him. It's good practice for handling the bees later on in the day – firmly but delicately.

That's the way Madame handles the household. She won't hesitate to point out a missed piece of dusting to Sarah, but the next day she'll compliment her on how well she looks in her new Sunday dress.

Monsieur often says he's the luckiest of men to have such a wife.

But when he said it yesterday I happened to catch Madame's

eye and there was a sudden odd look, almost like complicity. It made me feel uneasy, disloyal in some way, though I'm sure I have nothing to reproach myself with.

Monsieur of course sees nothing of looks and glances. I realise how much we say without words, how an expression on the face may speak volumes (especially when all four women are together in the kitchen). Perhaps not being aware of this contributes to his equanimity.

1 August

The question of the moment: can worker bees, which are, after all, female, ever lay eggs? The question arises because sometimes eggs are found in hives which are known not to have a queen. M. Huber thinks they can, because we've seen workers adopt what seems to be a laying posture in the cells. Reim thinks they can, but M. Bonnet thinks there must actually be small queens present. We can't assert that workers lay eggs unless we catch one in the act. So every day for a month now I've been observing the hives and I've never seen it happen, although it would be easy enough to miss in that throng. But it means we can't refute the idea that they're laid by small queens.

While M. Huber is thinking about this I am thinking too: that the only way to know for certain is to use a hive which is guaranteed free of any queen, which means checking every single bee before it is put into the new hive. Generally I pass them through cold water if I want to examine them, because it makes them more docile and less likely to sting, but it also has the effect of stiffening them and slightly altering their shape and a small queen is so like a worker that the difference might be missed. So it would have to be done without them being immobilised, as it were.

Which will mean full and free stinging. And to have any serious results we can't rely on one hive, we'll have to use two. So at roughly fifty thousand bees for each hive – oh, the arithmetic's clear enough. But I don't see any other way to do it. It will be painful but it will yield a worthwhile result.

Fine words to write, when I'm not in the middle of it.

3 *August*

Today we were at the hives.

He said, 'So we still have the problem of finding out whether workers can lay eggs or not.'

'The only way to know that is to establish a hive that is guaranteed free of queens.'

'But to establish that . . .'

'I know what that entails.'

'Do you really?' He looked at me with his blind eyes and I nodded and said yes. He said, 'I could never ask you to do that.'

'But you're not asking me, sir. I'm offering.'

He sighed. 'It would be a great endeavour.'

'I know, sir. That's why I want to do it.'
'Then your offer's gratefully accepted. If you're quite sure.'
'I am, sir.'
Which is not to say that I don't know it will be painful.

10 *August*

M. Bonnet came to dinner and in the afternoon M. Huber
brought him down to the hives, both of them guided by Pierre,
for M. Bonnet's sight is near failing. Nevertheless he has enough
vision left to see the extent of my stings, as I could tell by his
reaction. He murmured something to Monsieur, whose face
contorted.

'I can imagine,' he cried out. 'Dear François, I can imagine
your pain, don't think for a moment that I take your devotion
for granted.'

'I know that, sir. The pain is incidental.'

M. Bonnet nodded. 'One day the pain will be gone, but
the knowledge will be there in its place, and that will never
go.' He made some graceful compliment about how lucky M.
Huber was to have me. I thought yes, you can say that for you
wouldn't do it yourself. Which is not true of M. Huber – I know
that he would willingly undertake the work himself if he had
sight and that's why I'm willing to undertake it on his behalf,
while I might not be for M. Bonnet. But he's an old man now,
I should take more account of that.

But sometimes, though of course I never say it, I'm angry

with M. Huber for caring so much for his approval when I think that Monsieur has a finer mind, and certainly he's the one who's actually thought out the experiments and done the work, while Bonnet simply thinks 'it might be interesting' to know something. And sometimes I worry that M. Bonnet might claim M. Huber's discoveries as his own (but this is unworthy, my small peasant mind at work).

After his guest had left, Monsieur came back to the hives. It was about three o'clock in the afternoon, very hot, and I'd just put another stroke through my tally – no idea how many it was so far, fifty thousand or so. It's Pierre's job to count them up at the end of each day. M. Huber, very unusually for a working day, had had wine with his dinner instead of small beer. I stopped for a moment to bathe my arms in cold water.

He sat down, sighing, not drunk, but needing to get the weight off his feet.

'François,' he said earnestly, 'I do understand what it is that you're doing.'

'I know, sir.'

'I know that my work would be impossible without you.'

'Not impossible, sir. Your wife has managed in the past and little Pierre will be able to help before much longer.'

He shook his head. 'I could never ask of them what you let me ask of you.'

This is probably true, because their need to know is not as intense as mine. And in any event, no husband could ask his wife to endure this. I said nothing, just continued with each bee one by one: seize her, turn her over and hold her between thumb and forefinger, peer through the magnifying glass (shading her from the sun) and examine her organs to ensure she's just a worker and that there's not a queen among them.

This is the fourth day. I work obsessively, mindlessly, stopping only to rest my eyes.

'I like the work, sir. I know there's a limit to it, and eventually, one by one, I'll get there. I like thinking about the proportions – how many done, how many still to do. I change from decimals to fractions and back again. I don't know why I find it so absorbing.' I felt as though I was revealing a weakness to him, but a human one, which he would understand.

'The joy of occupation,' he said. Then he looked towards me gently (and when I say 'looked' I am aware of his blindness, and still I'll say 'looked'). 'But you pay a high price for that, Burnens. Sometimes I can hear your silence when you're stung.'

I shook my head. 'The pain isn't so bad. It's a price worth paying.'

'Not all pain can be soothed with calamine lotion,' he said thoughtfully, 'but hard work is very helpful there. It's not just that troubling thoughts are forgotten while we do it, but afterwards we have a glow from time well spent. Without you I wouldn't have my occupation, François. That's a very great deal of my life.'

'Nor I mine without you, sir.' And I know that it would be hard to find another master who could both demand as much and teach as much as M. Huber does.

He said, 'I've never told you the story of how I learned of my blindness, have I?'

I felt a frisson, because I know he never talks of this, it's not an oft-repeated story, it's too personal, painful. And I know that he tells it as a counterpoint to my own pain. Tonight my hands are too swollen to write it all, I will just make notes until I have time to write at length. I know he won't tell it again.

19 August

When he told me his story he was sitting on his old familiar chair by the hives, seeming to let his gaze rest on the ground in front of him. He began without preamble.

'I was fifteen, and as thin and gangling as boys are when their bodies are struggling to be full-grown men. I was already going to lectures at the university and I was trying out alchemical experiments at my uncle's house, so absorbed I took no account of time. My parents were delighted with my studies. What they didn't know was that at night, instead of sleeping, I read romances by candlelight. I loved them, all brave exploits and beautiful maidens in distress. It seemed to me that I could be profligate of everything, there was no price to pay. So I was using my eyes for sixteen, eighteen hours a day, burning the candle at both ends as you might say, and then, not wanting to know it, and very afraid, I became aware that my sight was beginning to grow dim. I found that one eye couldn't focus properly and the other had a small spot in the middle where I couldn't see anything.

'At first I ignored it, and as it got worse I was too afraid to think about it, but it got so bad that finally it frightened me enough to tell my father and of course he was very concerned. We saw a local man and he sent us to Paris at once to see two of the eminent doctors of the day. The first was Dr Tronchin, a general physician, who said I was outgrowing my strength, and that was natural enough at my age. But he was worried that there was a tendency to consumption, and all he could prescribe for that was the heroic remedy of living in the country for a year, as a peasant, labouring in the open air and eating peasant food, to build up my strength. You know that life, François.'

'Indeed, sir, and it's a very healthy life if there's enough food to go round.'

'Of course, that's the first essential. In my case he added that I shouldn't excite myself at all or read anything for a year. I said I could manage that well enough, though I promised myself to smuggle in a few books.

'But the next day we had to see Dr Wenzel, one of the most renowned oculists of Europe, and every time I'd thought of seeing him there'd been a cold feeling in my heart. I was full of dread. I suppose that deep down I already knew.

'And then we were in his room; there were panelled walls and books and etchings of tulips. The bright light he used to examine my eyes hurt them terribly. But he spoke very calmly, very calmly and it was such a relief to me to tell him how bad things seemed.

'When he'd finished examining me he opened the curtains and I had my eyes fixed on his face as soon as there was enough light to see it, but it was completely impassive. Then he drew up a chair beside mine and that was when I knew. And then he put his hand on my arm and that was when I knew for certain.

'He said, "I'd so like to be able to give you good news. I'm very sorry that I can't."

'And I asked how bad my eyes were and he explained – so calmly – that one had a cataract and one had gutta serena. It was a rare and very unfortunate coincidence that each eye should be afflicted with something different.

'"I know what a cataract is," I said, "but what is gutta serena?"

'"A disease of the optic nerve," said the doctor.

'"What does that mean?"

'"If both eyes deteriorate at the same rate, which I think they will, you have about three to four years of sight left."

'"Blind at nineteen?" I shouted out.

'My father suddenly made a convulsive sound. He turned away, but kept his hand on my shoulder. He was crying. It was another nail in the coffin, making me understand it was real.

'I said, "But couldn't it be longer?" in my most winning way, as though that would make a difference, but Dr Wenzel said, "I have to tell you that in my experience it would be very unlikely."

'And I made for the door, but there were so many tears in my eyes I couldn't see the handle properly. Even so, I knew this wasn't blindness, I could still see shape, colour. I was somehow aware that Dr Wenzel had stopped my father from following me and I was grateful for that. When I was out in the street I didn't cry at all, but there were snowflakes on my face. My skin was hot and aching – the snow slid down and cooled me.

'When my father joined me, he took my arm but it was almost as though he needed the reassurance more than I did. In the carriage back to the hotel I could see the figures of women hurrying along and it was dusk and it was snowing so they were indistinct, but that was good enough for me. I told myself I could live without the detail if it came to it. The dim vision we all share in gloomy light would be enough.

'I saw a shapely woman walk past and I wanted to seize her, hold her fast.

'Dr Wenzel hadn't actually said it was impossible for it to take much longer. And reading, surely that would be possible? Good light, the best quality candles, soft, no glare. Restrict it to the essentials. But then everything's essential at fifteen, so much to learn and see, the whole adult world before you.

'I pulled down the carriage window and leaned my face out, so the snowflakes would fall on it. I wanted to feel a sensation that didn't depend on sight.

'I determined to put my faith in Dr Tronchin. If a heroic remedy was required then I was ready for the fight. My body and my eyes all belonged to the same person, didn't they? So it was only a matter of common sense that if my general health improved, my eyes must improve as well. Who could argue with that?

'And then Marie-Aimée. I could picture her so clearly that

afternoon at the Candolles', before all this happened, moving so gracefully in her white muslin, teasing me unmercifully, yet later on when we stood looking out of a window together at the sunset it seemed there was some sort of wordless understanding between us. Her eyes were so kind, all I wanted was to be with her, to give her tender looks in return. We were both very young, but it was as though there was something between us already that was beyond our years.

'But now . . . she could have her pick. Why should she choose a blind man? So, one more reason not to go blind.

'Of course I knew in my heart that Wenzel had told me the truth. I sat in our hotel room which was over-decorated in that French style and for half an hour or more I sat staring at the gilt scrolling on a chair, following its pattern over and over – even today I could draw it for you in the smallest detail. And the strange thing is that the pattern was meaningless but at the same time strangely satisfying. By the time I stopped looking at it, the truth of my condition had begun to embed itself in my mind and I knew – though I didn't want to – that time spent on false hopes was time wasted. Though natural enough. Who wouldn't clutch at straws at such a time?

'My father was sitting at a desk writing to my mother with the news. He couldn't speak to me. He would put a hand on my shoulder in passing, but it was as though all his customary bons mots died on his lips and he couldn't find any words in their place. It made me terribly lonely, worse than if I'd actually been alone, that this man I loved – my father – was in the room and neither of us could find a word to say to the other, of consolation, of anything at all. I was terrified that this would be my future life, shunned by the people I loved, or hoped to love. In fact to this day we've never spoken of the thing itself. Arrangements, yes, and incidental things, but never the thing itself. Even with Marie-Aimée. It causes them unbearable pain, I can't . . . I never have.

'We had our supper sent up to us that night and we decided to ask Dr Tronchin to put in hand the arrangements with the farming family he knew. We both felt the need to retire early. Being together felt awkward.

'When I was in bed at last, alone in the dark, I gave way to my feelings and began to cry, and I cried until I thought I'd die of grief. It was pure anguish. Nothing else existed. I was so far sunk in it that I didn't think I'd ever have the strength to rise from that bed.

'But sleep came in the end, thank God, and the next day was bright and clear and I knew that I'd got through the worst night of my life and it could never be quite that intense again. So I knew that I could get through the next one and the next, on and on, just keep putting one foot in front of the other.

'In the meantime we were in Paris, I was fifteen, I still had plenty of sight and they say Parisian girls are the prettiest in the world.

'My father clearly felt the need for something to distract us and suggested we went to look at the pictures in the Louvre Palace. I said I'd rather watch the ladies walking in the Tuilerie Gardens, which delighted him for it showed my spirits rising. In the end we did both. You can imagine how intensely I looked at the pictures, trying to etch them into my brain. But afterwards, sitting in the gardens, I was watching a young governess – and she was well aware of me watching her, wagging her rump and glancing over her shoulder coquettishly – and it seemed to me there was no competition between a real woman and her pale imitation on a canvas.

'And I also thought that in the dark, with a woman, in bed, it wouldn't matter if you were blind because the feel of her, her smell, would be the same whether you had eyes to see her or not. But that brought me back to who would have a blind man, in particular, Marie-Aimée, and I couldn't bear to think I was losing the love of my life just as I thought I'd found her.

'It was too troubling and I suggested we go and arrange things, like buying me a pair of tough boots and warm clothing. My father was relieved at this. He put all his mind to finding the right shops and we discovered perfect establishments tucked away in little streets. Strong boots, but such good workmanship. I wore them for years and years. And then a seat booked on the coach and it was done.

'I set out the next day. I felt as though I'd arrived in Paris as a boy and left it as a man. It was a very sudden transition, but truly nothing was the same any more. My childhood had ended at the moment when my father burst out crying in Dr Wenzel's office. And I felt that I'd lost both my sight and the father who could make everything right. That was a heavy loss.'

'Yes, sir.' I have only suffered one of those things and I know how much that weighs.

20 *August*

Now that the work of guaranteeing the hives are free of queens is done – it took eleven days in the end – I feel a great relief because I think I acquitted myself well. The pain of my stings is receding. Anna's calamine poultices have been very effective but in the pain of my stings during our experiment I believe I have paid some tribute to M. Huber, to the pain of his blindness.

21 *August*

Today I found eggs in one of the hives – our proof that not only queens but sometimes workers, too, can lay eggs. Monsieur was delighted, but it seemed as though I had only a few moments to enjoy his approval before he was wondering whether it wasn't possible to obtain the absolutely final proof by catching a worker in the very act of laying. So I shall transfer our precious, pure workers into the new glass hive whose measurements allow reasonable observation at last, and I shall watch them until we catch one in the act.

1 *September*

For over a week now I've spent pretty much every hour of daylight observing their activity and I have seen nothing that could be described as laying behaviour, the insertion of the posterior into a cell. Monsieur is disappointed but still sanguine. I think I feel the disappointment more keenly, for I want very much to present him with the final proof of his idea.

I began to be discouraged, always reporting nothing. Besides, it seemed to me that we had enough proof already – we'd found the eggs, for goodness' sake, and we knew for certain there were no queens present. No reasonable person could argue with the conclusion he drew from our experiment. I said nothing of this, of course. Strange, then, the turn the conversation took when he joined me this morning, the sun still very warm but beginning to be lower in the sky.

'I was thinking about music,' he said. 'Learning a piece for the harpsichord, say. Do you know what they say is the difference between the man who plays for his own amusement and the man who plays for his living?'

'No, sir.'

'The man who plays for himself practises until he's got the piece right, but the man who plays for a living practises until he can't get it wrong.'

I knew at once what he was telling me but I took a little time to put it into words. 'So it would be that in this experiment finding the eggs is getting it right, but finding a worker laying would make it impossible to be wrong?'

'Just so. Keeping bees is not my pastime, it's my work. But I know I make great demands on you, François.'

'None I'm not happy to fulfil, sir.'

He smiled and I resumed my observation in a more patient frame of mind, determined to persevere. A week can be a long time day by day, but it's a short time in a whole life.

4 September

Today I saw a worker laying an egg. I seized her at once – a sting of course, but barely felt. I examined her and found that her ovaries, although not as well developed as a queen's, contained eleven eggs ready to be laid.

'Most gratifying,' Monsieur said, and all day long his face kept breaking into a smile. Tonight, in the library, as I made anatomical drawings of the specimen, he passed by me and said, 'Well done,' and I felt deeply content.

10 October

The season is all but over. We've observed that in hives with no queens the workers will seek to replace her by feeding worms in common cells with royal jelly, which will turn them into queens. In the process worker worms nearby receive a small quantity of the royal food, by chance, and these become the workers who can lay.

We marked my birthday with wine and cake. I still thank God for my position, though sometimes I wonder if this will be all of my life.

30 October

Jacques thinks it's time for the pig to be killed. Anna thinks it could go a few more weeks. Its feed is household scraps and costs next to nothing. But Jacques has it in his mind that now is the time. M. Huber, hearing of this, says that since Jacques must do the killing he's the one who must decide the moment. They both accept this.

Early one morning Jacques took her to the wood and fed her acorns and tickled her belly as he slit her throat. He brought her back to be dismembered (his job) and salted and cured (Anna's responsibility).

'She died happy,' he said. We eat good fresh meat every day, knowing there's bacon and ham in plenty for the months to come.

1789

20 January

The family has an English habit which I've never seen before: making 'toast'. On the coldest afternoons, as daylight fades, they sit together on the hearthrug and Monsieur roasts pieces of bread in front of the fire. He uses a special brass toasting fork with a very long handle, brought back by his aunt from her years in London. First one side, then the other, and he can smell the moment it's done and passes it to Marie-Aimée who pulls it off the fork – gingerly, because it's hot – and spreads it lavishly with butter and honey before cutting it in half and giving the pieces to the children, who devour it as fast as he can make it.

'More?' he cries out. 'More? It's like feeding a nest of gannets.' The children laugh, Marie-Aimée smiles tenderly.

They're such a picture of ease and affection, all four of them on the floor together, their faces glowing in the firelight. I leave them at such times and join Anna in the kitchen, where there's always a piece of cake.

'Not the simplest way in the world to eat bread and honey,' she says. 'And sitting on the floor, too. But they enjoy it, so God bless them.'

4 *May*

We've overwintered two late-fecunded queens to see whether they would continue laying only male eggs. They stopped laying last November and started again in April, but still all drones. We wanted to follow them indefinitely but today we found that all their workers had deserted them. The hives were empty and both queens were dead.

'You see,' Monsieur said sadly, 'no new workers have been born. There are more and more males to provide for, and the poor females have simply lost heart. They know their queen can't lead them out because she has no royal nymphs to leave behind. They must transfer their allegiance to a new queen. So they've joined a neighbouring hive.'

'And without them to feed her she's starved to death.' I could speak of it quite calmly but for an instant I felt as though she might equally have died of a broken heart. I don't know whether Monsieur felt anything similar – certainly he was subdued. It's strange the hold these little insects have on our affection.

We observed that there were far too many drones in the hives, and some were even laid in royal cells. The queens' instincts must have been utterly impaired. The result was that the organisation of the hives was distorted and devastated, leading to its abandonment and the queens' deaths.

20 May

Beyond our world of bees, the great subject of interest to everyone is what the summoning of the Assembly in France – for the first time in 170 years – might mean. It's only summoned in times of great crisis, although this time it seems to be about no more than taxation. I believe Madame has some investments in Paris, so she always makes a point of following the news from there.

(Note: It might be fanciful, but I can't help thinking that Huber's idea of 'too many drones' and the consequent devastation of the hive finds an extraordinary parallel in the events in France that began in this year. A. de M.)

25 May

Our first swarm has flown out – led by the old queen whose thorax we marked with red paint last year. Further proof, if it were needed, that the old queen always leads the first swarm. But since then the weather has been cold and unsettled with few days fine enough, or at least sunny and calm enough, to cast a swarm. M. Huber said 'alarmed' was not too strong a word for the bees' reaction when there's a prospect of bad weather, for they'll fly home if a cloud passes over the sun.

In the absence of the right weather to make experiments,

he has been speculating on what we know already. The queen leads a swarm out when the royal larvae in the hive are ready to transform into nymphs. Why at this particular moment?

'There can't be two queens in the hive at the same time,' he muses as I watch raindrops beating the glass of the library windows. There's even a fire lit, in late May.

'Reaumur, Schirach, Hattorf all agree that in order to prevent two queens inhabiting the same hive, nature has inspired them with a mutual hatred. If the queens are the same age, the combat between them is equal and chance decides the outcome, but if the old queen is pitted against a new-born queen I don't give much for the younger one's chances.'

'So, if she chose to stay, the old queen could destroy her rivals one by one, as they're born, until there are no emergent queens left.'

'And then the colony won't feel able to swarm and if they don't swarm they won't thrive. Their old queen will get older and older, she'll become weak, the colony will become open to predators and it will end up dying.'

We know that a strong hive will send out three or even four swarms in a year, starting four new hives. A very weak hive may not even send one out, so their queen grows a year older and the brood is not invigorated with new blood. Slowly they become unable to replenish their resources. We deal with this by smoking and drowning them and introducing a new swarm into their hive. I have no compunction about doing this. The workers' lives are very short in summer – no more than two months, and by then they'll have broken legs and torn wings.

To make such effort for no effect is hardly bearable. Hives need vigorous young queens if they're to thrive.

Monsieur was pacing gently backwards and forwards, as he likes to do when he's thinking. Six steps in each direction. There's a pattern of wear in the carpet, for this passage is always clear of obstacles. I think he values being able to move without feeling his way or needing assistance every few steps.

'We know they won't abandon her. We've seen hives where the queen is very old, infertile, and the bees hide her away in the darkest recess, the widow. They don't kill her but the hive may die because of her. That must be why in a healthy hive the queen leads out a swarm – so that what is left has the best chance of making new life.' He frowns. 'Tell me again what you've seen of the workers' behaviour after the old queen has gone.'

'I've seen that they have a royal nymph who's perfectly mature and ready to be born. I've described to you, sir, how they keep capping her chrysalis with more wax to delay her birth.'

'Very good. I dare say you have your own thoughts about it.'

He doesn't often invite me to speculate. Mostly I'm aware of his need for my rigour in observing and I satisfy that as best I can.

'Well, sir, it seems strange to me that just at the time when they seem to be most in need of a queen they should choose to imprison their best hope.'

'I agree. It seems unnatural. But it's just when their instinct seems defective to us that it would most reward investigation. I can't think of an experiment that would explain it. We know they cap the nymph and when, and how, all we don't know is why. But patience, patience, we'll find out. There's certainly a reason, it's just that we don't know it yet. In the meantime, let's take stock of everything else we've discovered that we know to be true.'

15 July

Pierre has been reading the story of Echo and her hopeless love for Narcissus and he was very keen to try out the echo in the rocky valley. He and his father and I walked up the valley yesterday in the early evening when the weather was calm and clear, the best conditions for hearing an echo. It was difficult for Monsieur because the track is steep and rough and he stumbled quite often.

'Oh, damn,' he said when it happened for the third time, but that was as far as he let his frustration intrude.

I've noticed that some men, particularly as they get older, become apoplectic with rage at minor inconveniences. Monsieur is at the other extreme from this, thank goodness. Obviously his blindness involves inconvenience at every turn and if he bellowed at each one of them there'd be very little energy left for anything else.

Halfway up we stopped and directed our voices at the huge cleft rock on the other side of the valley. Pierre tried,

'Come out, come out, wherever you are,' and it came back distinctly. Monsieur and I both tried yodelling but neither of us is particularly accomplished at it and Pierre held his sides laughing at our attempts.

As we walked back, Monsieur remarked that most people would regard an echo as harmless enough but Virgil had the idea, for some unknown reason, that an echo was injurious to bees.

'I thought insects can't hear,' Pierre said.

'There are no known organs of hearing, certainly,' his father said. 'But beekeepers look for their lost swarms by tanging, making a huge noise with a stick on a bucket, and it works. Even if they can't hear the sound I think they must feel the vibration.'

A family friend has given Pierre a speaking trumpet – somewhat misguidedly, Monsieur and Madame seem to think, since they have to suffer calls to meals and announcements of general interest throughout the day. ('Jacques will be departing for town in five minutes. Anyone needing errands performed please step forward at once. Anna is about to make an apple pie. Anyone who thinks it should be a strawberry blancmange instead, please tell Anna of your opinion.')

This evening I realised after we'd finished our work at the hives that I'd left my workbook behind and I went back for it.

In the twilight I saw Pierre, roaring through his speaking trumpet at the hives. 'Come out, come out, you bloody old bees.' He jumped when he saw me. 'Just trying to see if they can hear,' he said defensively.

'And what do you conclude?'

'Nothing really. Doesn't seem to make much difference to them.'

'How do you know that they're not disturbed?'

'Don't.'

'So it might be better to leave the experiment until you have a more definite object?'

He sighed. 'Yes. I'm not that interested in bees anyway. You won't tell Papa?'

'No. But remember that your father is very sensitive to sound and the speaking trumpet does make your voice very loud.'

'All right.'

I feel sure that he'll tone it down now. He has a great capacity to be reasonable.

I think of how it would be to talk to my own son like this.

20 *July*

We have heard of a terrible riot in Paris where the mob stormed the Bastille gaol and released the prisoners, mostly old men who had offended the King. They say mobs are roaming the streets and the army does nothing to stop them, being infected itself with republican ideas from fighting in America. The only soldiers certainly loyal to the King are the Swiss mercenaries.

M. Huber says mildly, 'I'm glad I saw Paris when I was a young man.'

I reflect that I've never seen Paris. Perhaps, one day . . .

We stick to our work. We describe the things we have observed. He wants to write a letter to M. Bonnet summing up his discoveries so far, a letter that M. Bonnet might commend for publication in a journal.

15 August

How we have worked at this letter. I read out the observations we have made. He comments on them and I incorporate the comments and read the letter out again. He listens and makes more comments. I redraft the words and read them out again. He comments again. It's been going on for weeks but we're on the fourth draft now and I'm hearing a natural tone at last. With so much modification and alteration this might seem the least natural of things, but all I can say is that it seems to take great effort to produce a piece of work that reads without effort at all.

18 August

We walked to the little lake in the early evening heat of a hot summer's day. We set up our rods but there was little activity from the fish.

After a while Monsieur said, 'They say the smell of a young woman will bring the fish out. Perhaps we should call for Sarah.'

'Women don't fish,' Pierre said sternly, perhaps avoiding more complicated ideas about Sarah. Then he shook his head of these notions and said, 'But can fish smell?'

'I don't see why not. Why shouldn't water hold an odour as well as air? I don't know if an olfactory organ has been discovered yet.'

Pierre said, 'You could discover that by putting them in a dark tank, pitch black, so they couldn't see anything at all. A big tank. Then you could put some bait in it, and if they swam straight to it, even though they couldn't see it, you'd know that they could smell it.'

'Very good,' his father said. 'It would be a strong conjecture, at least.'

It occurred to me that if the fish were truly in total darkness it would be impossible to observe their behaviour, but I didn't say this because I was as delighted as Monsieur at Pierre's philosophical thinking, and I didn't want to dampen his enthusiasm.

Monsieur didn't quail, however. 'Of course if the tank were really dark it would be impossible for the observer to see how the fish behaved.'

I thought there might be some disappointment here but Pierre took it on the chin. 'Yes, that's true.'

'Good experiments take a lot of thought to set up. Sometimes thinking how to do it takes longer than doing it. Although not always, as dear Burnens knows only too well.'

'I'm not that interested in fish anyway,' Pierre said. His father laughed and we fell into silence, watching our rods. Occasionally there was the sound of a fish leaping and Monsieur sighed with contentment. He's a good fisherman. He's used to sitting very still, concentrating on what he hears so that when a fish leaps and makes a sound in the water he doesn't need sight to know its whereabouts. His touch is so sensitive that he feels the slightest twitch on his line.

I described the multitude of bats flying over the water, drinking as they skimmed the surface, eating the insects who also wanted to slake their thirst.

He told of a schoolboy friend of his who had a tame bat and how he'd watched it alight on his friend's hand and tear off the wings of flies it was offered as food before it would eat them.

'That's very particular of the bats,' Pierre exclaimed.

Monsieur shrugged. 'We don't eat bones.'

We walked back with only a couple of grayling to show, but with a sense of peace, quiet, time well spent.

30 *September*

Monsieur has finally completed a beautiful essay on the mode of fecundation of the honey bee, proving that it occurs outside the hive, written in the form of a letter to Charles Bonnet.

This letter, three pages long, has taken three months to write. Monsieur decided he'd like to try to print it himself, using a handheld press with wooden letters. I understood his longing not to be dependent, although it was painful to observe him feeling for each letter. It took many laborious attempts, and I had to read out to him the almost incomprehensible results.

There was a spasm of pain on his face and I felt the pain myself. I so much wished for him to have that independence, in the way that a parent does with a child, I suppose. And then he sighed and said, 'Ah, Burnens, there's no point in me wasting my time doing something you can do so much better. You're my amanuensis and I count myself lucky. It's time I let you get on with making the fair copy we shall send.'

'Every word is yours sir.'

'I know, my man, I know.'

1 October

Dramatic events are taking place in France. These days whenever the newspaper arrives Monsieur asks what news there is and either I read it to him at once or Madame does, or she comes and listens as I read it out. The third estate has formed a National Assembly. Feudalism has been abolished. There has been a declaration of the Rights of Man. The authorities in our own cantons are nervous but most people readily support what looks to be a much fairer form of government in France, even if it's taken unrest to get it.

10 October

Today Monsieur received M. Bonnet's response to his letter on fecundation. It was both encouraging and muted. He urged M. Huber to conduct many more experiments and then publish the result of several years' work as a book.

'I know what he's saying,' Monsieur said. It was a grey day by the hives. 'He's thinking of my father.' He sat there quietly, very little activity by the bees. He leaned his head back. 'My father's work on the flight of birds of prey was certainly a contribution to the study of natural history. But a small one. Nothing followed. Monsieur Bonnet is afraid I'm going down the same road. He doesn't say it, but he's afraid I'll be charged with dilettantism, unless I can produce a large, rigorous body of work. All the more so because I'm challenging received opinion. And all the more so again because I'm blind, so my observations will be doubly doubted.'

I felt indignant on his behalf. 'Let them check, sir. You have your ideas and your experiments; I have the eyes to make the observations. Let them come and see if they can find fault.'

He laughed. 'Oh, they'll try their best, I'm sure of that. That's why we must always be more than sure.' He put his arm on my shoulder, finding it unerringly. 'I trust you, François. We'll do it together. We must take the hard with the smooth on the way.'

'But we still haven't seen the direct fecundation of the queen by the male,' I say.

He smiles. 'The point is that we've done the work, we know what happens. It may be that we'll never see it.' He stops and shrugs. 'Which will be a great disappointment. But it won't invalidate our work. We've done the experiments, we know the results, there's no argument.'

I'm glad to think of it in this way and not have to dwell on his disappointment.

The second piece of news today was of more universal significance. The Paris mob has marched on the King at Versailles, demanding he recognise the National Assembly and asking for bread for the starving people of the city. The King refused to recognise the Assembly and his Queen, Marie Antoinette, just shrugged and said, 'Why can't they eat brioche instead?' These words have resounded throughout Europe. Not a peasant in the fields has not heard them. The result, predictably enough, was that the mob invited the royal family to accompany them back to Paris, to the Tuileries, where they now live as the guests of the revolution. Their personal safety is guaranteed by the presence of the Swiss Guard.

We feel as though we're living in uncertain times, as though what has always seemed the natural order is beginning to turn upside down. The Paris mob dictating to the King of France! It would have seemed unthinkable even a week ago.

In the middle of this uncertainty Pierre has created his own oasis of calm. He's arranged some old wooden boxes on their sides to be his cabinet of curiosities. Inside there are oddly shaped stones, a dead stag beetle, the skin of a grass snake, dried flowers, foreign coins and pieces of broken clay pipes. Everything is neatly labelled.

Madame is delighted by it and calls Monsieur and describes the curiosities to him and he gravely feels the bumps on the stones. This little, ordered world Pierre has made makes us all more cheerful at this time.

4 November

An old friend of Jacques' came to visit. They sat in the kitchen with their pipes after dinner and Monsieur and I were welcomed to join them. The old man told the story of the bee boy who lived in his village long ago.

He was an idiot boy whose only interest was in bees, but it was a consuming interest and all his little wit was devoted to this end. His knowledge of their habits was prodigious. In the winter he never moved from his father's fireside, as though he was hibernating, but in summer he was as busy and excitable as the bees themselves. Honeybees, bumblebees and wasps were all his prey and he was adept at finding their nests in the fields. He would seize the insects with his bare hands and tear out their stings and suck them for their honey.

Sometimes he kept them under his shirt, next to his skin, sometimes he kept them in bottles. He'd run around wildly, making buzzing sounds. The beekeepers hated him, for he'd steal into their gardens and tap the hives to call the bees out. Or he would overturn the hive to get the honey out. He was passionately fond of it. When the beekeepers made their liquor from fermented honey he'd haunt the tubs and beg for a drink of 'bee-wine'.

When he grew into a tall youth he was sent away to a distant village and died before he reached manhood.

'Doubtless he fell into a quarry and broke his neck, or into a lake and drowned,' Monsieur said drily. 'His own village, the people who'd known him since he was a baby, couldn't do it so he was sent to strangers. They didn't have the same feeling for him. Accidents happen.'

'He was sent to another village and he died,' the old man said stoutly. 'That's all I know.'

'What a great shame that he was an idiot,' Monsieur said. 'If not for that he might have been a great natural historian.'

I thought of my own experience, counting out a hundred thousand bees, and thanked God that it resulted in a piece of worthwhile knowledge, for it would have been madness otherwise.

'I wonder,' Monsieur said, 'what would have happened if the boy had been fed with as much honey as he desired. Were his antics a means to get honey, or was getting the honey simply an excuse for his antics?'

'I think the bees were his friends,' Pierre said. 'If he was an idiot he wouldn't have had any other friends.'

Monsieur nodded. 'And perhaps he needed companionship more than most.'

'Isn't it true that a bee kept on its own dies, no matter how much food or warmth it has?' I said.

'Indeed. We might venture that it dies of loneliness.'

'Horses are the same,' the old man said. 'A horse on its own in a field will never thrive. They need companions of their own sort. I know a man who found himself with only one horse in his field and the horse was in a sad way. Well – he was an unfortunate man – he also had a solitary hen, and she found her way to the field and she and the horse found a respect for each other. She'd rub herself against his legs and he'd move them very carefully in case he trampled her. And he thrived.'

'So with the boy and the bees,' Pierre said.

'And then the man, after the floods, was it in sixty-five or sixty-six? Whichever, when the waters went down he found, all perched in the branches of the one tree, a fox, a cat and a hen looking at each other, none attacking the other.'

'Sometimes the need for companionship is so great that even something which seems a world away can answer it,' Monsieur said. 'We're blessed to have friends of our own kind who can answer that need.' He raised his glass in a toast, and sitting round the fire with the shadows flickering, this fellow feeling was warming, and the country lore was a bulwark against uncertain times.

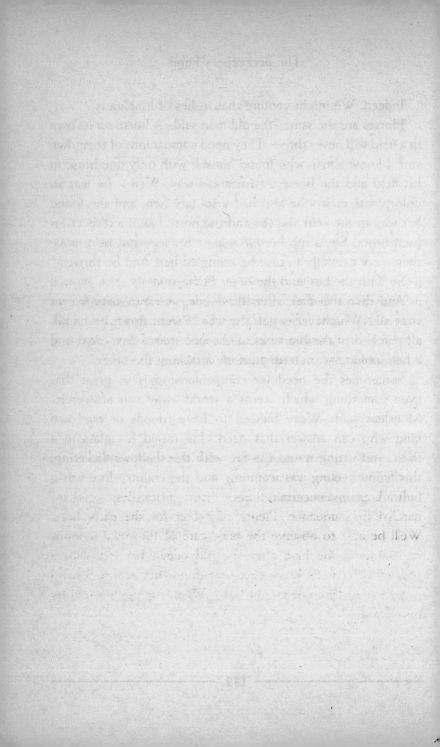

1790

(Note: This year was the beginning for the Huber family of the financial embarrassments of the French Revolution. Certain investments made in Paris on behalf of Madame Huber yielded less than their previous income. It was a period of belt-tightening, but one which the household seemed capable of accommodating with a certain grace. A. de M.)

28 April

We're working on swarms, we're working on old queens, we're working on young queens . . .

It's been a fine spring. Snowdrops, primroses, gentians, narcissi in abundance. Plenty of nectar for the early bees. We'll be able to observe the bees' care of the royal nymphs remaining in the hive after the old queen has left with a swarm. We already know that sometimes they seal in a royal nymph in order to delay her birth. What else can we find by observation?

14 *May*

We moved the bees from two straw hives into a glass hive. Two days later we introduced a queen who had laid freely in the past and she was well received and proceeded to lay in both small worker cells and large drone cells.

20 *May*

We found the foundations of sixteen royal cells.

27 *May*

We found ten of these cells enlarged, though unequally, with royal brood at different stages.

28 *May*

The queen's belly is much smaller but she begins to exhibit agitation. She appears to examine cells for the suitability of laying in, but then she will introduce just half her belly so the egg won't attach securely to the bottom of the cell. The bees that she meets in the course of her journey round the hive will stop if she stops, as though to consider her. Some of them climb on her back, but she continues. None of them give her any honey, but she helps herself as she passes the open cells. They no longer make circles of deference round her.

The first bees aroused by her follow her, excited, and in their turn excite the other bees. She visits every part of the hive until the agitation is universal. She drops her eggs anywhere, while the workers stop caring for the young and the bees returning from the field neglect to deposit their pollen. They all run over the combs wildly, finally rushing for the entrance with the queen and swarming out of the hive.

In order to keep this hive very populous we removed the old queen as soon as she flew out. As soon as the swarm realised they had no queen (which took only a very few minutes) they flew back to their old hive. We wanted to know whether the old queen always behaves in this way.

30 *May*

I've introduced a new, year-old queen who is well received and lays appropriately in small worker cells and large male ones. The bees enlarge some of them into royal cells.

1 June

The first royal cell from the previous queen is sealed by the workers, meaning there is at least one royal nymph maturing in the hive.

2 June

A second royal cell is sealed. At eleven o'clock everything is quiet and orderly in the hive, but at midday the queen suddenly becomes immensely agitated, running all over the combs and the workers become greatly disordered in response. Within a few minutes they mobbed the entrances and all flew out with their queen, settling on a branch of the hazel tree.

Again Monsieur told me to remove the queen so the bees would fly back to the hive. I did this without too much difficulty – perhaps they're too preoccupied with the question of where they'll spend the night. We retained the queen and the bees flew back. They were still excited and seemed to be looking for their queen, but by three o'clock all was calm again.

3 *June*

The bees have settled to their accustomed labours. They are without a queen. They close a third royal cell.

7 *June*

Over the past few days they have sealed several more royal cells. At the same time they've been abrading the wax of the older royal cells. They remove it in a pattern of wavy lines until it's almost transparent. The bees time this so that the cell is almost completely unwaxed on the seventh day, when the nymph is ready for her final metamorphosis into a queen. The thinly waxed portion is over her head and thorax, probably to allow for the evaporation of her great amount of bodily fluids.

All day we waited for this first queen to be born but it seemed the bees didn't wish it yet, for they covered the point where she would emerge with extra wax, thus keeping her prisoner inside.

'This is what we've been waiting for,' Monsieur says. 'They need a new queen, yet here they have one ready to be born and they keep her captive. Let's see what happens next and we may learn the reason.'

He had a look of the most intense concentration on his face, his head turned to one side, close to the hive. 'Listen. Do you hear anything, Burnens?'

'Nothing in particular, sir. Just the usual humming.' But already I was considering that blind people famously have sharper senses in other ways.

'Listen. Listen carefully. A kind of clacking sound coming from the oldest nymph's cell, the same notes in rapid succession, almost like the sound of knitting needles. But higher, more like piping.'

I really couldn't tell whether I could just make it out, or whether I wanted to believe I could.

'We'll come back tonight when they're quiet and see if we can hear it more distinctly.'

We went down to the hives again at ten o'clock. I stumbled a little, even with my lantern, in the darkness, but of course it made no difference to Monsieur who followed the rope path with his usual equanimity. It was a still, early summer night. I looked up at thousands of stars and the Milky Way lying in its multitude along the length of the sky. I thanked God for the gift of seeing it all. We listened to the hive and Monsieur heard the sound again, more distinctly.

'It's insistent,' he said. 'As though she's telling them she's ready. Commanding them to let her out.'

Again I wasn't wholly sure of it myself, but just as Monsieur trusts my eyes I'll trust his ears. He's mentioned in the past that he can't hear bats any more at his age – neither can I, at twenty-four, though Pierre still can at thirteen.

I saw him walking round the garden the other night, when he thought himself unobserved, banging the ground with a stick and saying, '*You* can't see them and *you* can't hear them,' referring to his father and me I supposed. I was amused. He's most tender and respectful to his father, as his father is to him, but it's important for him that he marks out his own world as well. I envied the way he used the stick and the words so easily, boyishly. I think I'd lost my boyhood by the time I was his age.

8 June

The nymph's piping has had no effect on the bees who remorselessly continue to cap her cell. But now we hear the same sound from a second royal cell. Another one ready to be born. Several bees keep guard at each cell.

9 June

At last! The first cell opens and what emerges is a slim, lively young queen (Q1), of a good brown colour, certainly strong enough to fly out at once, if she wishes.

'Two days extra maturity,' he says. 'They've delivered a strong queen. Is that why they made her wait?'

But she shows no inclination to fly out. Instead she's fascin-ated by the other royal cells. There cannot be two queens in a hive and her instinct is to kill each rival as she emerges, but whenever she approaches a royal cell the bees on guard bite her and pull her and chase her away. She can only find tranquillity a long way from these cells. Twice during the day she 'pipes' and each time it renders the bees motionless – with fear?

10 *June*

There are now twenty-three royal cells, all heavily guarded. It's hard for her to avoid them but whenever she goes near them the bees mob her, driving her away. She can't find anywhere tranquil and her agitation throws the bees into confusion. Quite soon they rush the entrances and swarm out, but, unusually, she can't lead them because she's trapped between two royal cells, too badly bitten to move. I took her out of the hive and when the bees realised their queen was not with them they returned. This was the second swarm of this hive. Once again they have no queen. There are now four sealed royal cells containing fully developed females.

11 *June*

Q2 has been sealed in for three days beyond her due day.

12 June

Nine o'clock. We found Q2 liberated and strong, but subject to the same cruel treatment that her older sister (Q1) had received. We didn't expect anything to happen at once and went back to the house for a good breakfast. When we returned we found the hive almost deserted, with a huge swarm clustered in a pear tree. We also found that the third cell was open and the queen (Q3) gone.

'They'll both be in the swarm,' Monsieur said, and so it proved. It was easy enough to see them by their size as I shook the colony into a basket. I removed them and the colony returned to the hive.

While we were engaged in this, Q4 had taken advantage of the confusion to liberate herself and when the bees returned they found her fairly agitated and attempting to approach the remaining royal cells. They resumed their guard: there were still eighteen royal cells to protect. At 10 p.m. Q5 was born. So there were now two queens in the hive.

I said I would stay up all night to see what the two of them did, hoping that my lantern light would be sufficient. Monsieur Huber sat up with me for a while.

'I expect the stars are good tonight,' he said. 'It feels as though there's a clear sky.'

'Yes, sir, they're very bright. And more shooting stars than usual.'

He sighed. 'I spent my very last hour of sight looking at

the night sky. I could just make out the moon, an occasional shooting star. When I woke the next morning there was no sight at all, not even a glimmer. But what was worse, it looked as though there was thick smoke. I sniffed but there was no smell of burning. Then I knew it was inside me and there was no escaping it.'

'That must have been a terrible moment, sir.'

'Do you know, it wasn't. Oddly enough, I felt a great relief. I'd been living in fear and now here was the thing itself and there was nothing left to be afraid of. It was as though a great weight had been taken from me.'

At this moment the two queens began to fight each other but without result. Monsieur retired and I went to bed at 4 a.m.

13 June

Q5 killed Q4. The victorious queen now approached one of the royal cells and began to pipe, striking the bees motionless. We thought that she would be able to take advantage of the dread that she inspired in the workers to succeed in opening the royal cell and killing the young queen inside, but she had to stop her piping in order to mount the cell to attack it, and as soon as the noise stopped the workers regained their courage and bit her and tormented her until they drove her away.

14 June

Q6 emerged from her cell. At eleven o'clock a huge swarm was thrown. The disorder was such that too few bees remained to guard the royal cells to prevent them from opening. We found Q5, Q6 and Q7 in the swarm and we removed them. The colony was returned to the hive. In their absence Q8, Q9 and Q10 had escaped from their cells and were in the hive. The bees resumed their duty around the royal cells that were still closed, mistreating any queen who tried to approach them.

Again I stayed up most of the night to observe their activity. There was a fight between two queens which resulted in the death of Q8, but Q11 hatched during the night so there were still three queens in the hive.

15 June

There was another duel to the death so now there were two queens left alive and they were both very excited, either wanting to fight each other or to attack the remaining royal cells. At noon they both led out a huge swarm and unfortunately it flew too far away and we lost sight of it.

16 June

The hive is now very thinly inhabited. The only bees left are those few who weren't affected by the agitation and didn't swarm, and those who were out gathering food at the time and returned when it was all over. There are too few of them to guard the royal cells: several queens escape and successively fight each other to the death until only one remains.

19 June

The last remaining queen has been indifferently treated by the bees.

20 June

She flies out and returns with all the signs of fecundation. She's treated with the greatest respect.

22 June

She lays her first eggs. There is a wonderful sense of a process completed. And seen by us in more detail than has ever been known before.

Monsieur is very pleased with these observations. 'Now we

know the extent of the new queens' murderous instincts we can understand better why the bees keep the royal nymphs in captivity. Suppose every queen emerged when she was ready, and then there was a spell of poor weather, too bad for any queen to lead out a swarm. What would happen?'

'The queens would slaughter each other successively until there was only one left,' I answered. 'And the last one couldn't lead out a swarm because there wouldn't be any emergent queens – they'd all have been born and killed already.'

'Exactly. So the multiplication of the colony would be left to the chance of fine weather. But nature is no fool. It ensures that if the queen can't fly out at once, her rivals will be imprisoned until it's safe to emerge. That way she can lead a swarm at the first opportunity, knowing there are royal nymphs in the hive. Good observations, Burnens, very good observations.'

30 *June*

Pierre has been ill for a week with a high fever. The doctor has visited every day, and yesterday his temperature started dropping and today he is declared to be on the mend. Monsieur has hardly left his bedside but now he's able to think about his work again and we walk to the hives.

We're still looking at swarms. One of our 'natural' hives threw its third swarm today and although we caught the first two and put them in new hives, this one barely settled on a tree for a few minutes before rushing off into the distance.

'Three swarms, and still enough left behind to build up a strong colony. Nature is prodigal sometimes.'

'A testament to the mild weather this year, sir.'

'And to your management of the hives, Burnens.'

'I remember that was one of the first things you taught me, sir. Never to take too much honey out for it will dishearten the bees. I hadn't thought of it like that before. If I'd thought about it at all it would just have seemed a mechanical business. Leave them enough to get through the winter and there's an end to it.'

'That's what many of our country beekeepers think. And it does well enough, providing the winter isn't too severe, or the spring too late. But they'd do better if they took the longer view.'

'I wonder, if the bees are disheartened when their hive is pillaged, do you think they feel the opposite when they're treated generously?'

'I think if we suppose the one we might suppose the other. We know that if we treat them like a dog, say, or even a child, gently and firmly, the colony thrives.'

At these words I had a sudden longing to be walking through spring meadows with a small boy beside me, his hand in mine, my son. So much to teach him and such delight in doing it. It seemed the simplest, most natural thing, and yet impossible because I don't have the wherewithal to support a family. I save what I can, but it's not a great deal after I've sent my mother the money for her extra comforts. And even worse, it seems as though my sister has repeated the pattern of her childhood by marrying a man who has turned to drink. I can't bear to think of her suffering as my mother did, so I have to find money to give her as well, to ensure that the rent is paid and my little niece Alise is clothed and fed. I went to see them and talked to Jeanne and urged him to change his ways and he promised he would, but I know what those promises are worth.

(Note: It's strange to read these words about myself and my family. There's pain of course, but also a great delight in this proof of my uncle's early affection for me. A. de M.)

1 July

'Now then, Burnens, let's use your observations to make a note on how the hive is replenished after a swarm. So many bees go. How is it that the hive re-establishes itself so quickly?'

'First of all, sir, there's plenty of brood left which will hatch in the next few days.'

'Yes. And what about the weather?'

'The hive will only swarm on a warm dry day. But then at least a third of the workers will be out foraging, and by the time they return all the excitement is over, and the newly hatched workers will still be too weak to fly out.'

'Anything else?'

'In the case of absolute delirium, when they all rush for the entrance at the same time, the bees at the bottom of the heap will be drenched with the sweat of those above them and they'll be too heavy to fly and will drop down to the bottom of the hive until they've recovered, and by then the swarm has gone.'

'Make a note. We must include it.' This means we'll note it in Monsieur's collected letters to Charles Bonnet, which are assuming an early form.

'But even given our kind management, see how dependent they are on fair weather. Last year, when it was poor, only one swarm despite all the provisions we'd left them for winter.' He was still tugging at his question of the moment, like pulling at a beard. 'How do the bees know so precisely the age of the nymphs? It must be the piping. But you don't hear the changes in the sound, do you, Burnens?'

'I'm not sure, sir, but I trust your hearing.'

I know he believes the intensity of the sound changes as the nymph matures. We presume the sound is made by one part of the body striking another, but after both observation and dissection we have found no organ that seems capable of producing this sound.

M. Huber takes this, as so much else, calmly. But I can see the disappointment on his face that what he hears can't be confirmed.

2 *July*

Something rather unexpected has happened. Dr Wenzel, whom Monsieur consulted in Paris a quarter of a century ago, is about to retire and has written to Monsieur to recommend an oculist in Geneva. As I read the letter aloud I couldn't help my voice becoming excited. Dr Wenzel explained that surgery on the eye had improved immeasurably in the last few years. There might be the possibility of an operation to partially restore the sight of the eye with the cataract. The cataract can now be removed whole instead of being needled.

I know that there was excitement in my voice. It seemed the most wonderful news to me. To see again, albeit only a little – what could be more wonderful than that?

'Shall I write for an appointment, sir?'

To my surprise he didn't share my sense of urgency. He tapped out his pipe. 'There's no hurry. I'll talk to Marie-Aimée about it.'

And, again to my surprise, she was not particularly excited at the prospect either. 'It's as you wish, dear François.' Her hand to his cheek, a kiss, his hand on hers.

Eventually they decided it would do no harm to consult the new doctor, but the appointment was made as just one incident in a day shopping in town. When they returned, the excitement was all in the beautiful doll they'd bought for little Marie and the fine compass for Pierre. I noticed they'd bought nothing for themselves.

Nobody spoke of the consultation with the oculist.

9 *July*

Sitting by the hives, he said, 'I'm not going to trouble with the operation. I expect you find that rather strange.'

'Well, sir . . .'

'It's not certain it would work, though it seems there's a chance of a certain amount of sight.' He raised his hand helplessly. 'I can't do it, Burnens. It's taken me twenty-five years to resign myself to my condition. And I think I truly am resigned now. I don't want to lose that. I had enough of false hopes as a youth, it would be foolish – I can't do it again, at my age.'

'I can understand that, sir.' And I could. But . . .

He smiled. 'Besides, if I could see again, how could I appreciate how much I'm loved? Her guiding hand that lights my darkness. I remember her, you know, as she looked at seventeen, that's always my picture of her. Her voice even then was so touching – it could only be that there was a sensitive heart beneath it. And today it's still the same, still as gentle to me, and her face is even softer now than then. What more do I need to see?'

Your children? I didn't say this aloud of course, but he answered the question himself.

'Of course I miss never having actually seen my children but I can imagine them so well, looking the picture of their mother. And I *can* see them. I've felt their features, I hear their voices, I *can* see them. I feel their movements – children's movements, not like ours. Somewhere inside myself I feel all this so strongly. And it doesn't depend on anything outside that could let me down like my eyes did. I've carved out that niche, slowly, over the years. I'm not going to desert it now, it's taken too long to make. I can do well enough there. Well enough is good enough.'

There's nothing I can say to this. I haven't been through the things he has. I wonder, because Marie-Aimée copes so well with his blindness, might she find it difficult if he could see again? They're both forty this year, an age when, as I understand it, a man sometimes no longer has the passion for his wife that he felt when she was a young woman. (Although her vitality makes her seem much younger than her years.) But does the happiness of their marriage depend in some unspoken way on his remaining blind? He needs her ministrations and she needs him to depend on them. In that way they're both happy.

10 July

And so we continue with our work on swarms.

It's understandable that a young queen should choose to lead out a swarm; her life inside the hive is made miserable by the workers' violent frustation of her instinctive desire to kill her rivals. However, hives with a queen who's been there for over a year behave differently, and will allow her to kill the young nymphs if she wishes.

But even so, still she doesn't always kill them all. Perhaps it's horror or aversion at the sheer number of them, eighteen or twenty to destroy. Her courage fails her, so many, too many, and she's seized by a terrible agitation. And if the weather's fine, she seizes the moment and goes, taking the bulk of the workers with her.

It's understandable that the bees, accustomed to her, loving her as their mother, finding her presence a necessity, should follow her out. But why should they follow out young virgin queens to whom they seem at best indifferent?

We have thermometers in the hive and there's an easy answer: to escape the heat that rises from 90°–97° F to above 104° F as the queen runs deliriously over the combs, exciting the whole colony. Exactly the temperature at which a human being might become delirious, as happened with Pierre.

11 July

Pierre, fully recovered, has found a nest of young hedgehogs, only a few days old, I judge. He brings one to his father. Its eyes are still closed. Monsieur feels it gently.

'Its spines are already hardening. They must be soft when it's born or how would the poor dam deliver her litter?'

The little creature is only two or three inches long and he strokes it softly. 'Do you see how it can't roll up into a ball yet? It must be that the muscle isn't strong enough while it's so young.'

'Can we keep it, Papa?'

'No. Animals rarely thrive if they're separated from their own kind. A bee will die of loneliness if she's on her own. This little hedgehog may survive if we feed it by hand, but then it will never survive in the wild. That's not fair. It's a wild creature. Take it back to the nest. It may live, it may not, but either way it's better without our intervention.'

Pierre nodded. 'But with Annette? That will be different? She's not wild.'

Annette is our house-dog who's about to pup.

Monsieur sighed in resignation. 'We'll look after Annette's pups if she can't.'

12 July

Monsieur has been considering what happens when a strange queen enters the hive. One of the two dies, that's undisputed. But while Reaumur conjectures that there's combat between the two of them, the German observers, Schirach, Hattorf and Reim, claim that the worker bees kill the invader with their stings.

'I don't believe it,' Monsieur says. 'Their observation hives are so crude and bee fights are so fast, running between the combs, that they can't possibly have made accurate observations.' We, however, have our flat glass hives.

13 *July*

We observed a hive where there were five or six royal nymphs. Within ten minutes of the first being born she was tearing at the tip of another royal cell, and when she couldn't break through at the top she turned to the bottom. She managed to make a big enough hole here to introduce her belly and strike her rival several times with her sting, killing her. The bees, who had been watching her, enlarged the hole and drew out the body of a young queen, which they ate, as well as the pap at the bottom of the cell.

Two virgin queens emerged from their cells at the same time. As soon as they saw each other they rushed together, appearing very angry, and each grabbed the antennae of the other in her own mouth. Their heads, corslets and bellies were opposed to each other such that each could sting the other to death, simultaneously. But it seems that nature does not wish this, for when both of them are vulnerable in this way, they back off and run away from each other.

We've seen this phenomenon many times.

'Now,' Monsieur says. 'It's a law of nature that there can only be one queen in a hive. So what happens when a second queen is born, or enters, the hive? One of them has to die. But nature can't leave this to the workers, for it might be that one group of bees would pounce on one queen, while another group, unaware, might attack the other, leaving the hive with no queen at all. So the queens have to fight each other, in single combat. But, when they approach each other front to front, it's possible that each could kill the other. Again the hive would be left without a single queen. This so alarms them that they flee.'

We see our queens approach again, and retreat. Then we see one dart on her rival from behind and seize the unfortunate creature at the base of her wings and – with no risk to herself – position herself above her rival to pierce her at the base of her rings. Very soon the vanquished queen dies.

These observations pertain to virgin queens. We want to see if the same is true of fertile queens.

15 July

Annette has had four healthy puppies, of which we will keep one and the other three are already spoken for. Pierre and little Marie are content with this and play with them in endless delight.

22 July

We observe a fertile queen destroy three nymph cells. While the old queen still remains, we introduce into the hive a new fertile queen. We observe that the guards cluster round the new queen – balling her – so thickly that within a minute she is an absolute prisoner. But strangely enough they do the same to their reigning queen, though to a lesser extent, and by this means they keep the queens apart, until they feel inclined to fight each other, at which time the bees fall back and see what happens.

We've observed this many times, enough to be confident to contradict Messrs. Schirach and Reim and assert that, in a natural hive, the bees never sting the intruder to death. In fact they kill her by balling her so tightly that she dies of suffocation, unless she's strong or agile enough to take on combat with the reigning queen.

Only once have we seen them sting an intruding queen – and that was my fault, for I was moved with pity for the young queen who had perhaps lost her way and ventured into another queen's hive. The guards at the entrance identified her as a stranger so quickly, and summoned reinforcements so speedily, that she had no chance of escape, and foolishly I tried to remove her from the middle of the ball. The bees were incensed at this and stung both her and me indiscriminately (and several of themselves were stung to death in the process as well, which could not have been their intention).

We were interested to know how the bees would receive a strange queen when their own queen had been removed. We have read M. de Reaumur's account of how they will receive a new queen well, as soon as their old queen has gone.

M. Huber says, 'I don't think so.' And he knows he's right, but the reputation of M. de Reaumur is such that we must make observation after observation until we know we can't be wrong. M. de Reaumur based his assertion on an experiment where he induced four hundred bees to enter a glass box where they could be observed. At first they were much agitated, but when he introduced a new queen the disquiet ceased and they welcomed her.

'I don't contest the results of this experiment, but I don't think it justifies his conclusion. He's taken out a few hundred of the seventy thousand or so in the hive. These bees are not in their natural circumstances. He himself has noted that too few bees together lose their will to work, so their instinct is modified. To make such an experiment conclusive it's necessary to conduct it in a fully populated hive.'

And so of course this is what we've done.

At first the bees don't notice that their own queen has gone and they continue with their labours, but after a few hours they become agitated and run all over the combs. If their own queen is then reintroduced they recognise her (feeling her with their antennae) and calm is restored. But if a strange queen is introduced within the first twelve hours they reject her, despite their lack of a queen of their own. They ball her and she generally dies of hunger or suffocation. This was what M. de Reaumur interpreted as a welcoming dance, whereas in fact it is the prelude to a deadly imprisonment.

If we wait eighteen hours to introduce a strange queen the bees still encircle her, but with less energy, and sometimes she survives to reign. If we wait twenty-four to thirty hours the strange queen will be well received, and reign from the moment she arrives – to the extent that the bees will destroy the large cells and royal grubs of their former queen in order to make way for the progeny of their new queen.

'And what can we say of that?' he asked. 'Have they forgotten their own mother so quickly?'

'Perhaps, sir, by then they're desperate for a mother – any mother.'

He nodded. 'Yes,' he said thoughtfully. 'People can become desperate, so why not bees?'

2 *August*

M. Jean Huber died a week ago after several months of illness. He had a cancer and his body was skeletal at the end. He'd travelled to Paris for an operation by a specialist but on his return it was clear from his gaunt frame that his condition had not improved but had considerably worsened. I should say, more accurately, that it was clear to me, as soon as we entered the room where he was lying, but the bed was too near the door for me to alert Monsieur to this fact in time and so the first he knew of it was when he bent to kiss his father. He cradled the shrunken face in his hands, and as his fingers found the little flesh remaining on the bones I saw his eyes widen and his fingers almost flew off his father's face. But he controlled the reaction at once and set himself to feeling the protuberance of cheekbone and brow, covered only by papery skin. He murmured words of endearment.

Having lost my own father when I was so young I always

find it touching that men of Monsieur's age have fathers at all, let alone fathers to whom they give respect and deference.

There was no need for the doctor to spell out the prognosis, although he did. Monsieur could tell it all through his fingers.

The funeral was well-attended, for M. Jean Huber had been a Councillor, one of the Two Hundred. The feast afterwards was held at Monsieur's brother's house in Geneva. As the mourners left and the numbers diminished, until only the closest family (of which I was counted one) were sitting in the kitchen, with the servants of the house standing around the walls, the conversation, influenced by wine, became both more affectionate and more disrespectful.

The talk was of M. Jean Huber's skill in the art of découpage with the dog, the piece of cheese, the profile of Voltaire. Or making it himself with scissors and paper but with his eyes closed – a piquant trick to perform in front of his blind son, I thought – or with his hands behind his back. Or getting the cat to do it. Or he could even do it by tearing the paper, not even using scissors. Many of these vellum pieces are now in cabinets of curiosities in England.

Undoubtedly it was done well, but was it worth doing at all? Nobody mentioned this, for it was a time for appreciation, indulgence. Just as, at my own father's funeral, only his military valour was discussed, not the sad decline afterwards.

But M. Jean Huber's skill gave him a reputation of sorts. He drew a series of portraits of the domestic life of Voltaire, whom he knew for twenty years. The great man delighted in

Huber's original conversation. The Czarina Catherine insisted on having the drawings, but Senebier arranged for them to be engraved first. Unfortunately the engraver stole one of the pictures, showing Voltaire getting out of bed and putting on his breeches while dictating to his secretary, and when it was published a verse had been added underneath that when Voltaire showed his arse, d'Alembert kissed it while Freran spanked it.

Then there was the joke he played on Mallet du Pan. He put an announcement in the public press that Kemplen's celebrated chess-playing automaton was coming to Nyon. He suggested to Mallet that they should go and see it for themselves but he didn't appear for their rendezvous so Mallet went on his own. He duly played a game with the automaton – and lost. Mallet returned home amazed and was about to declare his admiration to journalists when M. Jean, in fits of laughter, revealed that he himself had played the part of the automaton. What skill, to act the part so well that his good friend had no suspicion. (A good joke. And yet . . .)

Eventually, when over fifty, he settled to more serious work and his *Note on the Flight of Birds of Prey* was published in the *Mercure de France*, but it was too tentative to receive much notice. The next year he expanded it to a book of *Observations* with twelve (short) chapters and seven illustrations by himself. His theory was that birds of prey divided into two classes according to how they used their wings. The 'rowers' were the high fliers, like falcons, while the 'sailors' were the low fliers like eagles and vultures. He asserted that the tail did not act as a rudder, its only purpose being to assist in the bird's ascent or descent. These observations were fairly well received but he did no further work on the subject and never published again.

As the day drew to a close, Monsieur raised his glass and said, 'Let our toast be that we're the poorer without him.'

The family was well enough pleased with this as the epitaph to the day. We rode home quietly, each of us absorbed in our own contemplation of what it is to lose a father.

3 *August*

But the next day, while we were at the hives, Monsieur had regained his composure enough to make a more considered judgement, although one that he would not have mentioned to his brother, or even his wife, because it was too upsetting to look so soon at the whole truth instead of the comforting, partial truth with which the family could console itself. He banged his pipe quite violently against the leg of his old wooden chair.

'Are we poorer without him? Yes. Did he use his talents to the full? No. What was squandered, that's the painful part. The sense of what might have been done that was not done. Is he clicking his fingers in irritation now, looking at the waste?'

For some reason I was bold enough to say 'Yes, sir, I think he might be.'

He looked at me keenly. 'Your own father, I know, did not live up to his talents.'

'No, sir. But more prodigally than yours.'

He smiled gently, and I suddenly felt relieved for I had never admitted this as frankly before.

After a while he said, 'Fathers teach us things which will be with us for ever. How to spot a hawk coming in fast. How to tell one plant from another. How to judge the skies and the weather. How to pace your walking. How to greet a stranger, or a neighbour, or a friend.'

I agreed fervently, for I remembered each of those instances in my early years with my father, walking in the mountains. Lessons easily and naturally learned, and never forgotten.

'But it becomes more difficult,' he said. 'Once you know that if you only walk at one pace a·second you can walk all day, once you know what red clouds at night mean, once you can tell a crow from a rook, what do you do with this knowledge? That's where fathers become fallible. The point where they leave their own father's knowledge and have to make their own way. Some of them make that way and some of them don't . . .'

I said nothing. My heart was too full.

'For me, my father died in Dr Wenzel's consulting rooms when he began crying. There was still a man whom I loved deeply, but it wasn't the same.'

'For me I suppose it was the first time I heard him beat my mother for complaining when he came home drunk.' I'd never said this before in my life.

'Ah, that's a harder case,' he said. We were quiet.

'But they can't stop teaching us.' He smiled again. 'They teach us by example. At first it may seem a problem that it's a negative example. But by seeing them live their lives we learn how not to live our own. This might make us downcast at first, we might envy the man who has a father he would be proud to emulate in every respect, but in fact it makes us stronger. We know all too clearly the path we don't want to go down, so the fruitful path is all the better lit.'

He got to his feet, a man of nearly forty, pushing his palms down on his knees to help himself up. 'And tomorrow that path needs some careful observations of the bees to keep it well-lit.'

I agreed with all my heart.

14 *August*

We've been looking at the way the bees make their cocoons, particularly the queen. Starting out as an egg, three days later a worm hatches which grows for five days. At the end of this time the bees close up her cell and the worm immediately begins spinning a cocoon, which takes her twenty-four hours. For almost three days she is in complete repose before she begins transforming into a nymph. Four days after that she reaches the state of perfect queen.

'And how is the queen different? Does she cocoon herself just like the workers and drones?'

'No, sir. They always spin themselves a complete cocoon, closed at both ends and completely surrounding the body. But the royal worm does it differently. She spins an incomplete cocoon, covering only the head, thorax and first ring of the abdomen.'

'Are you sure? How many have you observed?'

'Just one so far, sir.'

'Are you sure this isn't just a defective instinct in one queen?'

'No, sir, I can't be sure of that. I'll observe more.' Which is what I've been doing, over many days in different hives.

20 *August*

I've repeated this observation with other queens, many times. Some people might consider this a trifling matter but Monsieur was delighted by it, for it shows the art with which nature manages the bees.

'From our work on the young queens we know that the firstborn seeks to kill the others before they emerge from the cocoon. But she couldn't do this if they were completely enveloped in a cocoon. Why?'

'Because the silk it's made from is so strong that her sting couldn't penetrate it. And if she did manage to sting she wouldn't be able to withdraw it because her barbs would be caught in the mesh.'

'So she'd die herself, a victim of her own fury. Nature doesn't wish a queen to die while killing another. If that happened there'd soon be no queens left at all. So to enable her to destroy her rivals, nature decrees that the royal nymphs only spin themselves a partial cocoon.'

We were quiet as the implications of this settled in our minds.

He sighed. 'Many times we're called on to marvel at the care nature gives to preserving and multiplying the species, but here we must admire the equal care she gives to exposing some individuals to death.'

'That's a sobering thought, sir.'

'But not really a surprising one. Should we expect it to be otherwise? Should we expect something as rich and varied as nature to exclude deliberate destruction?'

For some reason I thought of my father's death, although he, at least, had had the chance to procreate two children, unlike the vulnerable royal nymphs.

21 August

The prospect of procreation begins to make itself felt at home, for Martha has become betrothed to a fine young man, an apprentice watchmaker who has visited the house and whom Monsieur has approved of. Having no parents, only an older brother away serving in the Swiss Guard, Martha and Sarah regard Monsieur as the head of their family, a role he accepts with grace and due responsibility.

I was present at Monsieur's interview with the young man.

'And who is your master?'

'Monsieur Tissot, sir.'

'Ah, a master craftsman. He'll teach you well. And your intentions towards Martha?'

'To make her my wife, sir. To support a family by my work.'

'You know that Martha has been one of my family for a long time now. I stand as the father she doesn't have. If anyone were to neglect her or harm her I would feel it as a father would.'

The young man looked alarmed. 'I assure you, sir, I love her and all my intention is to provide for her as best I can.'

Monsieur rises from his chair, smiling, at peace. 'Then let's drink to it.'

And everyone is called into the library and toasts are drunk to Henri and Martha.

I wish her well with all my heart. I think they'll make a strong married couple. He will work hard and she will run a neat, orderly household, for she's learnt a great deal from Madame over the years. There's a warm feeling of new possibilities, but still at a comfortable distance, for he's three years away from finishing his apprenticeship yet.

22 August

Monsieur wanted to know whether spinning an incomplete cocoon was instinctive or simply the result of royal cells being too wide at their base for the nymph to get a purchase. We proved that it is the size of the cell that dictates the royal cocoon being left open, not an instinct. Royal worms enabled to spin complete cocoons in small cells undergo all their metamorphoses equally well. Leaving the cocoon open is not necessary to their development. Nature's only object is to expose them to death, and the hive colludes in this.

What an example of the subtlety of nature: that all bees have the instinct to spin a complete cocoon but the workers have in addition the instinct to build the royal cells too big for the royal worms to be able to do so.

24 *August*

'But let's continue,' he says. 'We often find males that are smaller than usual and queens as well. Bonnet suggests we take out all the worker cells from a hive and leave only the larger cells, which would naturally be for males. If the queen lays females in them which grow larger than usual we can conclude that cell size has considerable effect on growth.'

I duly set up this experiment, but within a day the dreaded death's head moths had invaded the hive. Those bees that survived the attack were discouraged by this, and so were we, for it's no small effort to identify and remove every worker from a well-stocked hive. It takes the bees a long time to rediscover their usual round after this sort of event, so we left that hive aside and I removed all the small cells from another one, leaving only the larger drone cells, and put in more comb of drone cells to fill it up.

25 *August*

'What are we expecting to see?' Monsieur asks.

'That they'll start repairing the damage from the removal of the worker combs.'

'Have they started yet?'

'Not yet.'

27 *August*

'Still no activity. They just stay clustered on the comb, they're not generating any heat.'

'They're discouraged. Their attitude to the queen?'

'All the usual respect. But none of the usual activity otherwise.'

'What's the queen doing?'

'She's groaning with eggs but she's dropping them anywhere rather than lay them in the large cells.'

A few mornings later, we woke to find that the hive was quiet, cold and dismal. Those bees that flew out at all came back with no supplies.

'Let's try to animate them. Put in a comb of small cells filled with male brood. Let's see if that will make them work at joining the new comb to the existing one.'

30 *August*

'They have not joined the combs, sir, but they've not been idle. They've cleaned out all the small cells of male brood and made them empty and ready to be laid in.'

'Have they indeed?'

'And now, sir, the queen is laying in the small empty cells, sometimes as many as five or six eggs in one cell.'

'Then take out the other combs of large cells and replace them with small.'

This I did, and the bees seemed entirely restored to their usual activity.

2 *September*

'Interesting, then,' he mused, 'that the queen can only lay certain eggs at certain times of year. If it's her time to lay females, she can't choose to lay males just because there are only male sized cells available. She'd rather drop them haphazardly than lay them in the wrong sized cell. It seems that the common worker bees show more intelligence here, for instead of caring for the brood of young males as they would generally have done, they cleared them out to leave the cells free so that the queen, bursting to lay females, might have the chance.'

'We know from our dissections, sir, that the queen's brain is tiny compared with her ovaries.'

He sighed. 'The workers do the thinking, as they do every-thing else. The queen can't overcome her instinct only to lay females in small cells, so they solve the problem by clearing the male brood out of the small cells, leaving them free for her to lay in.'

'And to do that they have to overcome their instinct to care for brood, of whatever sex.'

'Indeed. And they make more work for themselves. If we grant them intelligence here, we might also see evidence of their affection for their queen.'

1 4 *September*

I gather the problem is continuing with Madame's French investments. The effect of the revolution seems to be that the currency is worth a little less every day and taxes aren't being collected. Apparently there's a highly revolutionary group of Swiss Patriots in Paris supported by Vaudois refu-gees. I have to say I think my sympathies lie more with the Swiss Guard.

10 *October*

Monsieur and Madame are planning a supper party with dancing for their friends and family to celebrate their fortieth birthdays. They've inherited some fine plates and serving dishes from Monsieur's father as well as some good rugs and furniture and paintings.

The house seems more substantial now. Monsieur loves the things that remind him of his childhood. In particular there's a very old, low oak chest and every time he passes it he stoops to run his fingers along it with a smile. Pierre asked him why he was so fond of it.

'One of my earliest memories is of being too small to see inside it and even though I saw the maids taking linen in and out I still imagined there was something mysterious and exciting inside, that only I would be able to see.'

'Were you very disappointed when you realised there was only linen?'

'It was worse than that. One day, I must have been three or four, I found I was strong enough to push the lid up by myself, but after a few inches it was too heavy for me and it fell back down on my fingers. I howled. Of course it was very painful but what hurt more was the notion that it had bitten me for trying to find out its secret. I couldn't put that into words although my father guessed something of my distress. He picked me up to see inside while the maid emptied it of every piece of linen.

'"Now you know what's in it you don't need to look again," he said.

'He needn't have worried for I had no intention of doing so. When I got a bit bigger, tall enough to clamber up on it, I'd sit on the lid with my legs crossed and I felt like the king of the castle because I knew it couldn't bite while I was sitting there.'

I could see the thirteen-year-old boy smirking at the picture of his father as a young boy. 'You're not frightened of it any more, then, Father?'

'No, I'm not,' his father said straightforwardly, and Pierre had the grace to look ashamed. 'Now I know it's just a chest, but I'm very fond of it.'

Today, when he ran his hand across it he was startled to find little Marie sitting on it, cross-legged.

'Marie, get off the chest,' her mother said.

'No, my dear, let her stay. Why are you sitting here, little one?'

'I don't know. I just like it.'

'I used to like it too when I was a little boy.' He didn't explain the history of it, just picked her up to kiss her forehead, and she kissed him back and he put her on the floor where she happily followed her mother, while he and I made our way to the library.

I love these family scenes, and am envious of them too.

6 November

Preparations are seriously in hand for the party. Anna has been ferociously busy with pies and pâtés, and jugged meats, anything that can be made ahead of the day. Jacques was gloomy. 'I don't know what they're going to do for flowers. I know Madame doesn't want to spend money on them. If anyone had told me in the spring I might have managed something, but as it is there's only greenery and berries.'

'And very suitable too for this time of year,' Anna said stoutly, putting a list in his hand for the second trip to town that day.

Martha and Sarah have been running hither and yon, but at last Martha was allowed to leave the kitchen to attend Madame and dress her hair.

As I passed her dressing room, carrying fresh clothes for Monsieur, I overheard her saying to Martha, 'You just begin to notice that when you pass a gentleman in the street he looks at you and then politely looks away. His eyes don't linger, as they would with a young woman. It's something you don't really notice until it doesn't happen any more.' She sighed slightly.

'You're still the most beautiful woman in the world to Monsieur.'

'Yes, that's true, that's true.'

Monsieur has not the same reservations about his age. Indeed, he finds himself well, with a wife and two children whom he adores, and a settled establishment. He knows he's in the prime of life.

In the event Madame descends to meet their guests dressed in the finest of the family jewellery, looking – I can't say – such an elegant, beautiful woman.

There's eating and drinking and merriment. We're all included. After the food is cleared away, the rugs are rolled back and the fiddlers who've been summoned for the occasion start up their music. Martha and her young man dance up and down the aisle. Sarah looks wistful. I ask her to dance, safe in this company. There are quadrilles, and the old country dances, which we all know, guests and servants alike, and which are received with the greatest enjoyment.

Monsieur joins in on the harpsichord, picking out lively tunes. There's a late supper from Anna, who's forsaken the jollity in order to produce the next meal. We eat and it's time for our guests to go home.

Nobody mentions that Madame has made it clear this will be the last time there'll be such a celebration unless things improve very much in France, which doesn't look likely at the moment.

1791

3 February

Throughout the long winter months indoors a young woman
has been visiting Monsieur, one of many visitors. She is greatly
interested in natural history, as most of them are, and perhaps
more to the point she is also blind. This gives ample occasion
for the innocent touching of faces and hands. Marie-Aimée
is always present at their meetings, watching stony-faced. Of
course neither of them can see her expression. But it's clear to
an observer that the camaraderie of the blind is the one thing
she can't give her husband and she doesn't care to find herself
in that position.

I always open Monsieur's correspondence in the library in
the morning, sorting it into work or personal matters When
I opened the young woman's letter today I hesitated for a
moment as to which pile to put it on. Marie-Aimée happened
to be in the library at the time, which was unusual. Generally
at mid-morning she's immersed in her own domestic world.
Perhaps she was on the alert for something. In any event she
took the letter from my indecisive hands and – I can only say
– devoured its contents.

She threw it straight on to the fire where it was a cinder in seconds. She looked at me defiantly. 'He has enough to think about already. He won't be interested in that.' And with that, her rival was dispatched.

She gave me a challenging look and I raised my eyebrows slightly and turned to one side. With that gesture it was understood that I wouldn't tell Monsieur of the letter and his wife's destruction of it. But I don't feel at ease and I feel rather sorry for the blind young woman, even though it was intended as a farewell letter on her family's moving to Basle. The irony of the matter is that he asked me a few days ago for my opinion of her appearance and I told him she had a plain but good-hearted face. He nodded in satisfaction and said he knew she wasn't a beauty because her voice was too strident. So in fact Marie-Aimée has no grounds for jealousy anyway. I won't mention it to her though, for I've no wish to be a go-between, drawn into things that are none of my business.

Sarah walked in on the end of this, bringing wood for the fire, and at once sniffed something and looked pert. She's flighty, she hasn't grown up to be a responsible young woman like Martha.

Madame ignored her in a marked manner and Sarah quailed a little and left the room quickly.

The Beekeeper's Pupil

20 *February*

There's been severe frost for several days and all the lanes were filled to the tops of the hedges with snow. All of us able-bodied men have been out digging the tracks free. Monsieur works like a devil, spadeful after spadeful, hour after hour. There's no noise, the snow deadens everything, which might be thought to be a blessing but is actually eerie and uncomfortable.

When I asked Jacques whether he had young plants that would suffer, he said snow was the kindest mantle for young plants. 'As long as it doesn't melt too fast, they're safe.'

Monsieur said much the same about our hives, that as long as they stay cold they'll stay healthy, unlike hives that are carelessly placed so as to catch the first sun, so often succeeded by a bitter frost.

There's been a thaw and a freeze, a thaw and a freeze. The result is that the ice on the lake is now perfect for skating.

The sky was a vivid blue, the ice wonderfully smooth. I love to skate, the way that thought and movement come together so perfectly.

First Madame and then Pierre led Monsieur around the outer circuit. I helped Marie who, at six years old, isn't fully confident yet. As I supported her with my hands lightly round her waist she began to find her balance and she improved very quickly. It was immensely satisfying. Pierre challenged me to a race, his voice breaking gruffly halfway through his words. No longer a little boy, that's certain. I won, but only just. Next year he might manage it.

Monsieur and Marie made a little dance at the side, where they were out of the way. Then Marie-Aimée skated into the middle, twirling and sweeping on her own, a beautiful ice dance, unencumbered. (But I wish Monsieur could have seen her.)

Afterwards we were all red-cheeked and bright-eyed and when we came home Anna had perfect fondue ready to eat. We all ate together at the kitchen table.

'These small moments are the great moments in our life,' Monsieur said.

10 *April*

We've observed the scarcity of thrushes and blackbirds, killed by the frost.

20 *April*

The revolution in France proceeds apace. It's proclaimed there that the queen bee is now to be called the laying bee.

Monsieur shrugs in amusement. 'Changing her name won't change her nature. The bees are hardly going to decide they can do very well without her. I think we may still call ours queens.'

Here in Pregny we continue quietly with our work, although

some of Monsieur's discoveries may be called revolutionary, for they upset established notions. We've been investigating why we often see workers with their head and thorax inserted in cells containing eggs, and remaining there motionless for several minutes. Is it, as many observers believe, because they're caring for the newly laid eggs?

'Is it impossible to see what they're doing inside the cell?'

'Yes, sir. Though if we can get them to establish cells along the glass in the observation hive, there might be a chance.'

'So let's try it the other way round and see what happens to the eggs if the bees can't get to them.'

I put newly laid eggs into a box with air holes too small for the bees to enter and placed the box in a strong hive where they would have sufficient heat. They've hatched today at the usual time, just as if they'd been left in their cells.

'So it's clear they don't need care from the bees to hatch. But what have you seen?'

'I've seen them enter cells with nothing to attract them, no eggs, no honey,' I told him. 'They'll remain absolutely motionless there for twenty minutes at a time, so still they could be dead.'

'What do you think they're doing?'

'They're resting, sir, I'm sure of it.'

He nodded. 'They work so hard they have to rest hard too, as though they were dead. But the drones will rest that hard for eighteen hours at a time.'

'They pay for it in the end though.'

'Ah yes, nature always rights the balance.'

30 *June*

News has arrived of the French royal family's attempt at escape, in disguise and with false passports. They were hoping to reach the Rhine frontier, where Marie Antoinette thought they could recruit an army to march on Paris. They made quite a distance but then they were recognised and pursued to Varennes where they were caught. They were escorted back to Paris and now they're effectively imprisoned in the Tuileries, whereas before they lived there 'at the request' of the Assembly. There's an appalling fascination with the events, already far removed from the optimism of two years ago.

'You can't make an omelette without breaking eggs,' is Anna's surprisingly revolutionary view. Jacques sighs. Sarah attempts to give him a commiserating look, but he chooses not to see it, sensible man.

2 *July*

Our own labour is intense at the moment for, while we continue with our observations, we're also writing up five years' work in the form of letters to Charles Bonnet.

Monsieur is avid to publish. It's as though his father's death a year ago has freed him in some way so he can be more openly ambitious without belittling his father's achievements, such as they were. He's ready to stand alone now. It's strange how some men can enter fiercely into competition with their fathers in their youngest manhood while others must wait until he has left the scene before they can stretch their wings.

I've noticed this because my view of my own father has begun to change. Even though he died so long ago, it's as if I've only paid my respects, to some extent, in the last year. I've begun to realise the price he paid for his life in the army, which kept us warm and fed for many years.

I can see that it gave him the habit of drinking, and a need for robust drinking companions, a habit which was never going to sit well in our small (and small-minded) village. I can feel some sympathy now for the isolation he felt. He ended up ostracised – a miserable fate for a sociable man. I understand now that the impulse which led him to escape the village was just the same feeling which made me jump at the chance to serve Monsieur, rather than serving out my days in farm labour.

We've both escaped our fathers' rule at last. For Monsieur the consequences are fairly clear. For myself I'm not so sure.

4 *July*

The letters we're working on, based on our observations over the years, are in the form of essays: 'On the Fecundation of the Queen Bee'; 'On the Formation of Swarms', and so on.

I write a draft and read it to Monsieur who stops me frequently to rephrase something or to dictate further observations. I write a second draft and again he stops me as I read, though less frequently. I write a third draft which receives only minor modifications. He's pleased. 'This is worth Monsieur Bonnet's time,' he says.

I know that M. Bonnet's reputation will ensure that the work gets a serious reception and so his good opinion is very important to Monsieur. But there's something, I don't know, too much deference perhaps, that makes me uneasy. Bonnet's too keen on mutilation for my taste, though I know it's necessary sometimes.

For example when Monsieur wanted to understand the purpose of the antennae, the only way was to remove first one and then both and observe what happened. When only one antenna was removed the queen still behaved naturally, but when she had none at all she ran wildly over the combs, dropping her eggs anywhere. When a second such mutilated queen was put in the hive they showed no malevolence towards each other, and neither did the bees to the stranger queen.

Could it be that without their antennae the queens can't be distinguished and the bees get an equally pleasant sensation from them? Certainly when an unmutilated queen was put in the hive the bees attacked her very fiercely. We concluded that the antennae are not a frivolous ornament, as some have thought, but possibly the organs of touch or smell. This was a worthwhile discovery but once it was made we felt no need to repeat the experiment.

M. Bonnet is still very keen for us to observe an actual

fecundation and has urged Monsieur again to mutilate the queen's wings as he did a couple of years ago so the queen can't fly as high or as fast.

So we cut her wings to satisfy M. Bonnet's curiosity. (And as I began to perform the operation one day I could swear I heard Monsieur say, 'Sorry.')

When I cut off a little of the queen's wings she flew just as fast as before. When I cut off a lot she couldn't fly at all. After quite a few tries Monsieur said, 'There may be a medium ground but we haven't found it. This is not how we're going to prove it. We'll stop.'

I was glad that his respect had limits. But when Monsieur told him of our results, M. Bonnet suggested rendering their sight less acute by covering their eyes with an opaque varnish. His own sight had almost gone, but then he was nearly seventy. Monsieur was blind.

'I think we must try it,' he said. 'Just once.'

Today I applied the varnish with a heavy heart. She squirmed as I touched her eyes. I know that we both felt compassion for that queen – impelled by instinct to fly out, perhaps not realising that she had not the wherewithal to find her way back home again, and meeting a lonely death.

The varnish made no difference to the virgin queen flying out fast and high. But she never came back.

He said, 'That's enough of that experiment. It doesn't work. We don't need to do more.'

And in the meantime we hear of a dreadful massacre in the Champs de Mars in Paris, and that Marie Antoinette, despite her imprisonment, is able to make clear her approval of the National Guard shooting so many citizens. She must be the most hated woman in France. I think of our queen bees who destroy their rivals ruthlessly, but never, ever, turn against their workers.

2 *August*

Today we discovered something that was never known before. Simple words to write, but such pride.

We know that semen exposed to air coagulates, and we had always assumed that what we saw in the vulva of queens returning from the flight of fecundation was coagulated semen. So, accepting at last that we'd never see an actual fecundation and in order to neglect nothing, Monsieur decided to dissect returning queens, to observe what condition their organs were in at that moment.

'Why has it taken me so long to think of doing this?' he said.

I set up the microscope and the dissecting board in the library and we sat by the hives to catch returning queens. (I've observed incidentally that sometimes impregnated queens may still be infertile. When this happens the queen flies out again in a day or two. 'Shows some drones are more fit for mating than others,' Monsieur says. 'Not unexpected.')

But today the very first impregnated one that I caught showed us, without dissection, something we hadn't even been looking for. I had seized her by her wings and examined the underside of her belly. Her vulva was partly open and showed the oval end of a white body which by its size and position was too big to allow the lips of her vulva to close. We took her to the microscope and I was about to kill her with bromide smoke when I noticed that her belly moved incessantly, stretching and shrinking with convulsive effort. At last she managed to reach her posterior with her legs and pull out what was inside her vulva. It dropped into my hand.

I looked at it in astonishment. 'Sir, it's not coagulated semen. It's not a shapeless mass.'

'What is it? What do you see?'

'It's a part of a body. It must be part of the body of the male that fertilised her.'

'Use the magnifying glass, quickly.'

When I had examined this white substance from all sides, I could say without question that it was the generative organ of the male. It was torn off at the root of the penis. It was what Reaumur called the lentil, a kind of bladder which holds the seminal liquid, and now I could see that it passes whole into the body of the female.

When I examined the male organ I found that there were scaly plates on the lentil, serving as hooks to attach it to the vagina. It certainly took the female a great deal of effort to rid herself of this attachment.

'So now we know how they stay together during fecundation. It isn't as simple a matter as him gripping her with his legs, unfortunately for him.'

The root of the penis had broken only half a line away from the back of the lentil and we were tempted to believe nature had made it fragile at that point in order to ease the separation of the female from the male. 'Or perhaps,' I wondered, 'to make it mercifully quick for the male.'

'I don't think we can talk of mercy and nature in the same breath here,' he said. 'The queen's interests are paramount.'

3 *August*

When I dissected the lentil I found a small white cylindrical body inside it. When I then examined a live bee and pressed the lentil, a similar white body emerged, retracting like the horns of a snail when I stopped pressing. When I pressed the seminal vesicles, white fluid flowed to the lentil which became engorged and the white body appeared from it. I described this to Monsieur in detail.

'That's good enough. The white body is the penis, without question.' He was shaking his head in wonder. 'Ah, Burnens, do you realise no one has ever seen this before? We're the first to observe it.' It was as though my description had been graphic enough for him to believe that he'd really seen it, to the point where he would swear to it on the family bible. Both of us wore great smiles. And it's true. He has made a great discovery.

'So we know that instead of returning with coagulated sperm in her vulva the fecundated queen actually carries the penis of the successful male. So what's become of him?'

We looked at each other. (I mean that sometimes I look at him and he lifts his eyes to me and there's an understanding between us that is stronger than sight.) We are both men and we are each possessed of a penis. We know that the male bee, losing his sexual organs, must die. We don't dwell, for the moment, on the fact that his penis has been torn out by the root. We talk about it as naturalists rather than men.

I said, 'The next proof would be to find the body of a male mutilated in this way.'

'Yes indeed. He'd have to live long enough to fly back to the area of the hive for us to find him.'

We're silent again. If I find such a body it means his death is by no means as fast as we might have imagined.

'I'm sure I can recognise one with this particular mutilation.'

'If you can, that would be helpful.'

20 *August*

I've been examining the ground near the hives day after day, long hours bending over in the sun, picking up and examining the body of every dead male, always fruitlessly. Until today, when I found one. And I saw half of the long root of his penis extruding from his body and the penis missing. We have no answer to the question why nature requires such a great sacrifice from the drone. (And as intact males neither of us felt, at this moment, inclined to penetrate the mystery.)

Despite this final observation, we've still never managed to see the instant of impregnation. It's always a source of regret, though I think we know in our hearts that we never will.

'Four years,' Monsieur said, 'since we discovered that fecundation occurred in the air and assumed the queen came back with semen. And I always wanted the final proof of observing it, I wanted it so much that I didn't think of other ways of going about it. It took me four years to think of something as simple as dissecting a returning female. Because it wasn't in my mind. I was too full of wanting to see the moment of copulation and if I couldn't have that I wouldn't have anything else.' He sighed. 'I think I've learnt a lesson.'

'But you did think of it in the end, sir. No one else has.'

'Oh François, dear man, what would I do without you?'

He embraced me so tightly I couldn't make an answer, even if I'd had one.

(Note: Although M. Huber and my uncle always regretted the absence of this final proof it's difficult to imagine how a momentary conjunction 40 or 50 feet in the air can ever be observed. Later naturalists have found no difficulty in regarding M. Huber's impressive array of circumstantial evidence as conclusive in the matter of fecundation. But M. Huber clearly wanted, in his experimental work, to dot every 'i' and cross every 't'. A. de M.)

10 *October*

At last the Letters to M. Bonnet are finished. They go under the title of *New Observations on Bees*. M. Bonnet has given them his approval and accordingly they've been sent to the printers.

'And so I cast my bread upon the waters,' M. Huber says.

15 *October*

'Done with paperwork for the moment. No more observations this year. Let's go out and about. What about a day in town next week?'

Marie-Aimée has been patient enough at the long hours we've spent closeted together working on the letters but I would have expected her to welcome some diversion and was surprised at her cool response. At that moment, though, she saw Jacques walking past the window and she opened it and called to him.

'You were telling me about the mushrooms, Jacques, in the forest, and your friend who has a pig who hunts truffles.'

'Yes, Madame, Michel.'

She turned back into the room, animated. 'We could go out gathering mushrooms. All of us. We could take a picnic and make a day of it. Would Michel be our guide, Jacques?'

'He'd come along right enough. Whether he'd guide you to his truffles I greatly doubt.'

'Oh, we don't need truffles. Mushrooms will be plenty. As long as we know what we can safely eat.'

She goes to the kitchen to instruct Anna about the picnic.

After supper, when Jacques and I are quietly smoking our pipes, Anna looks at her list and says, 'If anyone asks my opinion, a picnic is ten times the work of a grand dinner.'

But Martha and Sarah were excited about it and promised her lots of help and she ended up sanguine enough.

18 *October*

After a lot of cramming in of provisions and people, all of them grumpy at the early start, the cart and the trap finally arrived at our picnic spot not long after nine in the morning. Michel was there to meet us.

Jacques immediately set about making a fire to boil water for coffee. We walked about a bit, stamping our feet in the early chill. Anna unwrapped warm bread from linen cloths. When the coffee was ready, Monsieur called for a nip in it and I fetched one of the bottles of brandy he'd told me to bring. Marie-Aimée looked slightly askance but I chose not to catch her eye and she seemed reconciled to it soon enough. When I poured a tot into Jacques' coffee, he gestured discreetly at Anna and I found the chance to pour her one as well.

There was a low mist on the ground and the beginning of sun breaking through the last few leaves. Michel had his sow on a lead and a fine animal she was too. He said he'd take us to an area with plenty of mushrooms. There was no mention of truffles. His knowledge of their whereabouts would be his son's inheritance, and his alone.

Anna stated firmly that she had no intention of walking through the forest in this damp and she'd stay and tend to our dinner. Nobody objected to this and we set off through fallen leaves, the children kicking them up, a musty smell. We began to find mushrooms almost at once among the tree roots and Marie-Aimée urged us to pick all we could, once Michel had identified them as being safe.

Pierre held the pig's lead as she snuffled around in her own manner and he described to his father how her snout was sometimes on the ground, sometimes quivering in the air. Marie-Aimée was walking arm in arm with her husband but at this description he got down on all fours and cried 'Like this?' and pretended to be a pig and little Marie cried with delight and demanded to go on his back. Of course she was lifted on and he lumbered off on all fours heading straight for a tree trunk. I managed to get there first and head him off. I was laughing, but when I looked up I saw a strange look on Marie-Aimée's face. Concern, of course, that they were going to injure themselves, but something else as well. Pain perhaps? Impatience?

We came back to a fine spread: anchovies and gherkins, a fish pie, a roast rabbit, quiches, potted beef, salami, cheese. Potatoes roasted in the fire. Anna was solicitude itself to everyone, even Sarah. I wondered if she'd had a nip or two of her own accord while we were away.

Then we cleared up and had a little wander and suddenly the day was short and there was a damp chill in the air. By the time we arrived home everyone was cold and there was that melancholy mood which always follows an excursion.

But Anna bustled, setting out a very good supper of the leftovers. I became more certain that she'd had several nips. Madame came in and gestured to the baskets of mushrooms.

'We can't possibly eat them all now, but they can be dried, can't they, Anna?'

'Yes, Madame. They *can* be.'

'Do you know how?'

'Yes, Madame. I know how. Whether I know whether they should be, well, that's a different matter.'

'But Michel says they're good.'

'I don't doubt he knows his truffles,' Anna said majestically.

'And he knows his mushrooms too,' Jacques said.

'But does he know his onions?' Pierre said and almost fell off his chair at his own wit.

His mother ignored him. 'I think they can all be dried.' She swept out of the room. Pierre was sent to eat with his parents.

When he'd gone, Anna said, 'We've never dried mushrooms before in this house. Fruit and vegetables, we've stored all sorts of those; jams and preserves and pickles, we've made all those, but we've never dried mushrooms before.'

'It's free food, isn't it?' Jacques said.

'Yes, but it's all very well Michel saying he knows. Some say if the water turns black when you cook them that means they're not poisonous, some say if the water turns black then they are poisonous. I'm just going to keep to what I know.' She started sorting the mushrooms and threw half of them away before she got out a needle and thread to string the safe ones up to dry.

She shook her head. 'Mushrooms. Mushrooms aren't the answer.'

Sarah and Martha looked alarmed and asked her what she meant but she wouldn't say any more and very soon went to bed. The rest of us picked over the remainders. I think I know what Anna meant.

27 November

The cat has died giving birth to her first litter. Little Marie had been thrilled at the idea of Emily having kittens but when Madame peeped into the drawer that Emily had chosen, she saw that things weren't right and sent Marie down to the kitchen on an errand. Did Anna have enough flour to make the cake they needed for Sunday? Anna's eyes narrowed and she suggested Marie help her cut rounds out of pastry, always a favourite job.

When Madame came into the kitchen there were significant looks and then Madame took Marie into the library to see her father. After they'd told her and she'd had her cry they planned Emily's burial. The question arose of where it should be. Jacques was uncommonly agitated and drew Madame aside at the first opportunity. The upshot was that the cat was buried at the bottom of the sweet pea trench. There's no finer food . . .

A rough cross was erected with Emily's name and dates and the epitaph, 'A fine mouser'.

While they were outside conducting the funeral ceremony, indoors Anna filled a bucket with water.

'Madame's quite right, we can't care for two newborn kittens.' She took one in each hand and held their heads firmly under the water. They were too weak to struggle much and it was over very quickly. Pierre walked in on the end of it. Although he looked startled for a moment he made no comment.

A bit later, little Marie came into the kitchen asking where the kittens were so she could look after them.

Anna said, 'They have to have a mother so they've gone to live with a cat whose own kittens have died and she'll look after them like her own.'

Marie was satisfied with this, though still sad, but when she told her parents they'd gone to a new mother, Pierre couldn't stop himself crowing. 'No they haven't. They've been drowned.'

His sister was gratifyingly distressed at this. He put his arm round her guiltily. 'It was the best thing for them. It was the kindest thing.'

'No it wasn't.' She wept inconsolably.

Monsieur sighed. 'This is why it's better to tell the truth from the beginning. When it comes out later, which it generally does, there's the pain of deception to add to the pain of the thing itself.'

He took his daughter on to his knee. 'The kittens were killed very quickly and painlessly because without a mother they would have died anyway, but more slowly and missing their mother terribly. They would have been very unhappy and none of us wanted that.'

She put her arms round his neck and sobbed. He rocked her gently, meanwhile 'looking' at his son.

'We must tell the truth,' he said, 'but we can choose to do it lovingly, or otherwise.'

Pierre looked ashamed and retreated to his own room.

1792

1 *January*

The beginning of our year is still overshadowed by the news
that came at Christmas of Wolfgang Mozart's death from
typhus at the age of thirty-five. Monsieur wept when I read
the announcement to him for he loves his music with a passion.
'So young and so much work done. And there might have been
so much more.' He moved to the harpsichord and softly picked
out a tune. After a while he said, 'Thank God that at least we
don't have to reproach ourselves with wasting our time.'

'Amen to that, sir.' As I listened to him playing, my gaze
wandered to the microscope, to the drawing pens and dissection instruments so neatly arranged beside it, and then to a jug
of bright-berried holly on a polished table, to the soft gleaming
of glass and wood in the firelight. It was a room that breathed of
loving care. And yet the music, in a minor key, found something
poignant in it. One day we, and even this solid room, will all be
dust. Even Sarah, bringing in coffee, had the grace to keep her
eyes down.

3 *February*

We were all greatly heartened today because the proof sheets of *New Observations on Bees* arrived. I guessed what the parcel was and told Marie-Aimée and Pierre what had arrived, then took it into the library and suggested that Monsieur might want to open it himself. He knew at once what I meant and sat at the table opening it carefully, with an expression of the purest joy. Marie-Aimée looked at him with great tenderness. Pierre looked from his mother to his father, and then at me, and we smiled. When Monsieur opened it he slowly lifted the whole bundle to his face and buried his nose in it and sniffed the printer's ink. And again, and again.

There was much hugging and kissing and telling him how proud they were and admiring the form of the pages. Monsieur ordered wine and summoned all the household. Anna was huffing and puffing in an immaculate apron, while Jacques chose to take off his working apron. Sarah was fluttering her eyelids at the idea of drinking in the middle of the day whereas Martha quietly accepted it as her due as a young woman soon to be married. Pierre proposed a toast to *New Observations on Bees* in the grave manner of a boy learning to be the man of the house. Madame told Monsieur how very proud his dear father would have been. So then there was another toast, to absent friends.

Later in the day, when the excitement had died down, I sat reading through the proofs, not yet for detail, more to get an impression of the whole thing. I felt a delighted wonder: I could scarcely believe that all those individual moments, each day, each year, each separate sting, had assumed an order, a form, stamped with the authority of print. Monsieur was in the room and I felt I must express my feelings.

'Sir, I . . . It's almost impossible to tell you. Seeing it in print.' I know that this will point up his blindness to him, but it can't be helped. 'All the work. Sometimes I thought I couldn't see the wood for the trees. And now I see it here in front of me and I see a wonderful body of work. It's so impressive, I can hardly believe I had any part in it.'

'But you did, my dear François, and a great part. As to seeing it, I can imagine it well enough.' He shrugs, and then his face lights up. 'But as to the smell of the ink!'

5 March

I'm concerned about Sarah. It's as though the more she sees her sister sitting contentedly in the evenings, sewing her trousseau, the more she feels the need to escape from what might well be her future. And the other day she made – well, not quite an approach to me, but something that could have been interpreted in that way.

Marie-Aimée had asked me to go out and look for Pierre. It was seven in the evening and he should have been home. We were fairly sure he was out with his friends from the farm down the road, but they ranged all over the neighbourhood and it might take some time to find him. Sarah said she thought she knew where he'd be, and she'd show me the way. Somehow it didn't surprise me that this young woman would know where these boys were.

So we walked through the cold evening together and she guided me to the stream that runs between two fields. At one point it divides to form a small island in the middle, known as Martin's Island, after the farmer who owns the land. As we got closer I could hear laughter and someone coughing then more laughter and the smell of tobacco smoke. It was very dark by now but I could make out a rough shelter. I didn't bother to jump the stream, just stood on the bank and called his name. There was immediate alarm in the camp, urgent whispering and then Pierre jumped across and said he'd run home. He set off with the speed of a young man pricked by a guilty conscience. I smiled, but I wondered what else went on there.

I also wondered why Sarah had come with me when she could simply have told me he'd be at Martin's Island. Or rather, I didn't wonder, I had a very good idea why. She asked to take my arm for she couldn't see in the dark. She snuggled close to me. She said how much she admired my devotion to Monsieur. How I worked so long and hard and it seemed a shame that I didn't have a good woman to give me the comfort I deserved. I said that was for the future. That was well enough, she said, but there was no harm in a little tenderness in the meantime, and she ran her fingers down my face. How does she keep them so soft with all her cleaning work? Why, there could be some tenderness just now, for look, it's the field with the haystack, and hasn't she just tripped a little and hurt her ankle and needs to rest it for a minute.

I said that we were late for our supper already and we must hurry back. She sighed but held on to my arm.

(This is not to say that 'tenderness' with Sarah would be unwelcome – far from it – but it would be very unwise, for I have no intention of making her my wife.)

She didn't say anything more. When we got back, there was a searching glance from Anna. Sarah put on a smug expression, suggesting a secret, and went straight upstairs. I was annoyed and wanted to shout out 'Nothing has happened!' but of course I didn't. I think it must have been clear enough from my expression. A man who's just enjoyed sweet pleasure can't help a smile breaking out on his face. That was not my condition. I retired to my room very early myself, to engross myself in my journal here. And God grant me that now I can go to sleep.

28 April

Notices of Monsieur's work have been appearing in the journals. The first one was cautiously approving but the next made me rage with anger. It dismissed his work: his blindness was a very serious obstacle to successful study which threw considerable doubt on the accuracy of his experiments and the truth of his discoveries. His observations depended on the intelligence of an uncultivated peasant and were not entitled to be received without caution and distrust. My voice shook with indignation as I read it. Monsieur sighed and said nothing at first. Then he smiled drily.

'So, "A blind man aided by a peasant". That's an easy jibe. I can't argue with his description of me, but as for you, dear Burnens, you ceased to be a peasant the day you joined our household. If indeed you ever were one. Being a peasant isn't only to do with position and labour; it's also a matter of a very set way of thinking, narrow, we might say if we were being harsh. That was never your way. Whereas our reviewer – he is more of a peasant than he'd care to know.'

'Thank you, sir. And I hope at least I'm no longer uncultivated.'

'Good gracious, man, you've read me more books in the last few years, and serious philosophical books at that, than most men read in a lifetime.' He smiled at me. 'We don't need to concern ourselves with this, Burnens, because we've done the work, we've done it the right way up and back to front and inside out. We know that we've done it, we know that we haven't cheated or given short change. Let's hold our nerve, they'll come round. Given the circumstances, it was never going to be plain sailing.'

This was true tenacity, I thought, and moderation, and resignation. I learn from him every day.

15 July

Ever since I first came to Monsieur I've been in the habit of visiting the second-hand bookstalls by the lake and sometimes buying modest editions of interesting works. I was surprised and pleased today when I was offered a good price to sell back one of my earliest purchases, much more than I'd paid for it a few years ago.

I've learnt a great deal from having the freedom of Monsieur's library but I have always thought of it as purely for my own interest – and to assist him of course. The idea that my knowledge might enable *me* to turn the odd penny on my own account is novel and not unwelcome.

28 July

A great rumpus in the house. I walked in on (and straight out of) a scene where Sarah was sitting at the kitchen table, her arms folded on it and her head down sobbing as though it was the end of the world, with Marie-Aimée on one side, and Martha on the other, both with their arms round her. And Anna quietly busying herself in the background. I saw Jacques a moment later in the passage and he jerked his head towards the kitchen and raised his eyebrows and gestured the shape of a swollen belly.

Her pregnancy permeates the household without anything

actually being said. But of course Monsieur has to be told in words for he doesn't see the shrugs, the meaningful glances. After Marie-Aimée has talked to him I see an expression on her face towards me that I've never seen before. It's partly an accusation: might I be the father? But it's also an inquiry: could I be the father? As though she's never thought of me before as a man who might have physical relations, capable of fathering a child. As a man, in fact.

The truth of Sarah's situation comes out fast enough. The father is a young man working at his uncle's farm nearby. He has the near prospect of coming into a very modest farm of his own, just enough to support a small family with a great deal of work on all sides, but his family also have a bride in mind, a young woman who is not Sarah. Martha and Sarah's parents are dead, the girls are family. Monsieur summons the young man to the house. I show him into the library where Monsieur waits for him, insistent that he can conduct this interview on his own. When the young man leaves, his head is bowed and he doesn't look up at the window where Sarah is peeping out from the little room she shares with her sister. That evening the young man's uncle visits Monsieur. The next day we learn that Sarah is to be married. She says to Martha, 'Perhaps we could marry together?' but Martha says it will be another year before her man is his own master and free to marry her and she has no need to hurry him.

But Sarah isn't too cast down. I don't imagine this future was her burning desire, but she talks brightly enough about her plans to build another room on to the farmhouse and her intention that they should grow salads instead of root crops. 'Salads bring in far more than roots. I shall take them to market myself in Geneva. And flowers, we shall grow flowers as well. Flowers bring in far more than roots.'

'That's true,' Jacques says, nodding sagely. 'But you don't get something for nothing. They're much more work.'

She waves a hand airily. 'I'm strong enough.'

'Well, you know where to come for seed to start you off.'

'Thank you, Jacques.'

'And I'd better give you some cooking lessons while we're at it,' Anna said.

'I've learnt quite a lot already,' Sarah said.

'Mmm.'

Silently we all wish her well, but can hardly bear to think of her if luck's not on her side, how she could be worn out with childbearing and hard physical labour within a few years. But she's a lively sort, not easily discouraged, she might manage to build a thriving business. (Having seen the young man I can say pretty fairly that the energy and intelligence to do so would come from her, though he's obviously strong and a hard worker. She could have done worse, she could have done better.)

1 August

Monsieur is desperate to get on with some work. ('The bees, François, no unexpected pregnancies there. What a relief.') Many neighbouring farmers have come to consult him recently on a worrying devastation of their hives. Sometimes there is a strange noise near them and a mass of workers fly out at night, which they never do generally. In the morning there will be a great number of dead bees in front of the hive and often it has been plundered of all its honey and may even be entirely deserted.

We have had the same experience with one of our own hives. It's hard to describe the degree of anger and sadness I feel when I see the bees lying dead and their store of honey, so laboriously accumulated on so many trips, gone in one night. They're ravaged. Of course I accept it as nature's work but still it pains me.

Wasps, hornets, moths and mice are known for their plundering of hives, but there is generally some evidence of the bees putting up a fight. These current predations seem to be on a different scale. The farmers put it down to bats, but bats eat nocturnal insects in flight, plentiful at this time of year, and they're not interested in honey so why should they ravage a hive? And so Monsieur has put the farmers to observing their hives closely and collecting whatever is found in the vicinity and he has found them bringing him specimens of sphinx atropos, or as it is more commonly known, the death's head moth, from the close resemblance of its markings to a skull. There's been an invasion of them this year. It happens every ten or so years, presumably to do with the weather where they come from.

This is an insect without a sting, and with no defence against a sting, in victorious combat with thousands of stinging bees.

To protect our own bees we erected a tin barricade at the hive entrance with openings only just large enough to let the bees through and much too small for a large moth. This worked very well to deter the intruders. I spoke to farmers who had not thought of doing this and found that in their hives the bees had made themselves safe by making their own barrier of wax and propolis. It was a double barricade whose entrances did not overlap. There were narrow passages between them, just wide enough for one bee at a time to go through. Monsieur was delighted with this observation.

'And here the work of man and bees meets,' he said. 'If we don't think to provide it for them they'll do it for themselves. These barricades are only made at the last moment; they're not put up in advance of the danger, showing signs of forethought, they're thrown up in the face of the enemy. But see how the bees move from being simple soldiers to being engineers. These are not hexagonal cells created by instinct, they're improvised defences and their shape varies according to the circumstances. And when the danger has passed and it's time for swarming or intense honey gathering then they'll demolish them. I think we must allow them intelligence here.'

3 *August*

I was reading to Monsieur this evening when there was a terrified scream from the kitchen. I grabbed a poker and ran in, Monsieur feeling his way behind me. Anna was in the corner pointing shakily at a large moth fluttering around the lamp.

'Death's head moth inside the house,' she cried out. 'It means a death in the family for sure.'

'It means nothing of the sort,' Monsieur said kindly but firmly, while I abandoned the poker and caught the moth easily and released it outside. 'It means you had the window open on a hot dark night and a light inside the room.'

'But it does, sir. My sister knew a woman and a death's head moth flew in when she was in childbirth and that child who had been kicking for all it was worth just an hour before was stillborn. And the poor woman knew as soon as she saw it that the baby would die and she nearly died herself, demented with grief.'

'That was a terrible thing to happen, Anna, but none of the moth's doing.'

'I'm not saying the moth caused it. I'm saying it foretold it. It did.'

'Well, if you must have a death in the house for your moth, I'll give you one – mine, many years from now, of old age, in my own bed, please God. And speaking of bed, it's time for us all to retire, I think.'

Anna seemed reassured. 'Yes, sir. I'm sorry for screaming.'

'That's all right, my dear. But remember that superstitions are not generally very helpful as a guide to life – or death. Do you know what Voltaire said: that superstition sets the whole world in flames, and philosophy quenches them.'

'I'll have to leave the philosophy to you, sir.'

'You can safely do that, Anna.'

She went to bed, calm enough.

He was amused at the picture of me grabbing a poker to fight off a moth.

'But Anna's fear is very common among country people,' I said.

'And has been for a long time. Think of its name – sphinx atropos. Atropos is the oldest of the three Fates – birth, life and death. She's the one who severs the thread of life. The country people have forgotten that, but they have the same fear as their ancestors thousands of years ago.'

'I still don't see how the moth paralyses the bees so they don't attack. Surely the bees can't be superstitious?'

'There might be some sort of emanation perhaps, though it would take a great deal to paralyse a whole hive. What else might be significant?'

'That it never flies out until the night is dark, while other moths gather nectar at sunset.'

'So it can see in the dark, which is useful for finding its way round the hive. But not enough in itself to explain the effect.'

'And then the noise it makes – the death rattle as Anna would say.'

'And here I think we may have something. It's a harsh shrill sound – very like the piping of the young queens but louder. We know that piping makes the bees immobile, and with fear we think, though we don't know of what. Why shouldn't the moth's sound have the same effect? And even more pronounced since it's much louder.'

'So the bees are paralysed with fear and don't have the courage to fight the intruder.'

'That would account very well for its needing no defence against their stings. But it's only conjecture for now. Although if we could observe the sphinx making this cry during its attack and the bees then yielding without resistance it would add a great deal of weight to it.'

5 August

All our glass hives were in use with other experiments but Monsieur directed me to set up a glass box with a nest of bumblebees to observe what happened when we introduced an atropos. It had to be done at night of course.

'What do you see?'

'It's very quiet, staying in a corner of the box. It doesn't seem excited by the smell of the honey.'

Nothing happened for half an hour and then the moth began moving towards the nest. 'The bumblebees are attacking it, and furiously. Stinging it one after another. It's trying to escape, running all over.' At that point the creature made a violent effort and pushed off the glass top of the box and escaped.

I recaptured it at once and put it in another box and though it was quiet all night it didn't seem to have suffered badly from its wounds.

'There's no point repeating it. It's cruel, for it's clear that something has impaired its instinct. Captivity affected it perhaps, or the light of the lantern destroyed its one advantage, that it can see in the dark. Let's see what effect captivity has on their instinct.'

Accordingly, I've confined two moths beside a comb full of honey for a week but they haven't touched it. Today however I managed to catch a large one in the open air. On dissection – and it was strange to work on such a large creature instead of a bee – we found its abdomen entirely full of honey, enough to fill a large tablespoon. I was repulsed by this, so much food for one creature, stealing the labour of so many.

I said something of this.

'But atropos acts on instinct. Some men do the same thing and they haven't got that excuse. Your fondness for the bees makes you a little harsh on atropos I think.'

'I'm afraid sometimes my attachment to the bees means I'm not as impartial as I should be.'

'That's a question of interpreting their behaviour, and there's room for different views there. But your observations are completely impartial, I'm sure of that.'

'Yes, sir.'

'So what can we reasonably conjecture from what you have seen? When they were confined they didn't touch the honey, so we can say with certainty that captivity affects their instinct to gather honey. That's why it was cruel to put the moth in with the bumblebees – captivity had deprived it of its natural instinct.'

'So it wasn't a fair fight?'

'Exactly. Nature manages to keep an equilibrium between rival species, but when man takes them over, that's upset. Just as when we keep animals for our own use they're more protected and they become less vigilant. It's our duty to compensate them for this loss, by making barricades for the bees, or fencing in our chickens to protect them from foxes. And if we want to increase the yield of our bees we must do even more, but always taking account of their instincts. In the end we learn how to govern them from them alone. But I wonder if we have it the wrong way round?'

'Sir?'

'I was thinking that the moth's sound terrified them because it was like the young queen's piping. But it might be that the piping – from a queen who is not going to do them any harm, after all – terrifies them because they think that a moth has got in. Even if they've never experienced a death's head attack themselves there could be some sort of instinctive memory passed down over the years and that's why they react as they do to the young queens.'

'It sounds entirely possible, sir.'

'But no way whatever to verify it. It will have to remain conjecture. But an interesting one.'

15 *August*

Sarah was married quietly in our village church. The ceremony was enlivened by a large bumblebee, a slow, heavy, lazy queen climbing up the white altar cloth, falling back, climbing up again. I noticed Pierre watching it, fascinated. So much more interesting to observe the bumblebee's progress than Sarah's nuptials. He's fifteen, he must have his own thoughts on the matter. And whether her knowledge of his secret hideout and whatever may have gone on there had any effect on his thoughts I don't wish to speculate.

Only two cousins came from the groom's family. All our household went, of course, and Sarah's aunt and her uncle who've taken little interest in her so far, but evidently thought the propriety of the family required some effort to be made on this occasion. Her uncle gave her away. Her only other relative is her brother who's serving in the Swiss Guard in Paris.

She looked very pretty in a new muslin dress which I believe Madame paid for, but a little disconsolate at the small number of people.

Marie-Aimée squeezed her arm. 'My dear, when I married Monsieur Huber my only companions in the whole of Geneva Cathedral were my uncle to give me away, and Madame de Candolle to accompany me. It's only one moment in a marriage.'

I liked the way she was careful to say nothing of the very different reasons behind their similar situations. Sarah will continue to work here for as long as she can, living with her husband on her free nights.

29 *August*

Notices of the *Observations* have continued to come in and, as knowledge has grown, prejudice has melted away like spring snow. The Paris Academy of Science has admitted Monsieur as a member. It noticed the strong impression the work made from 'the novelty of the facts and the rigorous exactness of the experiments'. At last!

'What timing,' Monsieur laughs. 'I think there's little chance I'll take up that honour in person for the moment.'

For events in France are moving faster than a bee fight and no sane man would venture near to Paris these days.

30 *August*

News has come from France against which everything else pales. The fight has been between the moderates – the Girondins – and the extreme republicans – the Jacobins. On 10 August the Jacobins, supported by the Marseilles revolutionaries, stormed the Tuileries, where the royal family were living, protected by the Swiss Guard. The National Guard were detailed to protect the palace but in fact they joined in the attack. In order to avoid bloodshed Louis took refuge in the

Assembly and ordered the Swiss Guard to stop firing, which they did. But the mob took no notice of such niceties and massacred the eight hundred Swiss men who had laid down their arms. Then they ransacked the royal apartments. Such nobility of purpose.

The news of the massacre of the Swiss Guard causes a terrible anger to rage through every canton. All of us have had relatives at some point in the Swiss Guard, or known someone who did. It was as though, even if they didn't guard our own country, they guarded us *in absentia*. They were working men, ordinary citizens, our fathers, our uncles, our brothers, our sons. Literally a brother in the case of Martha and Sarah, who howled with grief.

Monsieur said, 'You remember what Louis XIV said? "All the money I've paid for Swiss troops would pave the road from Paris to Basle with Swiss pieces."'

And every Swiss child knows the riposte: 'And all the Swiss blood spilt would fill a canal from Basle to Paris.' But this was something different, it wasn't fair fighting.

We gave each other what comfort we could, particularly to the girls, who'd lost their adored, distant brother.

Within a couple of days the monarchy was 'suspended' and the royal family were in the Temple, prisoners of the Commune. Fascinated horror . . . continues.

15 September

I came across Monsieur instructing Pierre in the art of observation. 'You know how to distinguish a male. Are there any males coming in or out of the hive? We're past the season of the massacre of the males. Have any survived?'

Pierre looks with intense concentration. I'm reminded of my early days here. I understand now that it's important for Monsieur to be able to teach by question. How many? Where? Which ones? How often? What do they carry? What are they doing? What is the result? What is the cause?

I suppose these are questions that a sighted man might ask himself silently, but for Monsieur they must be asked in words. And I find myself glad that he asks these questions of Pierre, so that I'm not the only person trained to answer them. But I don't want to know, yet, that Pierre can do everything I can, because that will bring closer the moment when I will have to make a difficult decision. I'm twenty-six now. Monsieur was blind long before that. And I see things he never saw. I have more knowledge of some things than he has. Knowledge of favour and corruption. Things that he doesn't have to consider in his daily life.

And in the meantime, terrible events continue in France. The departure of many volunteers for the front meant that Paris was unguarded and Marat took the opportunity to guillotine some twelve hundred priests and aristocrats whose presence was alleged to be a danger to the civilian population. But then the killing went on to include common criminals and prostitutes. As though no one knows when to stop, how to recognise the moment when the experiment is finished.

There's been great toing and froing over the frontier. The Prussians were within 140 miles of Paris. The French pushed them back to Valmy. And now the National Assembly has declared the abolition of the monarchy. I can hardly believe that it's come to this, yet it seems the revolution has its own dreadful momentum that grinds our former certainties to dust.

25 November

The French have fought the Prussians back to the frontiers of the Netherlands and the Rhine. The value of the assignat is beginning to decline very fast. Madame's finances are even more troubled.

The King has been standing trial and as a mark of his rank in these days he's addressed by his common name of Louis Capet. Robespierre accused him of being a traitor who'd planned civil war and ordered patriot citizens shot. If he lived he'd be a centre of intrigue, therefore public safety demanded his death. The Girondists claimed, without great conviction, that he was inviolable under the constitution. He was interrogated by the National Assembly. (This is the King of France, Louis XVI!) He was found guilty, almost unanimously.

Then the vote was for the sentence: exile, prison, or death.

There was a majority of one for execution. So now he lives under sentence of death.

There's little sympathy remaining here for the republican cause, though none of us are royalists either. We wait, appalled, for the latest news, whatever it is. All the Swiss Guard who were serving elsewhere in France have been dismissed and sent home. We know that many of them have switched sides, fighting for the anti-revolutionary coalition under Austrian command and British pay. Good luck to them, we pray.

10 December

I drove Madame into town last week to buy material for a new cloak for little Marie (now not so little, growing fast). I had some supplies to collect from Zwemmer's. As I was driving round to our meeting place I saw Madame emerge from a shop which dealt in paintings and fine art. I was surprised. I didn't think there was any money spare for that sort of thing.

Today she introduced to Monsieur a M. Braudel, a connoisseur of the fine arts, who was eager to see his cabinet of curiosities and his paintings. Monsieur was delighted to show him the objects in the cabinet, beloved objects that his fingers knew intimately. M. Braudel was clearly a man of refined taste. His fingers lingered over the knife and fork in the shape of Mars and Venus.

'As to the pictures, I must trust my wife to guide you for,

though I remember some from my childhood, I've no idea which is which any more.'

And so Madame showed him round: family pictures by Monsieur's father and brother and Monsieur himself when he was young, engravings by Hogarth and Piranesi, the pair of Canalettos, a Rembrandt drawing in poor condition, a de Greuze still life. Many others. He was most interested and appreciative and took a graceful farewell of Monsieur. But as I passed Madame's closet I couldn't help but stop and listen to her voice.

'Not the knife and fork. Nothing from the cabinet. He'd miss them.'

'Then the pair of Canalettos.'

'That's possible. Everything needs re-hanging anyway.'

I didn't need to hear any more to know what this was about.

12 December

'We must have a good clean-up before Christmas,' Madame announced. 'Take all the pictures down, clean them, sweep the walls free of cobwebs, wash them where necessary.' She's been very lax she says, and the house needs cleaning from top to bottom. There's great activity with brooms and dusters.

Madame herself wears a long white apron and steps up on to a stool, showing her stocking. She takes down the Canalettos. 'These need re-framing. I'll put them somewhere safe.'

M. Braudel comes to collect them for re-framing. No need to trouble Monsieur Huber. M. Braudel stows them safely in his coach and drives away.

I understand why she prefers her husband not to be aware of their financial trouble. It's a great love that they have. But again it demands complicity. None of us will ever speak of the pictures again, they'll be being re-framed for ever more. But it raises, on my side, a barrier between me and Monsieur.

1793

28 January

There was no reprieve for King Louis XVI. He was guillotined on 21 January, amid cries of *'Vive la Nation'*. Although we all knew he was under sentence of death the news of his execution was still profoundly shocking. Even more so in the case of Queen Marie Antoinette. The French have murdered, in her, the daughter of the Emperor of Austro-Hungary. What will follow? Nothing good, I fear. A strong France has always been our best protection against Austria. They say the Queen showed the utmost dignity as she was drawn along in the tumbril and that she met her death with composure. So, then, the shepherdess is dead.

It seems almost against natural law that there should be no King of France. And as is often said, nature abhors a vacuum. But who or what will take his place? And when will the killing stop? Fear of unrest and war flies over all of Europe. It seems as though France is in thrall to revolutionaries who can see nothing beyond revolution itself. The power of reason is impotent against their fervour. We shake our heads and turn back to our work with relief.

30 May

M. Charles Bonnet has died, aged seventy-three. It's been a very cold spring and it was too much for him after the long winter. Monsieur was deeply upset of course, although his death was neither unexpected nor tragically young. Still, M. Bonnet had been M. Huber's guide, his mentor, the authority to whom he appealed to endorse his discoveries. The older man (by thirty years) held for him the serious quality which his own father lacked. I accompanied Monsieur to the funeral, which was attended by many eminent men, and it was heartening to see the respect with which he was greeted, as the author of a serious work.

I, too, was greeted with respect. I feel I've come a long way from the young peasant of eight years ago and I know whom I must thank for it, which I do every day in my heart.

But if I think of eight years hence . . .

14 June

It's interesting that just two weeks after M. Bonnet's death Monsieur has decided that it's time at last to investigate the bees' production of wax. There is a small story to this. Bonnet had followed Reaumur and Miraldi in believing that wax was made from pollen, taken into the bee's stomach and regurgitated through its mouth as a pap. Reaumur wondered whether pollen was the only ingredient but his experiments were inconclusive.

In 1768 M. Schirach wrote to M. Bonnet about the work of a Lusatian observer who challenged the long-held belief that wax came out through the mouth and claimed he'd seen it extruding through the abdomen – a very different operation. M. Huber came across this letter many years later and proposed it to M. Bonnet as a subject of experiment, but Bonnet was dismissive and dissuaded him because he didn't think there was enough evidence to relinquish the accepted idea (to which he held). Against his better judgement, perhaps, M. Huber accepted this advice. But it seems that a death may give us a sense of liberty.

Accordingly, we followed the advice of the anonymous Lusatian naturalist to withdraw the bee from the cell in which she was working and stroke her body gently with the point of a needle – which didn't appear to cause her any pain, if anything the sensation seemed mildly pleasurable to her. In any event, her reaction was to stretch in such a way that I could see the scales of wax under the rings of her abdomen.

'So we've confirmed this beautiful observation. It's a great shame the author isn't known. He should have the credit for this.' Monsieur was greatly excited by this discovery, or rather confirmation. I extracted the scales and he called in Pierre to share the occasion. I let him heat the scales over a candle flame and we all agreed that it was indeed beeswax.

17 June

'We can publish,' he said, 'giving due credit to our anonymous Lusatian observer.'

I've written up the observations and we've been through our usual procedure of draft, draft and draft again, and we were ready to send it off today, when I discovered in the latest issue of the *Philosophical Transactions* an article by the Scottish surgeon John Hunter, whom Monsieur holds in high repute. His article described, in print, exactly what we had observed.

I read it aloud with a sinking heart. Monsieur listened in silence.

Eventually he said, 'Ah, well.' At such a moment there's both a high-minded delight that an observation has been confirmed by a third party, and a perhaps more human feeling of deep disappointment that the other person has got there first.

He sighed. 'It's a pity that I didn't start this observation five years ago.' It was not my place to say anything to this. But he laid no blame and gave every appearance of shrugging off his disappointment.

'Hunter's observation confirms ours. Let's see if we can work on it in more detail.'

So of course that's how we'll proceed, although I must confess I have less equanimity than Monsieur seems to feel. I'm still almost angry that the first published observation was not his, when it so easily could have been. A closed mind on the one hand and too much deference on the other have lost a prize.

But Monsieur's calmness about it is in tune with his resignation to his blindness. He spent enough time in his youth regretting what was lost, and now he simply looks to the next thing that might be done.

I admire this beyond words and I don't know if I could achieve it if I were similarly placed. But the (disloyal?) thought occurs to me that a state of absolute resignation to events might not be the best course for a man like myself who still has to make his own way in the world.

18 *June*

I've been continuing with our work and have found that the wax appears to come from a membrane attached to the body under the rings.

Monsieur is pacing. 'So we might assume that this membrane contains the organ for the production of wax, just as a breast holds the organ for the production of milk. Can we find it by dissection?'

'I've tried my best, sir, but I can't find the organ itself, nor the channel that must lead from it to the scales of wax on the exterior.'

'Take some specimens to Mademoiselle Jurine,' he said. 'I've heard she's highly skilled at delicate dissections.'

19 June

And so it was that I found myself today on the other side of
Geneva, at the house of Mlle. Jurine's parents. I write these
words so calmly. It was a modest, pleasant house with good
pictures and books. Apparently her father has published a
scholarly journal for many years, greatly worthwhile work,
but not such as to make his family rich. In lieu of riches he
has given his daughter a profound education in the natural
world, and this, together with her natural felicity of hand, has
allowed her to build herself a considerable reputation for being
skilled at the most difficult drawings and dissections.

For some reason I had in my mind a picture of a plain
woman, perhaps rather abstracted in her concentration on her
work. Instead, what I found was a very attractive young lady,
fully aware of her qualities, yet not in the least coquettish. I
liked her manner. I laid out my specimens on a long table.
At one end there was a microscope, a dissecting board, paper,
ink, a jar of scalpels, pencils, drawing pens. I loved the sense
of order, the possibility of serious work that the implements
contained. Two oil lamps stood ready to light the evening.

I explained what we were looking for. She listened carefully
and made a note. She said, 'I won't start yet.' But she leaned
over to look at the little bees as though they were the most
important things in the world.

I was impressed with her interest – but the way a stray dark
curl lay on her neck was at the front of my mind. There

was something about it that reminded me of the bumblebee crawling up the altar cloth at Sarah's wedding – something wonderfully natural, not in the least concerned that it was out of place, and all the dearer for it.

Her mother looked into the room to invite me to drink some coffee. Mlle. Jurine motioned me to go and said she'd join us in a moment. We had our coffee in the kitchen. Mme. Jurine had the slightly distracted air of a woman who manages a comfortable establishment on not quite enough money.

But where her daughter was fairly formal, she was garrulous. She made some inquiries about how long I'd been with M. Huber (whose family, it went without saying, her own family had known for many years). Clara, she explained, was perhaps too immersed in her work for her own good. She leaned forward, confiding, while her daughter was out of the room. 'At least I'll say for her she's not the sort to throw herself away on a fool or a wastrel. They've been round, of course, like bees to a honeypot—' She clapped her hand over her mouth. 'I'm sorry, that wasn't the right thing to say.'

I smiled. 'I understand exactly what you mean.'

'But she's had some very good offers as well, and she's refused them too. What can a mother do?'

At that moment Clara walked into the room – or as she still is to me, Mlle. Jurine – and I glanced at her and she smiled at me obliquely. I suspect she was well aware of the subject of her mother's conversation.

She said, 'It's going to be very difficult. I don't know if I can do it.' She frowned a little and I found myself feeling that

I couldn't bear her to be troubled by anything, least of all on my account.

'I know how difficult it is, Mademoiselle. I've tried it many times, and failed. If you can't do it either then we'll know that it can't be done for the moment and we'll have to trust to the theory.'

She nodded, slowly, gravely, and I wanted the moment never to end. I could have looked at her all day long. As I left she smiled warmly and I dared to hope I might have made a favourable impression.

I walked back and wild – impossible – thoughts whirled in my head.

And now I'm sitting here wondering how many days we must allow before expecting a result or making an inquiry about the progress. Three days? Four? Surely no more than a week, although I know she has other work in hand.

And then of course we must have other work to be done that requires minute dissection. And I fear my own dissecting skills are no longer what they were . . .

Am I a fool? Is her smile this warm to everyone? Am I just another bee buzzing round the honeypot?

25 *June*

While we were waiting for Mlle. Jurine's results Monsieur considered whether wax is a secretion, which makes it an animal product, or simply a collection of vegetable matter.

I know this is an important question but I find it hard to be particularly absorbed in it. I keep seeing a stray lock of hair in my mind's eye.

'Let's look at Reaumur again. What does he say?'

I forced myself to think clearly. 'That the bees eat pollen and regurgitate it as wax.'

'Which would make it vegetable matter. Whereas if we're right and it's secreted, then it's an animal product. Quite an important difference.'

'Yes, sir,' I said, trying to sound interested.

'As for making it from pollen, I don't believe that and neither does John Hunter. We've both observed that swarms in new hives need a great quantity of wax to make cells but they fly out to collect nectar, not pollen. On the other hand, bees from established hives who've built all the cells they need fly out to collect pollen, not nectar.'

So the first experiment was to see whether bees deprived of pollen but given honey would still make wax. I've confined a hive for five days with a store of honey and the bees have made plenty of fine wax comb. We have to make sure, though, that they hadn't originally carried enough pollen about themselves to make the experiment invalid. Today I took out all the wax they've made so far and continued to confine them with a supply of honey.

28 *June*

The bees continued to make wax so then we tried the experiment in reverse: we took away all the honey and left them only pollen. The result was that they made no wax.

'That seems clear enough, but let's assume nothing. Is it possible that the wax is already in the honey and the bees extract it as they need it?'

There are generally little parcels of wax in honey but when I put them under the microscope they proved to be old pieces from the comb, quite different from fresh secretions.

'Now what is it they find in nectar and honey that they don't find in pollen? Is it the sweetness itself, the sugar, that's important? Let's see what happens when we give them different degrees of sweetness.'

He asked Anna to make up a pound of white sugar syrup, explaining it was for an experiment.

She looked concerned. 'But I'd really want to clarify it with the white of an egg, sir. It wouldn't be clear otherwise. Would that make a difference to your experiment?'

He reassured her and she set to very happily – her contribution to important work. I've confined one hive with this food source, another with syrup made from very dark brown sugar, and a third with a supply of honey.

29 *June*

Ten days and no word from Mlle. Jurine. But with every day that passes the moment when I will see her again must come closer.

30 *June*

All the bees have made wax: the greatest amount from the brown sugar and the least from the honey.

Monsieur said 'How the bees make wax from sugar – or how a cow makes milk from grass – are subjects for the chemists. But so far our conclusions are based entirely on our observation in hives. We must find out if they do the same in their natural state.'

'So that plenty of nectar in the fields to make honey would mean plenty of working in wax.'

'Exactly so.'

'And it would be easy enough to see. The combs are almost white when they're new-made and almost black when they're old.'

'But we should see it over the spread of the countryside, not just in our own hives. Let's talk to our neighbours.'

3 July

And so we've walked or ridden to all the beekeepers in our vicinity, where I've measured the wax in their hives. After the incidents of the death's head moth last year it's touching to see how M. Huber is received by the small farmers. They never fail to offer him hospitality and he enjoys a drink of beer with them and swaps bee lore. Even the least knowledgeable beekeeper has his ideas and opinions on their welfare, just as a man who has a dog has his own ideas on dogs. The result is that I have access to sixty-four hives, scattered over several miles. It's a relief to ride out through the country instead of sitting at home, waiting, waiting.

4 July

I was in Zwemmer's, enjoying, as always, the array of everything I could possibly want for writing and drawing – and things I hadn't thought of wanting. I saw a woman's back as she watched her parcel being wrapped and I knew it was her even before I saw the loose tendril of hair. She glanced round as I approached the counter.

'Why, Monsieur Burnens, I think.' She smiled calmly.

'Why, Mademoiselle Jurine. What a pleasant surprise.' I matched her for calmness but it was far from how I felt underneath.

'Not so unexpected. You make drawings of Monsieur Huber's work, I believe. Where better to come for supplies?'

'Indeed. Although I find I always spend far more time here than I intended. It's hard to just step in and out.'

'I think it's my favourite shop in the whole of Geneva. There's something about the smell of fresh paper and the new wood in the pencils.'

'And varnish and paint.'

'And Monsieur Zwemmer is so knowledgeable, so helpful.'

'He knows all there is to know on the subject.' I had almost gabbled this and then there was a pause. She picked up her parcel.

'I must be on my way now. I still have work to do on your bees, Monsieur.' A little smile, bright eyes.

'Let me carry your parcel home for you, Mademoiselle. It looks heavy.'

'It's not so bad. But it's a very hot day. Yes, thank you.'

I went to take it and she said, her mouth teasing, 'But did you not come to buy something for yourself?'

'Only some ink.' I picked up the first bottle I saw and began to count out coins as though my life depended on it. She smiled and I grew calmer and was able to thank M. Zwemmer as he handed over the little wrapped bottle. He glanced at Mlle. Jurine then looked at me inscrutably. I put the ink in my pocket and she handed me her parcel of paper. It was light enough, it was nothing, it was everything, my ticket to walk beside her.

We walked in the shade of the lindens. I told her my story

of first meeting Monsieur and his testing my observation of the way the light fell.

'I think you must have learned a great deal from him over the years.'

'Yes, I have. And I think you must have learned a great deal from your father.'

'It's the greatest gift, I think. Not the knowledge itself, but how to find it.'

'Yes, knowing where to go, the sources to consult, the means to discover it for yourself.'

She looked up, nodded, smiled. And so we walked on in the dappled shade, talking so earnestly about knowledge. But I was thinking of Monsieur, the day he heard of his impending blindness, wanting to clasp every woman whose form he could make out. I wanted to clasp only one.

We reached her house. She took her parcel from me. 'Thank you, Monsieur. As I said, I'm still working on your bees. I haven't had any success so far, but I'll write to Monsieur Huber as soon as I do, or don't.'

'I know that he has every confidence in you.'

She raised an eyebrow. 'But I'm not infallible.'

'Nobody asks that of you, Mademoiselle.' I wanted to say so much more but I didn't have the nerve. She smiled goodbye and went indoors. I walked back both light-hearted and heavy at the same time.

For some reason I didn't mention our meeting when I got home.

Is it an idle dream to picture her as my wife, gracing our

own establishment? It's very far removed from my situation at this time. Impossibly far? I know nothing of her feeling for me, except that she likes me enough to be civil in public – a very small foundation to build these wild hopes on. And how many other men have carried her parcels home? I can't measure and consider as I do with the bees. This is a different world and I feel all at sea.

5 July

In France, the Jacobins, as we may have suspected all along, finally have what they've always wanted: absolute power. They've taken over the Assembly completely and the Girondin leaders have all been arrested. Which means presumably they'll all be executed, and sooner rather than later.

6 July

The fields are awash with orchids, campanulas, larkspur, daisies. Today I inspected the hives and found the bees had taken full advantage of the abundant nectar to store honey and pollen in the old hives, and make wax in the new ones.

Monsieur wants to know how the bees feed their young. Is it from honey or from pollen? If we're sure they use honey to make wax, then it would seem pollen must be the food for the young, for they won't have built up supplies of it without a reason. John Hunter thinks so and has made preliminary experiments.

9 July

We confined bees in a hive with combs filled with brood of all ages, both eggs and young larvae. We gave them honey and water, but removed all the cells containing pollen. For the first two days they seemed to take their usual care of their young, but tonight on the evening of the third day there was a great commotion and they tried most desperately to fly out.

I was afraid they'd all perish if we thwarted their instincts any longer and Monsieur told me to set them free. It was too dark for them to go to the flowers so they flew in circles near the hive until the coolness of the night air drove them back in. They were calmer now, and I closed the hive again.

11 July

Their consternation has continued and Monsieur has decided that five days is long enough. I pulled out the brood comb and found all the cells empty and no sign of the pap that feeds the worms or the jelly for the queens.

Next we confined the bees with new brood cells full of eggs and worms, but this time we gave them comb with pollen in it. I scattered some over the hive stand and they discovered it immediately and ate it voraciously. I dusted some of them so I could follow their progress and found that when they had gorged themselves they went straight to the brood cells and would put their head in the cell and stay there for some time while they regurgitated the pollen as pap.

13 July

There's been none of the frantic activity they showed when lack of pollen meant they couldn't feed their young. When I removed the brood cells I found everything at its proper stage of development. Order has been restored to the hive. We can conclude that pollen is the food of the young.

And we can perhaps deduce from their behaviour the intensity of their love for their young, and the care they take for them, and how, if they're prevented from doing this it drives them to unbearable distraction.

14 July

There's been a human counterpoint to this: Sarah has come to visit with her new baby, a fine boy called François. And what can we say? He's evidently been fed on the finest pollen, a robust, healthy little chap. She paid a graceful compliment to Monsieur, who said he was honoured and delighted to have the baby named after him. In the passage outside the kitchen as I stood back to let her pass she looked at me sideways with what I can only call a married woman's smile. Someone who knows things that unmarried women aren't privy to. And now that she was safely married, I could return her smile.

She said, 'Of course there is another François who is equally remembered.'

But my mind was full of how Clara would look, holding a baby.

Sarah had brought Jacques a bunch of sweet peas, grown from the seed he'd given her as a wedding present, the seed he'd been cultivating for years. We all knew it wasn't just any bunch of flowers. He examined the blooms very carefully: shape, colour, scent, and then he nodded, but didn't speak and we realised there were tears in his eyes.

'Good, good,' was all he could say.

Sarah hugged him while Anna looked on, smiling, rocking the baby in her arms.

'But you know, Jacques,' Sarah said earnestly, 'I've been thinking. I'm going to sell my flowers at market, so I could just as well sell your seeds for you. When people see how beautiful the flowers are they'll be willing to pay well for good seed.'

'I don't know about that,' he said. 'And strictly speaking, the seed belongs to Monsieur.'

'That's true,' Anna said, 'but it's your work over the years that's made it valuable. You could have just saved what seed there was, but instead you worked hard to make it the best possible seed. You went on hour after hour in the evenings, while darkness fell. Our supper was late because of it. I know,

I was here while you did it. And if I know Monsieur, he'll see the fairness of that.'

Sarah continued, with a young person's candour, 'And if you grow too old to work all the time, but you can still manage your sweet peas, selling the seed would bring you in some money.'

Monsieur walked in at this moment. 'Why, Jacques, you're not planning to leave us, are you?'

'No, sir, no,' he said vigorously, and explained Sarah's idea.

'Excellent,' Monsieur said.

'But strictly speaking, sir, they're your property. You paid for the original plants and they're growing in your land.'

'But it's your care over the years that has made them valuable. You've studied them, you've taken great pains. They're the fruit of your labour and they belong to you.'

'Thank you, sir.'

Monsieur nodded to him. 'But Sarah, is there not a danger that if you sell the seeds, people will grow their own, and stop buying your flowers?'

'I think there's room for both, sir. Besides, a young man will always want a bunch of flowers for his sweetheart, not a packet of seed.' She looked at me archly and I wondered if Mlle. Jurine and I had been seen in Zwemmer's or walking together back to her house.

15 July

It's warmer now and the chestnut and linden trees are in bloom. I've seen much activity by the bees, building comb. It's a pleasure to observe this because it distracts me from what matters most in my life, which seems to lie in ruins.

This morning a brief, polite note arrived from Mlle. Jurine saying she hadn't been able to find the wax-producing organ.

I turned this note over and over, opened it and folded it again and again, as though I might find some significant, hidden message. It's addressed to Monsieur, not me, which is correct of course. But it's so formal it seems to leave no door open through which I might see her again. She expresses no wish to assist again in the future. Does this mean our relations, hers and mine, extend no further than the work in hand? I've been living in a dream of so much more than that. Yet what more should she believe? I am M. Huber's secretary and I have nothing to offer on my own account.

I used to take an honest pride in my situation but everything is more complicated now.

22 July

The bees' activity has continued but now the warmth has become heat (over 77°F) and there's been no rain for a month. The flowers are entirely faded so there's no nectar for them to make honey, although they're collecting pollen in abundance. Without honey no wax is being produced so the new swarms are not lengthening their combs. This is a sad state for the bees: they have ample food for their young, but no resources to make cells to lay them in, so the colonies are not thriving as they might. Of course an attentive beekeeper would remedy this by giving the bees supplementary honey, but the whole purpose of our experiment is to observe the bees in as natural a condition as possible. So we do nothing to alleviate their condition. This is quite hard. We're both fond of them and it goes against the grain not to help them out.

24 *July*

We've heard of the death of the ruthless French leader, Marat, stabbed to death in his bath by a young woman called Charlotte Corday. Such a beautiful name – it's on everyone's lips. His bizarre death seems all one with the times. Who will be next? Their leader, Robespierre, has set up a Committee of Public Safety. It seems to me that no one is safe under this. Thank God I'm a Vaudois, not a Frenchman. Even though there's been some unrest here it's remained merely unrest, nothing like as terrible as what is happening in France.

11 *August*

Last night there was a great lightning and thunderstorm and it rained for the first time in six weeks – what a wonderful sound to hear – and it was heavy for several hours. I knew it would be beating down the plants and when I looked out of the window I saw Jacques standing in the garden in the pouring rain, shaking his head. It was too late to try to save anything not already staked.

Then suddenly there was a thunderous crash inside the house. I was shaken in my bed. I ran out from my room, and Madame rushed out from hers, in her nightgown, looking somehow more feminine than I've seen her before. I could hear Monsieur bumping, trying to be present, and told them both to stay where they were while I had a look downstairs. I found that a chimney stack must have been struck by lightning and had collapsed into a fireplace, spilling bricks all over the hearth. Thank goodness it was summer and there was no fire burning.

Jacques had arrived by this time and together we agreed that the mess was nothing that couldn't wait until the morning to be cleared up.

I returned upstairs and reported this to Monsieur and Madame who were much relieved. For some reason I couldn't get the picture of Madame in her nightgown out of my mind. But what made an even greater impression on me was the expression on her face when she saw me in my nightshirt. A sudden widening of her eyes, something involuntary. Something of the way she looked at me when Sarah fell pregnant. I don't want to dwell on it.

The buckwheat had yielded only pollen so far, but today, after the rain, its blossoms glistened with nectar. The bees came out in force and took it for food but they haven't made any wax yet. I record these facts so that I don't have to think about more troubling things.

30 *August*

The last two weeks have been drought again. I examined all sixty-four hives in our neighbourhood and found that the bees had made no wax extensions to their combs since the middle of July. They'd stored a lot of pollen, but the stores of honey had diminished considerably in the old hives, and there was none at all in the new ones. The new swarms haven't made enough wax cells to store honey to see them through the winter.

When the winds are southerly and the air is moist and warm the bees flourish, but prolonged heat and drought affect them severely, as does north wind and cold rain. Having observed very closely that the weather, collection of honey, and making of wax were inextricably linked, we have finished our experiment of observing the bees in their natural condition. Now we can intervene to save the new swarms by supplementing their supplies with honey or sugar syrup, and what a pleasure to do so.

7 *September*

I'm aware that this is work well worth doing, but it hasn't the intensity of our investigations of a few years ago, when Monsieur was having to challenge received opinion. We've confirmed Hunter's observations – and it's important that they're confirmed – and Monsieur's name carries sufficient weight to make his confirmation significant. But I no longer have the fervour which made light of the repetition and the pain.

And of course we're both much older now.

Perhaps I just mean that I feel the stings more sharply these days. In the past the work, the endeavour, the enterprise, was so intense that I couldn't imagine anything else.

But it's not just that. This morning I awoke wondering if I must resign myself to life in another man's service, albeit a man who has raised me to this point, so generous and unstinting of his knowledge. And a man who is greatly dependent on me. This is not the case of a manservant who can easily be replaced leaving an able-bodied master. This is difficult.

10 *September*

I've concentrated on our work and written up the observation that there are two distinct kinds of workers in a hive: larger ones which gorge themselves on nectar and return to make wax; smaller ones which bring home pollen to feed the young.

So we may call them waxworkers and nursemaids and I've coloured them both separately and never seen any interchange of function.

(Note: I believe that since the introduction of Italian bees it has been understood that this difference is determined by the age of the bee, the younger ones being the nurses and the older ones the waxworkers. M. Huber did not know this at the time. A. de M.)

30 September

I've been gently nudging Monsieur towards the idea that some of my earlier illustrations would benefit from being redrawn by Mlle. Jurine. This morning he agreed.

Just five minutes later a note arrived from Mlle. Jurine saying she had to go to Basle to care for an aunt who was very ill. She regretted that she wouldn't be able to undertake any more work for us in the immediate future. Again, correctly, the note was addressed to Monsieur.

'Very civil of her to let us know,' Monsieur said. 'Another person might not have bothered.'

I agreed. In that particular civility I find, perhaps foolishly, the smallest spark of hope, even though there is no acknowledgement of me personally.

Autumn has turned unexpectedly dank and sodden. Falling leaves and dripping rain mirror my feelings but I am restless too.

5 December

My mother died on 30 November.

We buried her yesterday. Her end, when it came, was mercifully quick. Her heart failed her and in a few minutes she had died.

My sister wept, but almost absent-mindedly, as though her heart was elsewhere. Her husband didn't accompany her but little Alise clutched her hand. Things didn't need to be spelt out – we'd shared a childhood.

When they'd gone, after the simple meal, the almoner said, 'She was very contented in her last years. She was so proud of how well you were doing with Monsieur Huber.' She hesitated and then went on, 'And she used to say how proud your dear father would have been too.'

It pierced me, as she had guessed it would. 'Thank you,' was all I could say, but it was heartfelt.

After a while I said, 'I'm sorry I wasn't with her when she went.'

'It was so fast she wouldn't have known it in any case. You'd done everything a son could have done. You wrote every week, you sent money. I'll give you a full account and you'll see that she spent hardly any of it.'

'Why not? It was for her.'

'She said if she was warm and fed she didn't need anything else. It was all for you. That gave her much more pleasure than a new blanket.'

My poor mother. Some happy years when we were young, and then some miserable years making shift but always doing her best for her children. I'm profoundly relieved that her last years were peaceful.

I'm determined to care for my sister and little Alise if things turn out badly there. I think that's the best testament I can give to my mother, and one she would be most pleased with.

20 December

It's interesting how having no parents suddenly accentuates feelings of mortality, of having only a limited time to accomplish things.

The money my mother saved over the years leaves me with just enough to furnish a modest apartment, if that were to be the case.

Might it be? Could it be?

I find my heart isn't in the festive season.

1794

(Note: My uncle describes a quiet family Christmas where Mme. Huber kept a rigorous but discreet eye on expenditure. M. Huber and the children appeared to have enjoyed it as much as usual but my uncle remained restless and he intimates that Mme. Huber didn't seem as wholehearted in her enjoyment of the simple rituals as she had been in years gone by. This feeling persisted well into the new year. A. de M.)

28 February

Winter ended today, for me. Suddenly I'm full of energy and boundless hope, all held in those sparkling eyes, the sweet smile. What luck – although it didn't seem so at the time – that I awoke this morning feeling even more than usually disconsolate and discontented. It being Sunday I decided to use my freedom to go for a long walk to wear myself out so that I might purchase equanimity through exhaustion. But while I would usually have headed up the valley, into wilder country, today I felt in need of more diversion, so I turned

instead towards the city. I had my dinner – and a good one
– at an inn and continued my walk into the park.

There was a group of ladies, perhaps twenty strong, promenading. I'd heard of these groups, though never seen one
before. They walked together, talking animatedly, and as I
passed them (with 'Good day, Monsieur' falling easily from
their lips) I saw in the middle a face that shone out.

'Why, Monsieur Burnens,' she said, stepping aside from
her friends.

'Mademoiselle Jurine. I didn't know you had returned to
Geneva.'

'Only last week.'

'How is your aunt?'

'I'm glad to say she's made a full recovery.' She raised her eyebrows. 'Although I have to say she took her time about it.'

'Perhaps with you as a nurse, Mademoiselle, anyone might
take their time.'

She laughed. 'You're too kind, Monsieur. I simply did my
duty.'

How I wished that I could be the subject of her duty.

The group was moving forward and ladies were looking
back at her, smiling inquiringly. 'I must rejoin my friends.'

'I don't wish to detain you, Mademoiselle. I'm very glad to
see you back in Geneva.'

'I'm very glad to be back, Monsieur. I've missed my walks
with my friends. We always meet in the park in fine weather.'
She looked at me demurely. 'We always meet on the last Sunday
of the month.'

'Do you indeed, Mademoiselle?'

She smiled and waved and rejoined her friends. I stood watching after her, holding to myself the precious gem she'd given me – to tell me when I might see her again.

10 March

Something unsettling at home. It seems as though my desire for Clara makes me more conscious of all women. And Marie-Aimée is here, all the time. I find myself thinking of her, unwillingly, as a woman rather than as my employer's wife. This isn't the problem though, for I'm well used to keeping my feelings to myself, and I believe I've given her no indication of any change.

But despite that, she knows. Or perhaps it's that her feeling for me has changed and she's less careful than I am about showing it. Small things – passing a little closer than absolutely necessary, a glance held for a moment longer than usual. The sort of thing where the first time it happens it might be an accident and the second time it isn't.

I don't respond at all, at least not in any voluntary way. I behave as I did with Sarah. I think of Clara. I think of how much I care for Monsieur, and the trust that he places in me.

Nothing untoward will happen, I'm determined. But there isn't the easy atmosphere of before. For instance, instead of being quite happy to accompany her on a walk, now I dread her asking me. And indeed she hasn't asked me for some time, as though it would be awkward for the two of us to be alone together.

15 March

I'm trying to concentrate on my work, hoping to keep other things at bay. Monsieur has been studying the wax cells, in particular the art the bees use in building them. Of all the possible patterns of storage they might have used, they've settled, with the hexagon, on the shape which gives the maximum amount of space for the minimum amount of materials and labour. It's the most perfect geometrical shape for their advantage. So how did they come to it?

I was reading aloud from Reaumur. He insisted we couldn't allow the bees the honour of deciding this for themselves. He believed it was ordained by an immense intelligence which saw infinite combinations of things in a way we can scarcely begin to comprehend.

'Now I'm not going to grant the workman the glory of the invention,' Monsieur said, 'but I wonder whether the bees might not think about it rather more than Reaumur allows. As for that fool, de Buffon . . .'

'The populariser.'

'Quite so. I can't believe that such a complicated organisation as a hive can be left either to stupid creatures or to gross animal machines such as he describes.'

De Buffon regards bees as automatons who find themselves

together as a condition of their life. Packs of dogs, for instance, gather together freely, which suggests some choice in the matter. Where there is choice there must be some degree of intelligence, but bees are born to their condition. This is a union produced by nature, independent of any choice on the bees' part. Certainly they organise themselves to ensure their existence, but they're compelled to it. And yet from this a partial observer grants them intellect, motive, geometry, order, foresight, love of the republic – all based on the observer's admiration, not the observable facts.

De Buffon goes on to argue that bees never planned to be born together, and their association doesn't imply anything at all; whatever the results of their work may be, it's clear that they haven't decided it for themselves and it proceeds only from the universal mechanism established by the Creator. Place together ten thousand automatons, all perfectly similar, all required to do exactly the same thing in the same place, and perfectly regular work will be the result.

In addition, he says, the much vaunted hexagon construction is nothing of the sort; the hexagon is very common in nature. Crystals and salts often assume this form. Take a simple example: fill a vessel with pea seeds and water, seal it and boil the water. All the seeds will be hexagonal because of their reciprocal compression. In just the same way the round bodies of the bees and their reciprocal compression can only result in their cells being hexagonal. Naturalists grant bees more intelligence than wasps or hornets because their work is more regular, but they blind themselves to the fact that this depends solely on their number and shape. The more numerous they are, the greater will be the mechanical constraint and the more perfect their regularity.

Monsieur laughed. 'Do you remember Bonnet sitting here and getting so angry at Buffon's ideas? I can hear him now: "Buffon's a physicist, not a naturalist. Perhaps we're supposed to be thankful that this great thinker is untouched by a sense of marvel and can show us the blindness of our ways." Frail as he was, stamping on the floor.'

'It's interesting how the same observations can lead to such different conjectures,' I said. Not to mention how two men approaching the same thing from different angles can have such contempt for each other's ideas. I think perhaps this isn't confined to the world of naturalists – certainly Rousseau and Voltaire hated each other.

'To be fair, the questions of foresight and the interests of the republic are difficult to decide,' Monsieur said. 'In our present state of knowledge there's little more we can do than conjecture. So let's see what we can discover as fact about the making of the cells.'

20 March

Reaumur admitted he knew little about cell construction. Even John Hunter, our most enlightened contemporary (and in my opinion Monsieur's rival in this field) admits he hasn't been able to follow how the bees use their scales of wax.

We know that the base of the cell is a pyramid composed of three rhombs, or lozenges, and from this base a hexagonal tube is extended. The angles of the rhombs are very precise and consistent – I've spent hours measuring them.

'Might there be some correspondence between the geometry and some part of the bee's body?' Monsieur speculated. 'The bee might measure the angle by using the joint of its leg, for example.'

So I've spent absorbing hours measuring bees. While I'm occupied I don't have to think of other things.

22 March

'There's no correspondence between the joints and the angles, sir.'

'And their teeth? That's what they use to carve the cell, after all.'

'Again no correspondence.'

'So the teeth are no more aligned to this geometry than a sculptor's chisel is to the work which emerges from his hands. What of the antennae?'

'More difficult to say. The twelve articulations make it easy to trace the shape of any object, but there's still no fixed pattern which would serve as a template.'

'We might think of the antennae as a compass then. Well, a chisel and a compass are effective tools for building a cell but can we say that the result depends on their intention, rather than blind instinct?' He was pacing now, the well worn path on the carpet. 'Think. If the workman doesn't have a model for his work, if there's no visible pattern outside himself, surely there must be some intelligence in his operations? So what can we say of our bees?'

'I don't think we can assert anything, sir, until we've observed them more closely at their work.' I felt like the prig, the spoil-sport, but Monsieur was pleased.

'Good, yes. The problem is that waxworking occurs in the depths of a cluster of bees. How are we going to see it?'

'Perhaps if we had a bell-shaped glass hive I could fix struts to it so they started their work at the top, where we could see them.'

'Excellent. Burnens, I'd be lost without you.'

I didn't have the words for a reply.

28 *March*

The last Sunday in the month. In the park. Waiting for her, to meet her in an accidental manner. I don't dare say she's looking out for me, but still, she sees me soon enough. She drops aside from the group and one or two ladies look backwards with knowing smiles.

'We meet again, Mademoiselle.'

'Why, what a surprise, Monsieur Burnens.'

'I don't wish to distract you from your friends.'

'No danger, I shall rejoin them in a moment.'

'I've heard of these ladies' groups but I don't quite understand . . .'

'It's innocent enough.' She smiles. 'When our fathers or husbands go to their clubs on a Sunday afternoon, to talk of weighty matters, we prefer not to be "widows" sitting at home, but to make our own club, on the hoof as it were.'

'To talk of weighty matters?'

She considers this seriously. 'At least not to chitchat. Not to gossip. Although, of course, sometimes . . .'

'I don't want to keep you from your friends, Mademoiselle.'

She smiles, teasingly. 'No danger of that, Monsieur.'

I curse myself for not having some excuse ready to keep her talking. I said lamely, 'There may be some more dissections to be done.'

'Bring them to me by all means.' She returns to her friends, turns round, smiles. Some of them turn round and smile as well.

I have nothing to offer but good intentions.

Buds are bursting open on every branch and the frost will soon be altogether gone from the ground.

30 *March*

We have the new hive in which to observe how they make their cells and I've fixed the struts. At first the bees formed a pyramid, hanging from the top. After twenty-four hours I could see signs of wax in their rings. They became less tranquil and suddenly one detached herself from the cluster and made a space for herself at the top by driving the others away with her head. She withdrew a scale of wax from her abdomen with a pair of her legs, brought it to her mouth and used her tongue to turn it round and bite it to shape.

'Shades of my father,' Monsieur sighed when I described this to him. Indeed, the dog, the cheese, the profile of Voltaire seemed more than ever a misapplication of intelligence when we looked at the efforts of the bees.

The bee stored the wax in the cavity of her teeth and then brought it back into her mouth, from where it came out as a narrow ribbon, impregnated with a frothy liquid, like pap. She applied these particles to the vault, where the pap seemed to help the adhesion. She used a second and third parcel of wax, always biting them to make a form. Although she applied these forms at specific points she didn't attempt to shape them further once they were attached.

Then she, the founding bee as we might say, disappeared and a second bee took her place, following the alignment of the founder in placing her wax. And then a third bee took over, again following the alignment. She was succeeded by another, and so on. The end result was that they produced a block of wax. This would be the foundation of the comb, but the swarm now became several inches thick so that we could not see further into it.

Monsieur was delighted that we'd seen the frothy liquid extruded from their mouths. 'Now we know the reason for Reaumur's opinion that they make the wax from their mouths. He was mistaken, but we can see why he thought that. This is a relief – I wouldn't want to reject his facts, such an observer as he is, without explaining the cause of his error.'

2 April

We still have difficulty seeing the bees do their work. I've made a four-sided glass hive but even so, looking through a glass pane alters perspective. And in order to make the observation accurate, I have to remove the glass pane and put my face very close to the work that's going on, which means the risk of stinging. I move gently and sit very still. And I hardly breathe at all – they never feel my breath on them – and they're not alarmed. And I'm stung much less than might be expected – which is not to say that I'm not stung at all.

Today, as I sat watching their activity, I couldn't help thinking of the time a few years ago when I was examining all the workers in the hive to see if by chance a small queen might have got in, and the stinging I endured then. The physical pain is less now, but so is the delight. I think I used to carry a burden from unhappy times and the physical pain was almost an antidote to it. But now, although I'm troubled and confused in my present situation, I feel as though I've laid down that burden and perhaps the same is becoming true of my work with bees.

These thoughts have difficult consequences, but I can't deny their force.

Monsieur said, 'I'm so glad that you're not stung too much.'

In truth I'm hardly stung at all. He said, 'I know the cost of your devotion,' and his face was wracked.

He's said such things before, and in the past I've counted my blessings at having a considerate master but now I find myself, reluctantly, counting the cost of his dependence on me – and mine on him.

He said, 'Your observations are so precise, and taken with such risk, they can only increase the confidence of our readers.'

I thanked him, but inwardly I sighed. The only thing for now is to continue with the work.

5 April

Buffon imagined, with his mechanical explanation, that the bees built a big block of wax and then made an impression on it with their bodies.

Monsieur was rubbing his hands with glee. 'But we've found that exactly the opposite is true. In fact they make a small block and then carve it into bases for cells.'

'And sometimes they make a mistake,' I said. 'A bee may lay one of the early pieces in the wrong position to make an even block, but as soon as the mistake is realised another one removes it and puts it in the right position.'

'This observation is so important, Burnens. It's one of the biggest arguments for intelligence as opposed to blind instinct. Automatons don't make mistakes. If the bees have the possibility of making a mistake and correcting it, then waxworking can't be a blind, unthinking process. We might conclude from what we've seen that geometry is the result of their work rather than the principle that causes it. Well done, very well observed.'

10 April

News has arrived of the execution of Danton, the last strong moderate in France. His last words: 'I have lived entirely for my country. I am Danton till my death. Tomorrow I shall sleep in glory.' All the world knows it was Robespierre's doing.

Everything is changing and the old certainties are gone.

The changes I am contemplating are not, thank God, that bloody, but there will be hurt, I can't deny it.

28 April

The de Candolles came to visit. After dinner the ladies sat out in the warm spring sun, talking in the amiable way of old friends. Pierre and Augustin were trying to juggle pine cones, laughing a lot. Pierre was more dexterous and clearly the older and stronger. The ladies watched them fondly, but M. de Candolle was in a different mood. He heard the boys laughing at the words 'watering can' and shouted at his son, 'You can laugh, sir, sitting in the botanical gardens, doing nothing all day. Do you think they call you the watering can out of respect? And doubtless you spout nonsense and they laugh all the harder.'

'I watch the plants grow,' Augustin said mildly.

'You mean you neglect your proper studies. You watch the plants grow. What kind of occupation is that?'

'I'm sorry, Father, I'm just more interested in botany than in medicine.'

'Botany is an interest, not a profession. People won't bring their gold pieces to your door so you can watch plants grow.'

Monsieur laid his hand on his old friend's arm, finding it unerringly. 'My dear friend, how I wish, how I wish with all my heart that I could sit and watch plants grow.'

It's very rare for Monsieur to make a direct allusion to his blindness and he hit his target. M. de Candolle covered his hand with his own and squeezed it.

Monsieur continued, 'Watching them is the beginning of studying them, and what a lifetime's study that could be. The man with such an interest is a fortunate man.'

'Yes, yes. Well, we shall see.' He wasn't prepared to embrace the idea yet, but without doubt Monsieur had built a bridge for them and the two of them might cross it one day and meet in the middle.

30 April

Winter has gone. Fat flower buds ready to burst. Sunshine with warmth in it. In the park this Sunday afternoon the ladies feign surprise when they see me. 'What a coincidence, don't you think, Clara?' She looks down demurely, and drops back and we walk together behind the group who resolutely pay us no attention.

She asks after my work and I ask after hers.

'And what is Monsieur Huber planning to investigate next?'

'I think he wants to look at gasses in the hive. Air composition.'

'That sounds interesting.'

'But I'm no chemist. I . . .' At this moment I hesitated because I knew that if what had only been private thoughts now became spoken words I would be committing myself to something. 'To tell the truth I don't find as much interest in the work these days.'

'You're not interested in chemistry?'

'It's not that exactly. More because I think the great work has been done. He's made some extraordinary discoveries, he's overturned established theories time and again. But now it's done.'

'Might there not be other things?'

'There could be twenty years' worth of work on wax. I don't think I want to do that.'

'I shouldn't think you do.' She laughed. And then, frowning, 'But Monsieur Huber is very dependent on you, I believe.'

'Yes, indeed. And I owe him a great deal.'

Neither of us spoke of the possibility of my leaving him.

We talked of events in France and at home. The ladies had completed their circuit. We shook hands and she rejoined her friends while I wondered how I had got to this age without any future prospects. Other than being M. Huber's secretary.

2 May

A student came to visit Monsieur by appointment. I'd assumed that he'd want me to be present to look out books, that sort of thing, but he insisted that he and the young man could perfectly well go to the hives themselves and we could see about books later if need be. I was quite content with this for I'm glad of any show of his independence from me.

'Why don't you take Madame to see the badger sett you told me about?' He turned to his wife. 'You've been complaining of a lack of exercise, my dear. It's a beautiful day, you should have a rest from your household duties and enjoy the afternoon. Martha can look after little Marie. You need some air.'

Marie has sprained her ankle quite badly, falling into a rabbit hole, and Madame has been sitting with her a lot, reading to her.

'I don't know,' she said. 'Perhaps I might just have a rest.'

'Oh, a walk, fresh air, it would revive you. Then you could rest when you came back if you were tired.'

'Perhaps Pierre might want to come,' she said.

'Yes, excellent.' He beamed and it was decided.

I knew from something I had overheard earlier, when one of Pierre's friends had visited, that they had plans to meet at Martin's Island in the afternoon and that there might be sisters present. Somehow I thought this would hold more interest for him than seeing a badger sett with his mother and me.

She came down after dinner and said, 'It seems Pierre has to make up some studies and he can't join us.'

'Let's have our walk anyway, Madame.' I hoped that it might in some way ease the awkwardness between us.

The student had arrived and we could hear him talking to Monsieur in the library.

We made our way along tracks that lay between fields and hedges. It was a glorious day with clear blue sky and a lark singing.

She said, 'Do you remember when we came this way to see the blackbird's nest?'

'Yes, Madame.' As if I could have forgotten it. The cold wind, her fine, fine skin, which I'd longed, despite myself, to touch, the tears welling in her eyes as she spoke of Monsieur's blindness.

'Pierre was still a little boy then,' I said, grasping at something which could be talked about easily. She pulled a leaf from a bush, sniffed it, slowly pulled it to pieces. She's always had beautiful hands. Monsieur loves to stroke them.

'Seven, eight, years ago.' Fragments of leaf fell slowly in the warm air. 'It's a long time. I've grown older though my husband doesn't see it.'

'He will always see you as the young woman he fell in love with, Madame.' I thought this would be reassuring but she frowned and shook her head.

'He thinks I've stayed the same age but it's he who hasn't

aged. His enthusiasms, his curiosity haven't dimmed over the years. But I feel much older. I have to decide things for us both that . . .'

She stumbled a little and I offered her my arm. The sweet scent of early summer blossom. The hum of bees flying out. Simple things that I couldn't enjoy because my heart was beating too fast. I had a fair idea of where this was leading and I dreaded it.

After a while she said, 'I look after him.'

'Madame, he's aware of that, no man could be more.'

'Yes, I know that. I know that a hundred times.'

And then she stopped abruptly, her hands casting around and tears in her eyes. 'But sometimes, sometimes, I want to be looked after myself.' And then she cried out, 'Oh François,' and I found her in my arms.

I held her, embraced her, but as a brother not a lover. Even so I said something I'd barely admitted to myself before. 'From the moment I first saw you I knew I must never think of you in any way but as Monsieur's wife, or . . .'

She put her mouth up to be kissed and I brushed her lips and stepped back with some finality. It was mild enough but I felt her shrink as though I'd done something brutal. She turned away and my arms weren't round her any more. She sighed and gave a great shrug.

She said, in the matter-of-fact way of soldiers discussing old battles, 'It was the night of the storm, when the chimney collapsed. Lots of things changed then.'

'Yes, I know.'

'I wonder if you do, François.' She didn't look at me.

We'd arrived at the ostensible object of our journey. I pointed out the sett. She barely glanced at it.

'Oh yes. How wonderful, home for the little badgers. Shall we go back now?'

We walked back together but each in our own world. She didn't take my arm. We didn't speak much, we were polite, cautious.

At home she went to her room with a headache and had her supper sent up to her.

3 *May*

We were in the library. I was writing up an experiment while Monsieur was smoking a pipe, cogitating.

He said, 'Sometimes we're so familiar with facts that we don't bother to observe them carefully.'

My heart was beating terribly and I could hardly bear to hear these words, but of course he was speaking of his work, not his wife.

'Nothing should be indifferent to us as naturalists. I was beginning to think we'd come to the end of our labour, that there were no more questions to solve, or doubts to clear up. But it's not so, and I'm greatly relieved. My life would be a poor thing without my work, and you to assist me in it.'

I smiled, but inwardly I groaned. There will never be an easy time to say that I must think of going. Marie-Aimée walked in on the end of this conversation, dropped her book on the library table and walked straight out again.

'Wasn't that Marie-Aimée?'

'Yes, sir, she was just returning a book. I believe she's called elsewhere.'

He smiled. 'But the blindfold has fallen from my eyes. I see what we must study next.'

I had a fair idea of what was in his mind and was happy to apply myself to it as well, for it's a pleasure to deal with theories and results in the physical world, rather than the other things that occupy me. I've been reading to him M. Lavoisier's account of his meeting in Paris in 1774 with the English chemist, Mr Priestley.

Joseph Priestley had observed that both animal respiration and the combustion of material had an effect on common air, diminishing its volume, and making it noxious. He believed that every metal was combined with phlogiston – the stuff of flammability. When a metal was burnt to its final residue its own particular calx remained and the universal phlogiston was released.

When Priestley met Lavoisier he'd just experimentally heated red calx of mercury and found that a new kind of air was expelled, in which a candle burned very brightly and mice lived longer than in common air. Common air, he claimed, was always partly saturated with phlogiston and couldn't absorb much more, but the 'pure' air was uncontaminated and all the phlogiston could escape into it, so the candle burned brighter and the animals lived longer. He called this pure air 'dephlogisticated' air.

Lavoisier was fascinated by this and repeated the experiment, finding that non-metallic elements like sulphur and phosphorus formed acids in this air, so he named it 'oxygen', meaning 'acid-maker'. But he rejected Priestley's theory that combustion is the result of the liberation of phlogiston; he deduced that in fact combustion is actually the result of oxygen combining with the burning substance.

Lavoisier's work has not been mainly in original experimentation, but in careful measurement of results, and the most astute analysis of them. We might say that Priestley has produced and observed this gas, while Lavoisier has understood its significance.

Monsieur says, 'But I like the way that Priestley has happy accidents, where he accidentally drops some mercury into his pneumatic trough and discovers a new gas. It reminds me of the way we discovered the male organ in the queen, when we weren't even looking for it.'

I remember the excitement of that moment. It seems a long time ago.

12 *May*

And now we hear that M. Lavoisier, aged fifty-one, has been held prisoner in Paris by the Revolutionary Tribunal for the last eighteen months. We didn't know anything of it – France is in such a state that it's hard to keep count of things there any more. But we can have no effect on that. As the world we've known all our lives collapses, we concentrate in our own little world on what seem such simple questions. Just now: how do bees breathe inside the hive, where the circulation of the air must be so poor?

'Try burning a candle in a bell jar.'

I put a bell jar over a board with a groove cut in it to simulate the hive entrance. It went out after a few minutes because the air wasn't entering fast enough to sustain combustion.

'So how do the bees manage?'

We'll think about it.

15 May

Our work has stopped as we try to comprehend the dreadful fact that M. Lavoisier has been guillotined. Madame rushed into the library with the news.

'There's a long notice in the newspaper.'

'Read it to me, quickly.'

'Why don't you read it to us both, François?' she said, rather too sweetly. She pulled up a stool to her husband's chair and leaned on the side, her hand on his arm, her dress becomingly draped. She looked at me, sitting opposite, with a kind of cold curiosity.

So I read it aloud, as became my position.

Lavoisier's father had given him a fine education, and as a

final proof of confidence in his son had bought him a title of nobility in 1772.

Monsieur groaned aloud. 'He couldn't have known what was to come. The Terror was still twenty years away. Oh God, if he'd known what a poisoned chalice he was giving. No man could have thought a title would mean a death warrant one day. God preserve Pierre.' His anguish was evident on his face.

Madame soothed him, stroking his arm and looking at me as though to say at least this was something she could do which I couldn't. 'Our situation is very different, my dear. Pierre is safe now and there's no reason he won't be safe in the future.'

I continued reading. M. Lavoisier had set up a model farm in 1778. When there was a famine he advanced money without interest for the villagers to buy barley. He became a Director of the Academy of Science. In 1789, as a member of the Farmers-General he was elected to the States General in Paris. He was largely responsible for the establishment of the metric system of weights and measures, which has been adopted very quickly all over Europe.

In 1792 the Convention ordered the arrest of the Farmers-General. On 8 May 1794 he and twenty-seven others, including his father-in-law, were tried by the Revolutionary Tribunal in the morning, found guilty within the hour and executed that afternoon. Their bodies were thrown into a common grave.

Joseph Lagrange, the greatest mathematician of our day,

paid him this tribute: 'It required only a moment to sever that head and perhaps a century will not be sufficient to produce another like it.'

We were all downcast. What is happening in France at the moment leaves no room for hope. It seems to be indiscriminate massacre, with no regard for the fine, the considered, the best of the generation.

Monsieur sighed. 'And in England Mr Priestley has had his house burnt down and his work destroyed by a mob because he's a republican. He's been forced to flee to America. What can we say?'

'That being a chemist is a dangerous business at this time,' I said.

'Indeed. I remember all those alchemical experiments I did in my youth. It seems like a golden age now. It wasn't a world where two of the greatest chemists who've ever lived could be killed or exiled. And not for their revolutionary work – which might be understandable, if not excusable, in an ignorant world – but for their political ideas.'

Marie-Aimée looked perturbed at this talk. 'Don't be downcast, my dear. Remember you live in the love of your family and friends.'

He patted her hand. 'I know, my dear, I know. Well, thank goodness for our bees, Burnens. There may be massacres there, and merciless ones at that, but they're not disproportionate. Everything is done in the interest of the whole hive, not one small faction of it.'

'We might all learn from them,' I said.

'Yes, that's it,' Marie-Aimée said. 'Study your bees.' Her tone was utterly impenetrable.

(Note: I find a certain piquancy in this conversation. None of them imagined that in four years' time Napoleon – a name unknown to them at this time – would have annexed Geneva to France. On the other hand, I believe that Joseph Priestley flourished in America. He lived in Pennsylvania for the last ten years of his life and the Chemical Society of America, an august body, was founded at his house. A. de M.)

27 May

Madame paces. What happens in France? How can we know? Are there betrayals, abandonments here at home? How can she know? She can hardly bring herself to be civil to me. If she's in the kitchen when I walk in, she walks out. Anna glanced at me oddly the last time this happened. Of course Monsieur sees nothing of this. I'm sure Madame regrets her actions on our walk. I wish there were some way to make peace between us but she's unapproachable and I don't know what I can say.

It's impossible to continue in this situation. I don't know what my future will be – and that's painful at my age – but I know that I must give notice to Monsieur. My days here are done.

Of course I shall give him plenty of time to find a replacement and I'll help him finish the work we're presently engaged on. It all sounds quite straightforward and yet . . . And of course

I can't mention the trouble with Madame to Clara. Tomorrow is the last Sunday of the month.

The last Sunday in May

She looked so beautiful in her light dress and shawl and my heart leapt when I saw that she was looking out for me. As always, the ladies smiled at me mischievously and allowed us our privacy.

I had so much to say but all the time I was deafened by the voice inside asking, 'What do you have to offer? What can you offer?'

'How is your work going, Monsieur?' she said, so polite, formal.

'Slowly. Neither of us knows enough chemistry. Monsieur is going to enlist Monsieur Senebier for guidance.'

'He's a good man in that field. It was very sad, the news about Monsieur Lavoisier,' she said.

'Indeed. What a terrible waste. We've been studying his work so it struck home all the more. Monsieur was deeply affected.'

She nodded. 'Being blind, these things must be worse in a way. I mean . . .' She shook her head, thinking, a little frown of concentration which always makes me want to smooth it away. 'If there isn't the consolation of sight, these things must be more deeply felt.'

'Yes. And that makes everything harder for me.'

'How do you mean?' Her voice was inquiring, but as though she knew the answer already. It was the easiest thing in the world to tell her.

'I've decided that I must leave his service.' There, I'd said it at last, and there was no thunderbolt, and the world hadn't fallen asunder. But her face had taken on a new, deeper expression and there was suddenly an intimacy beyond our previous politeness.

'That must have been a difficult decision.'

The way she spoke of it in the past tense made me feel stronger. It was a decision that had been made. The problems lay elsewhere now. (What to do? How to tell him?)

'Yes, it was. It's not because serving him has become more onerous, less if anything, but I have to leave if I'm to have a life of my own. I've been with him for nine years now. I'm older than he was when he married Madame, older than he was when he became a father. I don't think there was ever an understanding that my position would be for life.'

She nodded slowly. 'Nine years is a good length of time. Nobody could accuse you of disloyalty.'

'I hope not. I know how much I owe to him. Without him I might still be a farm labourer.'

'I doubt that, Monsieur. If it hadn't been Monsieur Huber, I think some other opportunity would have found its way to you.'

'I hadn't considered that.'

'Which isn't to belittle what he's given you. But I think you may have given him as much in return. It will be a great loss to him, there's no denying it.'

'I know, and he's the man of all men whom I least want to hurt. But instead of just being a man leaving his master I feel as though I'm a parent abandoning a child.'

'Does he know anything of your intention?'

'Not at all. I'm afraid it will be a very unwelcome surprise.'

We walked without talking for a while, through the dappled light on new leaves, looking at the bees out feeding on early summer flowers. Everything seemed more vivid, but more fragile.

'So,' she said, 'what will you do when you leave?'

'There's the difficulty. I'm not at all sure.'

She frowned in disbelief. 'Then what would you like to do?'

I hesitated. I didn't want to seem a fool but suddenly everything was racing forwards. What I wanted to do was so very far from my present position, seemed so impossible to achieve. 'I'd like to open a shop dealing in philosophical texts. All sorts of things, old books and new works, quarterlies and reviews, treatises and pamphlets.'

'That sounds like a good idea,' she said, straightforwardly. 'Why could you not do that?'

This dream has been unspoken for a long time. Suddenly to talk of it to someone else was almost shocking, as though I were revealing a nakedness, but it also brought it from the realm of dream to that of possibility. Her question prompted me to think of it quite differently.

'Well, there's the problem of capital. I would need quite an amount to buy stock and I don't have any.'

She shrugged. 'This is Geneva. People have money. They're always looking for good investments.'

But I can't leap just like that from being a manservant to being my own man. 'I don't have enough knowledge yet. I've learnt a great deal from Monsieur's library but that's mostly natural history. I need to broaden my knowledge in other fields.'

She nodded. 'That's more difficult.' She looked at me, such a smile. 'But I'm sure you'll find a way.'

'I believe I will,' I said, though I had no idea how – and that seemed the merest trifle because if she believed I could do it then so did I.

The ladies were near the end of their path. 'It's been very helpful to talk to you about this, Mademoiselle. Everything seems clearer now.'

She smiled. 'Good luck, Monsieur.' I kissed her hand. She rejoined her friends and they turned and waved

As I walked home it seemed as though something had changed for ever. But as I drew closer to Pregny I knew that I couldn't simply walk in and announce my resignation. Nothing was simple.

I still have not mentioned my meetings with Clara to anyone here. It's my own business and, anyway, what is there to say? If there is an understanding between us it's completely unspoken.

2 *June*

'Let's begin at the very beginning,' Monsieur said. 'Let's determine whether bees need to breathe air at all.'

Inwardly I sighed. If we start from such elementary principles
the work will take for ever. But I duly put them in a vacuum
flask and once the pressure had dropped they fell motionless,
as though dead. When I restored the air they recovered.
(Thank God.)

So we can assume they need air to breathe. This is not
remarkable.

I've decided not to say anything about my intentions
until after our work with M. Senebier. It's an important
occasion for Monsieur and it would be unfeeling to upset him
beforehand.

3 *June*

'Let's examine the air more closely.'

I set up, according to his instructions, three flasks. The first,
sealed so no air could get in, held workers, while the second
also had workers but this time with free passage of air. The
third had drones and it was sealed like the first.

12.00 p.m. Began the experiment. Hot, sunny day. Feeling
a little sick for some reason.

12.15 p.m. Bees in the first and third sealed flasks began to show signs of suffering: their rings dilating and contracting rapidly, breathing heavily and licking moisture from the sides of the flask.

12.30 p.m. In the first flask the cluster of bees hanging round a straw smeared with honey suddenly collapsed, and once on the floor they couldn't get up again. The same result with the drones in the third flask.

12.45 p.m. They were all asphyxiated. I took them out and put them in fresh air and within a few minutes the workers revived. None of the drones survived. The bees from the second flask with an air supply were unaffected in any way. I wondered whether the drones' death was any worse than what they would have suffered naturally, if they were massacred by the workers after the swarms.

I tested the air in flasks one and three and found that new bees introduced suffocated almost at once and a candle would not burn in it. Monsieur can confidently assume there was not enough oxygen.

This detail does, for now, calm the turmoil I feel about telling Monsieur, about my future prospects, about Clara, and of course Marie-Aimée who persists in her coldness.

5 June

While we wait for our appointment with M. Senebier, Monsieur is thinking about the breathing orifices that Swammerdam discovered on the thorax and abdomen of nymphs. Is the same true of adults? He asked me to immerse various parts of their bodies in water.

When only her head was immersed for thirty minutes the bee was not affected, but if only her head was out of the water she suffocated almost at once.

When the head and thorax were immersed she struggled for several seconds before suffocating. When the head and abdomen were immersed, leaving the thorax free, she suffered no ill effects.

When wholly immersed the bee quickly dies, but this is when we can see the air bubbles emerging. I confirmed Swammerdam's observation of the orifices and also found two more that he had missed.

Monsieur was very pleased. 'Certainly one to include in the next volume of *Observations*. Excellent work, Burnens.'

But I know that I won't be here to write it. I feel like a traitor.

10 *June*

Marie-Aimée brushes past imperiously and gives me cold looks. I don't know if anyone else has noticed. Obviously not Monsieur, of course.

Theoretically, if there were a little more money from the Hubers so that I could rent a small apartment, and counting what Clara could earn from her work, there could be just enough to live on if I continued as Monsieur's secretary. But there's no spare money here to pay me more and, even if there were, Marie-Aimée makes it impossible, makes me long to go even though I have nothing to go to.

12 June

M. Senebier visited daily for three days, bringing quantities of equipment and chemicals with him. We've learnt how to test the stale air with nitrous oxide, showing a complete lack of oxygen. We've confirmed it by observing that this air precipitates chalk from lime water. M. Senebier is interested in germination and we found that lettuce seeds would not germinate in this air.

In pure oxygen the bees lived eight times longer than usual but in the end they died, when all the oxygen had been converted into carbonic acid gas. In carbonic acid gas they asphyxiated at once but revived in fresh air.

Introduced into nitrogen prepared from sulphur and moistened iron filings they perished at once, and the same when introduced into hydrogen prepared from zinc.

I've found it difficult to observe their convulsions without emotion. In the past we've modified their food and dwellings in ways that sometimes proved harmful but it was an acceptable price for the richness of knowledge gained. Gas has such an immediately terrible effect that I find it hard to justify our results. When I describe the sight to Monsieur my voice is measured. This is one of the very few occasions where

I believe that he would behave differently if he could see with his own eyes. Mutilating their wings – he could imagine that vividly. But this death by gassing is unimaginable if you haven't seen it.

Tomorrow I will tell him I must go.

13 June

We were down by the hives, he sitting on his old chair, me on mine. So many hundreds of hours here over the years. And so many years.

He said, 'Do you remember how we used to wait for the swarms to fly out, or the fecundated queen to fly back?' There was something elegiac in his tone and I wondered for a moment if he was opening the way for me. In any event I seized the chance.

'Sir, I find myself in the swarm's situation. I mean that I must leave all that I hold most dear.'

I saw from the spasm on his face that he knew at once what I meant. 'This is the moment that's always been waiting to come,' he said. 'From our very first day together.'

'I'm sorry, sir.'

He turned aside and covered his face with his hand and I was dreadfully reminded of the day so long ago when Dr Wenzel told him he would go blind and he had to bear the additional weight of his father's tears. After some moments he regained his customary equanimity, but there was never a time

in all our years together when I was more aware of the effort
it took him to wear that face.

Then he shook his head and reached out to grasp my arm.
'I've always known it, though I was as ready as the next man
to let myself think it would go on for ever. But you had to
set the date. And as a master frees his apprentice, or a father
lets go of his son, you'll leave with my blessing.'

'That means all the world to me, sir.'

'You have to go away or you'll always be the apprentice,
never the master. And you'll make a good master.'

'Thank you, sir. If I do, it will be because I had the finest
example.' This was wholly inadequate to my feeling but as
usual words deserted me at the important moment. I resolved
to write him a long letter to express my gratitude.

He sighed. 'There'll never be another like you, François.'

'But there's Madame, sir, now the children are older and
make fewer demands on her. She helped you before I came.'

'Indeed, very much. But times have changed.'

'And your son, sir. Pierre is a gifted observer.'

'Yes, he is. He'll help with the bees, but he's not interested in
them in the way that you are. I know his main interest is ants.
And it's too late for me to turn my attention to them. I'm too
old to start on a new province – and anyway that's his field.'

'But he's interested in bumblebees.'

'Yes. Because I'm not.' He smiled. 'I'm proud he's chosen his
own path. He'd be a poor fellow if he had to dog his father's
footsteps without swerving.'

'You didn't do that, sir.'

'Nor you, François, and I think we're both the better for it. God rest their souls.'

'Amen.'

'Meanwhile young Augustin fights with his father. It's evident to everyone except the parties concerned who will win. He'd be a mediocre doctor but he'll be a superb botanist.' He stood up and paced a few steps. 'But why this particular moment, François? Why today and not six months ago or a year hence?'

'There's a lady involved, sir.'

'Ah, ladies always get things moving. May we know who she is?'

'It's Mademoiselle Jurine.'

A great smile broke over his face. 'My dear man. From all I know of her you couldn't have made a better choice. And from all I know you're immensely privileged if she's settled on you.'

'It's early days, sir, nothing is settled. I haven't made any declaration yet. I can't, I have no immediate prospects.'

'I must see what I can do for you.'

'I appreciate that, sir, but I know I have to make my own way.'

'Let's see, let's see.' He paced his habitual path between the hives. 'But didn't we do some work, François? Between us we made some observations, discoveries, things you can be proud of all your life.'

'I shall, sir. We observed things that can never be disputed.'

'What we did can't be done again. When you're gone, I won't be able to replace you. It's the end of my serious work.'

'That's not true, sir.' But I know that it is. And not just because of me, but because the radical work has been done. There'll be confirmations, and comforting ones, but nothing like the excitements of the past.

He smiles. 'Perhaps you should ask Mademoiselle Jurine if she can make drawings of the breathing orifices.'

'I'll do that, sir.'

'You won't leave at once, will you?'

'No. Of course not. There'll be time to finish our work on breathing, and time to find another manservant.'

'I don't know that I have the heart to train up someone else.'

There's nothing I can say to this. I think I would feel the same in his position. I'm just profoundly relieved for myself that I've cast my bread upon the waters.

16 June

Needless to say I found it necessary to go into town very shortly and I thought I might as well take the specimens for Clara to draw. When I arrived at her house I was disappointed to find she had not yet returned from an errand. Her father invited me into his study and we talked for a little while about his books. I was fascinated to see different editions of some of the texts I know so well. He asked how long I'd been M. Huber's secretary.

'Nine years, sir, although I was only a manservant when I began.'

'You must find the work very interesting to have been with him for so long.'

'It has been, sir, and I've learnt a great deal.'

'Do you ever think of doing something on your own account?'

'Yes, I feel I must.'

'But Monsieur Huber would miss you greatly, I think, if you were to leave him.'

'He will. I've told him I intend to leave, even though I have no particular prospect yet.'

'What, none?'

'I have my dream, but no way of realising it yet.'

'What's your dream?'

I suddenly wondered whether Clara had already told him. She had no reason not to mention our meetings to her parents. 'I want a bookshop, sir. To deal in philosophical texts. Monsieur has always allowed me free use of his library and I love the books. If that interest could be my livelihood I'd count myself a fortunate man.'

He nodded, and I was amused and moved to see it was in just the same way that Clara does. 'It's a good time for such an enterprise. So many discoveries at the moment, and they'll lead to more. It's a rich field and a knowledgeable man could do very well. So why is it only a dream?'

'No capital to speak of. I've built up a little stock of books over the years but not nearly enough for a business.

And although I know Monsieur's library intimately, it's not exhaustive. My duties with him mean I haven't been free to spend as much time as I'd wish in other libraries. I'd want to be more knowledgeable than I am now before I embarked on it for a living. After all, where a man can make money, there he can lose it too.'

'Which is not to be wished. Particularly if he has an establishment to provide for.'

'Yes, sir, just so.'

He sat behind his big desk, piled with manuscripts, books, notes. He had a chair which swivelled on its base and he turned gently in it. 'I believe you've chanced on my daughter once or twice on her Sunday walks.'

'Yes, sir.'

'She speaks well of you.'

'That's kind of her.'

'No more than you deserve, I'm told.'

(Has he been making inquiries?)

He hesitated, making a business of relighting his pipe. 'I don't want to come between you and Monsieur Huber. I'm glad you've already told him you intend to leave his service. It means I can speak freely. The fact is that an old friend of mine, a very wealthy man, died last year. His son has inherited a large library – fine books but in a dreadful muddle. He's asked me if I can recommend someone to serve as librarian, to put the books in order and catalogue them all. He estimates it will be about three years' work. I thought of you.'

'Thank you, sir. I'm most grateful. It sounds like an excellent opportunity.'

'It's a pleasant estate in Vaud, and there'd be a cottage in the grounds. He's a rich man, but very discerning. His main concern is to have the job done well. I think he'd be reasonably generous.'

Ideas were rushing through my head but one stood out above all the rest. If I had a cottage and a salary then I had something to offer a wife.

A note arrived from Mlle. Jurine via a small boy. She'd met a friend in town and they were having coffee so her return would be delayed. I thought I'd better not stay since I'd arrived without an invitation. I wondered if she, too, would be disappointed when she heard she'd missed me. I felt in my heart that she would.

I left the specimens with M. Jurine. 'I'm very interested in the position, Monsieur.'

'Good, good. I'll talk to him, we'll arrange a meeting.'

As I walked back to Pregny I felt the same exhilaration as I had that day so long ago when I knew I had the position of manservant. Then I was excited to be leaving Vaud while now I looked forward to returning in a new capacity. But then I knew my mother would be delighted with the news, whereas now Monsieur, despite his generous spirit, is bound to be more ambivalent.

2 *August*

Will this be the final paroxysm in France? For Robespierre himself has been guillotined. How much further can they go? In the six weeks before his death there have been nearly thirteen hundred executions. The National Convention ranged itself against his Committee of Public Safety. When he was charged, he, the greatest orator of the day, could not form the words with which to defend himself. People said it was Danton's blood which rose in his throat and choked him.

He was only thirty-six. Men live and die fast in these times.

I've said nothing yet of the prospect M. Jurine raised. Until it's settled it might be tempting fate. Marie-Aimée, perversely, makes the prospect of my departure easier for me. When he's not there, she throws the letters on to the library table so they slide along the polished surface to my chair. I pick them up impassively. I know Monsieur must have told her of my intention but she makes no acknowledgement of it at all.

I pray that the post of librarian will come to pass.

3 *August*

'Can we venture another experiment?' Monsieur asks mildly.

I know that he's asking if I'll see it through. 'Of course, sir.'

'Good. Now Monsieur Senebier has analysed air you've taken from the hive at different times of day and found that it's nearly as pure as the air outside. So have the bees themselves, or something in their hives, the means of producing oxygen?'

There was a poignant feeling of this being the last time we would go through experimental procedures together. His voice was firm as he asked questions, and mine was firm as I replied, but for both of us there was an undertone of times past.

'Put wax and pollen into a flask for twelve hours. See if it produces anything.'

4 August

The air in the flask was no richer in oxygen than before. Monsieur wasn't satisfied yet. 'If there's anything in the hive that might produce oxygen then it shouldn't make any difference to them if the entrance is closed.'

3.00 p.m. I closed the entrance to a hive so no air could get in. My heart was heavy. I felt as though this was my job, not my work. Monsieur was not without misgivings himself. 'I know what's going to happen,' he said, 'or I'm fairly certain at least. But I must do it anyway, so I can't be accused of neglecting anything.'

I can see that there is a scientific case to be made for doing the experiment but I wish in a way that Monsieur were more arrogant. I think sometimes his blindness blinds him to the depth of his insight.

3.15 p.m. The bees begin to show signs of discomfort. They stop work and within a few minutes there is an extraordinary noise as all of them, those on the combs and those clustered underneath, start vigorously beating their wings.

3.25 p.m. They're beating less vigorously. They're weakening.

3.37 p.m. None of them are using their wings any more. They're losing their grip on the combs, dropping to the floor. Hundreds, thousands, complete collapse.

'Are they still moving?'

'Some of them twitching. Now nothing. They're all suffocated. Time, three forty p.m.'

'Temperature in the hive?'

'Dropped from ninety-five to seventy degrees, same as the air outside.'

'Clear the entrance, give them oxygen.'

I worked as fast as possible. The effect was striking.

3.45 p.m. 'They're reviving. Rings of the abdomen moving naturally. Beating their wings. Some beginning to climb back on the combs.'

'Thank God.' He paces. 'So we can conclude that the bees don't have any resource in the hive to supply oxygen. It must come from the outside. So how does it get in? We know the dimensions of the hive don't allow for a free air flow, and we know they perish when the hive is sealed.'

'Sir, when they beat their wings they make a sound loud enough for us to hear. There's some force there. Might not that be enough to make the air circulate?'

'It's such a slight thing, a bee fanning its wings. Can it

really have that much effect? But it would be a simple, elegant solution. When we're near a fanning bee we can feel the current of air she produces. If there are thousands of them at it . . .' He paces some more. 'If they can create circulation inside the hive we should be able to see the evidence outside the hive. If we had a sensitive enough anemometer to measure wind pressure just outside the hive entrance . . : Let's see what we can do.'

6 *August*

It's a calm day. Hot, no wind. I fixed a feather over the hive entrance. It moved as much as one or two inches away from the perpendicular. So we have shown the existence of a current of air at the entrance to the hive, and we can assume that the air corrupted by the bees' breathing is immediately replaced by fresh air. And all of this is simply brought about by the bees' own efforts.

It's the end of the summer's work. This is my last experiment at Pregny, after so many years. Finishing with a simple observation is very satisfying. It recalls all those years of 'simple' observations, when we found out great things.

7 *August*

In response to a note from M. Jurine I met him and M. Duval in a coffee house. M. Duval is a shy, modest man. I liked him very much and we agreed terms easily and shook hands. Much more important was that we agreed on what mattered to us both: the cataloguing, and the way it should be done. He'd like me to start in the autumn, and I would very much like to move into my own cottage before winter. So now I have a date to set before Monsieur.

9 *August*

A note came from Mlle. Jurine saying that her drawings of the breathing orifices were ready to be collected. This time, when her father opened the door, it seemed she was upstairs and would be down in a moment. Once again we went into his study.

'Sir, it seems that my position with Monsieur Duval is secure.'

'I'm sure of that.'

'Sir, I can only offer my love and my good intentions and my hard work. Would that be enough for you to give me permission to court your daughter?'

He laughed. 'You have my permission, Monsieur, and the best of luck to you. You're not the first to try, but I think you might have more chance than the others, from what she tells me.'

At that moment Clara herself appeared and handed me the package of drawings and said she had to walk into town to buy some more ink.

I accompanied her. I found myself talking animatedly about the prospects of my new situation. She smiled. I told her how this position would give me the depth of knowledge that I wanted. She smiled.

I found myself telling her how I had left my village in some respects under a cloud because of my father, and how I longed to return to my native canton as a man of reputation, dependability, if not yet of substance. She nodded thoughtfully.

She stopped walking and we faced each other. 'It's clear enough,' she said, 'you need a wife.' With a smile. Oh, I could have got lost in that smile.

'Would you be that wife, Clara? Will you?'

The answer was in her lips, her eyes. I kissed her in the street in Geneva. Matrons walking past tut-tutted and we laughed.

15 *August*

After I'd told Monsieur of the date I would leave, something seemed to happen to Marie-Aimée. Of course my engagement to Clara became public knowledge at this time and it somehow made her cold rigidity collapse and she herself seem smaller and warmer. She decided there must be a farewell dinner. All the servants were invited, and to enable them to enjoy it fully she decided that she would serve it all herself. Martha was to come with her fiancé, and Sarah with her husband, and of course Clara as my fiancée.

In the afternoon she broke off from giving instructions to Anna and asked me if I would like to go for a walk. I was happy to agree and we set off on the path we've taken before: the blackbird's nest, the badger's sett. There was no tension any more. Things were resolved and I wasn't afraid of what she had to say.

'Your arm, François. Let me take it for the last time.'

I gave it willingly. We walked on the familiar path, the hedges dusty now in late summer.

'It's been a long time.'

'Yes, Madame.' I didn't know if she meant since we were able to do it easily, without tension.

'Many years, François. The prime years. Pierre's childhood, and little Marie. My husband's work. You've been very loyal, no one could have been more.'

'I hope so, Madame.'

She smiled, shrugged. 'All things must come to an end. Ah, we're all older now.'

'I wasn't much more than a boy when I came and I'm much more than that now when I go. It's due to you, Madame, and Monsieur of course.'

'Knowing you must go, that makes it all different. There was a time – it all seemed as though it would go on for ever, as though nothing would ever change. And now – I have to see that things do change. My husband will miss you very much.'

I noticed that she didn't speak of her own feelings. I said, 'I'll miss you – all of you – more than I can say. I'm so glad that you have Pierre. He's a fine young man. He's more than able to help his father now. And I know he'll be a great comfort to you.'

'Yes, he will. Until the day when he must leave too.' She looked at me and I looked her full in the eyes, for there was nothing hidden any more.

'Goodbye, dear François.'

And this time, when she raised her lips to mine, I was able to hold her tight in my arms and we kissed like cousins and then we walked home arm in arm, light-heartedly, laughing at all the 'Do you remember when?' stories.

I don't pretend to understand what has made her change her attitude but I'm very glad indeed to be leaving with good feeling.

16 August

And so we gathered together for the last time. The table was beautifully set by little Marie. Although Madame carried out as well as she could her intention of serving us all, Martha and Sarah raised their eyebrows at each other as she carried in the tureen of soup, watched anxiously by Anna. They managed, in the most tactful way, to take over this duty.

'Madame, we feel uncomfortable just sitting here. Please let us . . .'

She allowed them and we were all easier. I looked round at them all. Martha, who'd been a young girl when I arrived, chasing ducks. Now so dignified, with her husband to be. What an immaculately clean and ordered house she'll keep. Dear Sarah, doing very well in her business, with her pleasant, silent husband and little François asleep in his basket. Anna, solid as a rock, keeping the household victualled, whatever the circumstances. Jacques, Monsieur's eyes in all practical, everyday things, always seeing what needed doing. And as he will take the fruit of his work on his flowers, so will I take the fruit of my work with Monsieur. Little Marie, the apple of her father's eye. Pierre, now a young man of great promise.

And Clara, of course, holding my future in her white hands. Marie-Aimée had made a great fuss of her when she arrived. And Clara responded just as I might have imagined, naturally and gracefully.

Monsieur (who'd already told me privately that he knew by the gentleness of her voice that Clara was a beauty) was on his feet, talking of our work together over the years and my hopes for the future. 'One day, François, I shall visit your bookshop and you'll delegate your assistant to deal with business and you'll conduct me round your stock yourself. And you won't call me sir, you'll call me Monsieur.'

'No, sir, I'll always call you sir.'

'God bless you, François.'

Truly, this was the end.

(Note: My uncle describes his nuptials but there is nothing here about why he left M. Huber's service that is not already known to you. A. de M.)

20 *November* 1794
Parc Duval, Oulens, Vaud.

M. Senebier has written on behalf of M. Huber to ask me to carry out in winter the experiment we made earlier this year.

I'm touched that he still turns to me, although a little perturbed that he feels he needs to. I would have thought that Pierre would have filled my shoes now, although there is mention in the letter of him being immersed in his studies at the university. But there's a pleasing sense of completion that I, who performed the others, should also perform the last experiment in this series.

It was deeply satisfying to carry it out using my own hive of bees in our cottage garden. Indoors, my own collection of volumes is not yet enough to call a library, but one day it will be.

A bright clear day in late November, a few late leaves still clinging but most of them long fallen and swept away. Too cold – 43°F – for the bees to fly out but the hive is full of life and activity. Once again the aim is to establish whether there is an air current at the entrance, and this time in the certainty that it can't be caused by the entrance and exit of the bees. At the top of the hive I fastened a hook and from this I suspended a loop made from a single long hair from Clara's head. This loop was threaded with a small square of the thinnest paper I could find, placed level with the hive entrance and an inch away from it.

How many thousands of experiments there have been, and so often at this hour. Sometimes they merge one into another and I can't remember which one established whether workers could lay eggs and which one discovered the effects of late fecundation. I remember an endless succession of long afternoon hours, sitting in the dappled shade on the old wooden chairs, waiting, observing, recording. And a succession of winter days in the library with a fire burning, the smell of wood smoke, writing up observations and making drawings.

Just as I will note today's experiment and write to M. Huber with the result. My apparatus was in position and I had placed a small rule, graduated in twelfths of an inch of a Paris foot, to measure any movement. (We're not yet entirely metric in our measurements.) I observed the paper move backwards and forwards, up to an inch out of the perpendicular. When I placed the paper further away there were no oscillations.

I believe that from this observation Monsieur will be able to confirm his idea that the bees beating their wings inside the hive ensure the circulation of air, regardless of the external temperature or whether the bees are flying in and out.

I have a feeling that this is the last time Monsieur will ask for my assistance. Whatever work remains to be done will be done with the assistance of other people, not me.

It's my delight to keep bees. When I first entered Monsieur's service I made a great distinction between a man who kept bees for a living, and a man who knew about bees. That was a false distinction. The man who would know about bees has to keep them. The man who keeps them has to know about them. To keep them means to watch over them, to guard them, to care for them. My life would be the poorer without them. Studying them has taught me a great deal, not only about the bees themselves, but how to think about other things. It's second nature now to distinguish what I wish to be true from what is really true.

I have instructed the stonemason to make a headstone for my father's grave. All is understood now, and forgiven. I have come back to my native region with my dear wife and we're full of hopes. I love my work and I'm learning from it greatly. And God willing, we shall be blessed with children and I will teach my son the ways of the bees.

But that's in the future. For now I can only say that I miss Monsieur every day, his determination to grapple with every difficulty, his enthusiasm for a new idea but the stoicism to deal with disappointments, his utter commitment to his work, even his blindness to other things. Always I carry his voice in my head. I think, what would he think of this? And I know that I have brought away riches I can never lose.

(Note: Sadly, when I was seven my mother died and my uncle and my dear aunt Clara took me in and loved me as their own. He took great pains with my education and, always generous with his time, taught me as much, I think, as he would have taught the son he never had. I hope that my love for him and the care I was able to

give him after Clara died repaid him in some measure. I believe he felt that it did, and I believe that I can say he died as a man fulfilled. A. de M.)

24 rue St Jacques
Paris
18 December 1832

Dear Mme. de Moivre,

Thank you for sending me your uncle's notebooks, which I return, having learned a great deal from them.

I understand now why M. Burnens left M. Huber's service when he did although, as you intimated, certain details are not pertinent to my memoir. It's interesting that the straightforward reason – that he wished to marry – was always somewhat fudged by the family. Perhaps we see here Marie-Aimée's pervasive influence on the household and the fact that she herself was never very clear as to why he went when he did, or at least could not admit to it.

What is evident from your uncle's journals is that he had become very much more to every member of the family than M. Huber's secretary, and it is a testament to the place he held in their hearts that when he left they all felt in their different ways that they had been abandoned.

Certainly, he was never replaced.

I don't know whether you are aware that Marie-Aimée died fifteen years after the journal ends, in her sixtieth year. It was another great blow to a man not unused to enduring misfortune but M. Huber was blessed, as your uncle appears to have been, in having the services of a loving daughter to care for him. He died in her arms I believe, and, as you say of your uncle, as a man fulfilled.

I am at all times, Madame,

Your most humble and obedient servant,

Augustin de Candolle

SOURCES

Nouvelle Observations sur les Abeilles was published in Geneva in 1792 in one volume. A second edition in two volumes, partly edited by Pierre Huber, was published in Paris in 1814. The English translations of 1806, 1821 and 1841 are abridged and often inaccurate. *New Observations Upon Bees* published by the American Bee Journal in 1926 is a more meticulous and readable translation by Charles Dadant.

Other books I have found useful include:

Memoir of Huber, Augustin de Candolle (Edinburgh Philosophical Journal, 1833)

The World History of Beekeeping and Honey Hunting, Eva Crane (Duckworth, 1999)

The Origin of Species, Charles Darwin (Oxford University Press, 1998)

Sketch of the Life of Francis Huber, S. B. Herrick (Popular Science Monthly, volume 6, 1875)

Narrative of a Journey Through France and Switzerland, James Holman R. N. (London, 1822)

Memoir of Huber, W. Jardine (Naturalist's Library, volume 34, 1858)

The Life of the Bee, Maurice Maeterlinck (George Allen, 1901)

Heroes of the Darkness, J. B. Mannix (Partridge, 1921)

Biographie Universelle, Joseph-François Michaud (Paris, 1858)

Enlightenment, Roy Porter (The Penguin Press, 2000)

Delphine, Mme. de Staël (1802)

The Illustrated Natural History of Selbourne, Gilbert White (Webb and Bower, 1981)